Christmas in Cranberry Harbor

CANDACE HAMMOND

Sea Crow Press

To Frank, for being a fellow creative who understands the need to disappear and work, and is always there for me. To all my kids, from the ones I raised, the ones they married, the ones they've had, and the ones brought to me through partnership, thank you for not (to my face anyway) thinking I am crazy for pursuing this dream. To my brother, Mark, who has always supported me in countless ways, and my mom, Louise Allen Hammond, who I'm hoping knows, it all turned out okay in the end...

Christmas in Cranberry Harbor

CHAPTER 1

ANYONE WHO HAS SPENT any significant amount of time on Cape Cod can't help but have a moment as they cross the Sagamore Bridge. Lizzie hadn't lived on the Cape since she'd graduated from college, but as soon as she was on that bridge, looking down at the canal it grabbed her. That feeling of being home. Damn it. She didn't want to have that flip in her stomach, that same flip you get when you think you're over someone but clearly you're not. She was no longer a Cape Codder, she was a Bostonite, or rather a Bostonian now. But she had to admit, as she made her way down Cape, as the locals say, it even smelled like home, a mix of salt and trees that always stayed with her. Despite her efforts to not miss her hometown, she did.

Lizzie Martin had worked hard to land her dream job as a features writer at the *Boston Sentinel*, but the newsroom was more vacant than ever with most of her colleagues having been laid off, and it was not the cheery and fun-filled place it once was. The rows of empty desks were so depressing and sad. Her dad, owner of the last independent newspaper on Cape Cod, was a rare holdout, refusing to sell to the corporate folks, and never made a secret of how much he wanted his daughter to take the reins when he was ready to step down. She promised herself she would not be seduced by the charms of Cranberry Harbor over these next two weeks being home for the holidays. She loved her apartment, she got to work next to her best friend Sarah every day, and she loved being in Boston. Mostly she loved all these things. She did not, however, love her chilly editor, Margaret, or not getting to work on the kinds of stories she'd become a journalist to write. But life was full of compromises, right? No one gets everything they want. She knew this all too well. It was why she hadn't come home for Christmas in three years.

She'd made excellent time, rolling into Cranberry Harbor in under two hours, and before heading to her parent's house she decided to take a drive through town. She'd been home in the summer every year, but this was the real Cape, the one she still held dear, despite trying hard not to. This was the Cape Cod of the locals, and the people who'd loved it enough to make it their year-round home by choice.

Main Street in Cranberry Harbor was quiet. It was only four o'clock, but there weren't many cars around. She slows down as she rolls past Tall Tale Books, one of her teen employers, and a favorite since childhood. It was a shop that had spoiled her, and forever rendered it impossible to order books online without extreme guilt. A total sacrilege in her mind. She makes a mental note to stop in and meet the new owners while she's home. Well, not home, while she's here in Cranberry Harbor. Boston is home. Boston is home, she declares again. Don't go getting all sentimental remembering discovering Jane Austen for the first time in that shop she reminds herself.

Right next to the bookstore is Sea Coast Coffee. This was and is the perfect combination of locations: a great bookstore and a great coffee shop. The only thing that would have made it better would have been finding a way of connecting the two, something Lizzie had often fantasized about on slow days when she had worked at both the bookstore and the coffee shop all through high school and during breaks from college. Coffee and books were what kept her going then, and now. Before she even thinks about it she finds herself pulling into a parking space and grabbing her purse.

The scent of the sea catches her nose as she walks across the parking lot to get herself a chai latte. The bell on the door jangles, just like always–thank goodness some things never change–and it makes her smile. As she looks around she feels a little sad to not see one face she knows. She isn't the only local kid who's grown up and moved away. Cape Cod had gotten so expensive it was hard for anyone who'd grown up here to stay. She knows she is just like so many others from her graduating class who've left to start businesses, buy homes and have families elsewhere, it was a sad reality that the Cape was losing its young adults in droves.

She orders her tea and, unable to resist the case of cookies, asks for an oatmeal and dried cranberry one that is easily the size of three normal cookies. She finds a table, sets her treats down and slips off her coat.

"Is that who I think it is?" rings a cheery voice from behind her. Lizzie turns to see it's her former boss, the queen of teaching foam making, Hope. Hope Alden to be exact. As in her family goes all the way back to the Mayflower, Aldens.

"Yes, it is you! Oh, Lizzie, it's so good to see you!" Lizzie jumps out of her seat and gives Hope a big hug.

Hope was now in her late seventies but hadn't changed a bit. There might be something about eating a little bit of something sweet every day staving off the aging process. "Hope! It's so good to see you!"

"You sit down and enjoy that cookie! I just put those out, I must have known you were coming!" She sits down next to Lizzie and can't stop gushing. "Your Mom and Dad are so darn proud of you," she says. "They are always bringing in clippings and telling me all about all the exciting stories you're writing. This whole town is so proud of you, dear."

Lizzie can feel herself blushing. She'd forgotten what it was like to not be just one more writer, one more faceless person in a big sea, it felt nice for a moment to be the medium-sized fish in a small pond.

"Oh my gosh, I'm sorry they keep foisting stories on you! Dad's been doing that forever."

"They have every reason to be proud of you, honey. I love keeping up with how you're doing. We miss you around here. But I know, there's not enough to keep young folks like you here."

Lizzie suddenly feels bad about how resistant she's been to coming back here to visit. It was kind of nice to be looked at as special, and she feels a smidgeon of guilt at being just one more young person to abandon ship.

"It is really hard to make a go of it here for sure, Hope, but boy, you certainly discovered the golden ticket early on - ply people with coffee, cocoa, tea and your amazing cookies, and you will always have a steady stream of customers. Do you ever think of slowing down?"

Hope laughs, "Oh, I've certainly slowed down, honey. I can't keep the pace I used to. My granddaughter, Leah graduated from college last spring and she's taking over more and more of the business."

"Wow, if you'd asked me I would have said Leah was about twelve years old. How did she ever…"

Hope jumps in, "Oh, you and me both, Lizzie! But she's been a godsend, she's got us all online - I'm on Instagram! And she's really helping build our brand, I didn't even know I was a brand until six months ago!" she laughs. "We're even going to be starting to do our own coffee roasting off-site, Leah says it will make a big difference in the quality of what we're doing. And we're partnering with some other local businesses too, trying to help each other grow and create synergy."

"Listen to you, talking synergy! I never would have thought I'd see the day when you'd be all about branding and social media!" Lizzie is so delighted to see Hope still has such a spark and passion for Sea Coast.

"You gotta keep up!" She stands up and pushes her chair back in, "Speaking of which, I have to get another batch of cookies in the oven before I leave for the day. Leah insists I leave by five every day."

Lizzie stands too and gives her another hug. "I am so glad I saw you, I was hoping when I came in you'd be here. I'm so excited about everything you're doing, and how happy you seem."

"And I'm so glad you came in! This better not be the only time while you're home. We're closed on Christmas day, something I never used to do, but..."

"Leah? Good for her, you should close on Christmas!"

"Yes, she's young, but she's keeping me in line," Hope says, clearly proud of her granddaughter.

"Good! Somebody needs to," Lizzie says smiling at her. "I promise I'll come back, I'm here for a couple of weeks."

She gives her a hug goodbye, and Hope rushes back to the kitchen. Still standing, Lizzie pops the rest of her cookie in her mouth, puts her jacket on, and as she turns to leave, knocks over the remainder of her tea on the floor, sending it pooling everywhere. "Shit!" she says under her breath, grabbing a bunch of napkins from the dispenser on the table. A teen with a mop shows up and starts cleaning the small lake of tea on the floor, "I've got it, ma'am, don't worry about it."

'Ma'am'? I'm a ma'am now? Oh dear lord. "Thank you, I'm so sorry, I'm such a klutz." Jeez, I'm home for ten minutes and I'm already making a spectacle of myself, she thinks.

"Are you causing trouble here, Ms. Martin?" she hears as she's picking up the wads of soaking wet napkins from the floor.

She knows that voice. The person behind it is why she hasn't come home for Christmas in three years. She stands up and is face to face with Jack Cahoon. It's hard to feel cool while holding a soaking wet pile of paper napkins, but Lizzie is giving it her best effort. "Hello," she says, cooly, hand on her hip, quickly aware that the soaked napkins are dripping down her pant leg.

"Here, let me take those," Jack says, taking the napkins from her and throwing them in the trash. "It's good to see you, Lizzie, how are you?"

Lizzie's left leg is soaked, but she is doing a heroic job of not showing how awful it feels. "I'm fine, thank you."

"Okay..." he says, shifting his posture a little in response to her lack of cordialness.

"Well, my parents are expecting me, so, I, uh, I have to go!" She rushes out of there before she gets stuck in more uncomfortable small talk. "Nice seeing you," she says, lying, as she pushes the door open and escapes. "Ugh! Nice to see you!" She mimics herself as she walks across the parking lot in her wet, and now very cold pants. She hurries to her car and tries her very best to ignore the flip she just felt in her stomach.

CHAPTER 2

OF ALL THE coffee shops in all the world...Who was she kidding? Sea Coast was the *only* coffee shop in Cranberry Harbor, the run-in was inevitable. But what was he even doing here? Jack had moved away, headed to California, Silicon Valley to be exact.

After graduating from MIT he'd been recruited by the biggest companies out there but had turned them all down preferring to come back to the Cape and start his own company. He had built a small start up but it didn't go as planned. He'd hoped to be able to bring tech jobs to the Cape and stop the flood of young people fleeing to better opportunities elsewhere, but it didn't work and he'd lost all his savings, and money from several investors. So, when tempted by a six-figure job at one of the biggest companies on the West Coast, he left. Leaving everything and everyone, including her, behind. After four years together, having known each other since middle school, he left her and all their plans like they had never mattered.

Lizzie decides to play it safe and not stop anywhere else and heads right to her parent's house lest she spill anything more or run into Jack again.

She pulls into the driveway, she loves hearing the familiar crunch of the crushed quahog shell driveway. She smiles seeing the twinkly lights wrapped around the porch railing and the candles in all the windows. It was the way her parents had decorated the house her whole life and she never wanted it to be any different. She was happy to see in her absence these past Christmases that absolutely nothing had changed. Getting out of the car she smells the smoke from what she knows is a crackling fire in the fireplace, and begins to gather her things from the back of her car.

"Lizzie!" her mom, Gabby, calls to her as she comes running from the porch, followed of course by Daisy, the rescue dog they'd adopted last year. "Oh my goodness, I can't believe you're really here! I was so worried something would come up and you wouldn't be able to make it!" She pulls her daughter close and hugs her. "Never again, okay? You are never to miss another Christmas!" she says mock-scolding her. "It's not the same without you!"

"Okay, I promise, never again. Hi there, Daisy," she says, leaning down and kissing the excited pooch. She wasn't sure she could hold true to never missing Christmas again, but it was easier to agree right now. After seeing Jack she wasn't sure she even wanted to stay this year, but here she was. Maybe she'd just stay in the house and bake cookies and watch holiday movies with her mom the whole time. That could work.

"Let me help you with all this, honey. What did you bring? Looks like you're planning to stay a while! Hint hint..."

"Mom,"

CHRISTMAS IN CRANBERRY HARBOR

"I know, I'll stop bugging you, but a mom can dream, right? Come on, Daisy," she calls to the bouncing dog.

They head to the house carrying a suitcase, bags of gifts and all of Lizzie's work paraphernalia, which she still didn't know why she'd found it necessary to bring.

"What happened to your jeans?" her mom asks.

"Ugh, a stupid chai accident at Sea Coast, "I'm going to run into the bathroom and quickly change." She opens her suitcase and pulls out a pair of leggings. "Be right back." She peels off the wet pants, still feeling the stinging embarrassment of her meeting with Jack. She looks at herself in the mirror and can see her face is still red from the encounter."Change gears," she says to herself as she emerges from the bathroom.

"Here, give me those, I'll wash them," Gaby says. Lizzie happily hands them off. It's very nice to be home and have Mom taking care of her.

The house smells amazing, a combination of the warm fire, spices and the huge Christmas tree. Her parents never skimped on their tree. They used to drive to Vermont to cut one down as a family, but for the last ten years or so they'd taken to buying it from the local high school which sold trees to raise money for their music and theater departments.

"Oh my gosh, this smells incredible, Mom," Lizzie walks over to look at the tree. "It doesn't have as many ornaments as usual, or am I misremembering?"

"No," she says as she reaches behind the couch and pulls out a box. "We just saved all of the ornaments you and Matt made or have given us over the years for you two to put on the tree. We wanted to get it up and start decorating, but we need you to finish it. Your brother's coming over for dinner, so we can all work on it together. Maybe even string some popcorn and cranberries like the old days?"

Lizzie drops onto the couch and begins to relax for the first time in weeks. Suddenly the hustle of all her deadlines begins to fall away, helped by the big mug of hot cocoa her mother just put in front of her.

"Aw, you even put mini-marshmallows and a candy cane in it, Mom, thank you." She picks up the steamy mug, leaning back on the couch.

"Of course, I know how you like it," she takes a moment to survey her daughter. "You okay, honey? You seem tired, are things really stressful at work?"

She takes a sip of the hot and sweet beverage. "No more than usual, I guess. It's such a Catch-22, I'm being given more opportunities as more people have been let go, but I miss my colleagues and it's a lot more pressure. There are a handful of us now doing the work of what used to take a whole newsroom. I'm sure that's nothing new for you to hear. Dad's been going through this forever. He and Stan have kept the Cranberry Harbor Gazette going for years, just the two of them. I truly don't know how they do it."

Gabby sits down and motions for Lizzie to put her feet on her lap and begins to rub them. She had retired last year from her family medicine practice, but she was and always would be a caretaker looking after everyone. "It's so hard to see the two of them try to keep the paper afloat. But they both love it so much, I don't think they'll ever give up. And even though it's hard, and they have less advertisers, people still love that paper. It's really the heartbeat of the community. Everyone reads it, but it's still a struggle."

"Maybe it's a matter of a different business model, online and print?"

"Good luck trying to convince your Dad, he's very old school, 'You need to hold a newspaper, Gabby,' he always says."

"Well maybe I'll catch him in a weak moment and wear him down," Lizzie smiles at her mom.

"Wear who down?" laughs Matt Martin, Lizzie's brother

comes breezing in carrying a bundled up toddler whom he sets down next to Lizzie on the couch.

"Oh my gosh, who's in there??" She teases her niece. "Is it Santa?" The little girl shakes her hat-covered head. "Is it...an elf?" The bundle of hat, snowsuit, scarf and mittens shakes with giggles.

The little girl whips off her hat, "No, Aunt Wiz, it's me! Sophie!"

Lizzie hadn't been thrilled when she'd been named Aunt Wiz, a product of the L in Lizzie being a bit of a tongue-twister for baby Sophie, but now she'd grown rather fond of it. She loved this little girl, now a precocious almost-three-year-old. She hated how much she changed in between visits. Matt and his wife Shannon brought Sophie to Boston every few months, wanting her to experience the New England Aquarium, the Children's Museum, and all the city had to offer. But they were both so busy, Matt with his solar energy business and Shannon as the children's librarian at the Friends of Cranberry Harbor Library, it was hard to get over the bridge very often. Lizzie made a mental note to stop being so darn selfish and get herself back to the Cape more often.

"Where's Shannon?" Lizzie asks as she takes off Sophie's jacket.

"Mommy's working," she says as she slides off the couch and runs toward the kitchen. "Cookie!" she calls out as she rounds the corner, Gabby in quick pursuit, and Daisy right behind the two knowing there would inevitably be crumbs involved.

"Hold on there, little missy, just one, because we have to save room for dinner," Gabby calls after her as she chases her into the kitchen.

"Fine," Sophie acquiesces, giving in awfully fast for a toddler.

"She's so sweet, Matt, it almost makes up for naming me Aunt Wiz," Lizzie playfully chides her brother.

"Hey, that's all her!" he laughs, knowing full well he'd

encouraged it as much as he could. "I'm so glad you came home, it means so much to Mom and Dad. But we all know it's Mom who really loves Christmas."

Lizzie gets up and picks up the box or ornaments from behind the couch. "We're supposed to put these up, come on, help me."

Matt heaves a sigh and groans as he gets up off the chair he was just relaxing into. "Fine."

"Jeez, that was the sound of an old man getting out of that chair!" she teases.

"Stop bugging me! You may sit at a desk all day, but I'm climbing on roofs, hauling solar panels, going up and down ladders … you know, doing real work." he teases.

She throws some little stuffed bear ornaments at him. "Oh yeah? Well, I run all over Boston tracking down politicians, and all sorts of people getting them to trust me to tell their stories."

He throws some tinsel at her. "Well I, um I… fine, I give up. We both work hard."

"Yes we do, but I give you points for doing it while being married and having a toddler. I only have myself to worry about."

"We're lucky. Since Mom retired she's been a huge help, and Shannon's parents and her sister help us a lot too. We couldn't do it without family. I don't know how people without family around manage. I really don't."

"How's the business going?"

"It's been crazy busy. Everyone wants solar panels, which is great, but I need more help, and it's hard to come by," he says, doing his best to artfully arrange a bunch of ornaments that are so old they're held together with hope and scotch tape.

They both keep rummaging through the box finding old favorite ornaments from the past.

"Oh my gosh," Lizzie says, holding up a dilapidated paper reindeer, "I can't believe this is still intact!" She inspects it closer, "Well, sort of intact?" She places it carefully on some underbranches on the tree. "I've been reading in the Gazette how much the housing crisis here is impacting businesses finding help."

"Oh yeah, I'm having a really hard time. This isn't a business a sixty-five-year-old retiree with a second home here wants to try out as a part-time gig. I really need young adults," Matt says. "But I don't want to bore you with my problems. How's Boston?"

"Your problems are never boring to me." She puts her arm around her brother's waist, and hugs him. "Boston's okay. I pay an insane amount of rent for a tiny apartment, and work more than ever for no more pay. It's not wonderful."

Matt hugs her and then goes back to decorating the tree. "Do you ever think of going anywhere else? New York? L.A.? Back here?"

"No, no and really no," Lizzie says emphatically. "Too expensive, too far and no way could I ever live on the Cape again. I don't feel like I fit in anymore. And besides, I hardly know anyone here, and oh, you just said no one our age can afford to live here."

"So not true," he interrupts her. "But hey, you know us, you know Hope…"

Lizzie puts her hands on her hips and laughs, "You've got to come at me with more than a toddler, as adorable as she is, and my former boss who, while lovely, probably isn't going to be signing up for Zumba classes with me anytime soon, and you and Shannon who have your own busy lives."

"Okay, so we'd need to expand your circle beyond us. But there are some awesome new people in Cranberry Harbor. The couple who took over the bookstore are great, and under 40, and Ben Knowles is back. He took over the Marshview Inn from his parents."

Lizzie sits down on the couch to untangle some gold

garland. "Look, I know you love it here, and you've built a business and a wonderful life, but it's not for me. I'll figure it out. If the Sentinel lays me off, it might be time for a plan B." She gets frustrated and throws the garland back in the box.

Matt fishes it out and in short order untangles it. "How did you...?" Lizzie laughs at how quickly he undid what she couldn't do.

"I am the problem solver," he jokes. "Give me anything knotted up and I can untangle it."

Lizzie sighs and leans back on the couch. "How come you got that talent and I didn't?"

"I was always good with my hands, and you were always good with words." He shrugs his shoulders. "I can see the forest for the trees, and you can write about what the forest looks like."

Matt sits down beside her. "I hate seeing you like this. You don't seem happy. Is there something else going on? What about that guy you were seeing...Ted? Fred?"

"Ed, Edward. Nah, that's over. He traveled all the time for work and we didn't really like the same things. He didn't like dogs."

"You don't have a dog,"

"Yeah, but I might want one...someday."

"Okay, but still..."

"I might want one someday, okay?" she says emphatically. "And not liking dogs says a lot about a person. Seriously, what kind of person doesn't want to snuggle a puppy?"

"Okay, okay, I hear you. Someone who doesn't like dogs is not the right person for you. Got it."

"Thank you."

"Dinner's just about ready," Gabby calls from the kitchen.

Matt stands up and heads toward the dining room. "Jack Cahoon's back in town for the holidays. Maybe he's got a dog?"

He smiles, shrugs his shoulders and walks out, "Come on, dinner's waiting."

Lizzie rolls her eyes, and mimics her brother. "Maybe Jack Cahoon has a dog!" Of course he probably does.

CHAPTER 3

PETER DIDN'T MAKE it home from the paper until they were all well into dessert and Sophie was asleep with her head on Matt's lap, sprawled over from her own chair. by the time he came in.

"I am so sorry everyone! Deadline night," He rushes over to hug Lizzie who stands up to greet her dad. "Honey, it is so good to see you!" He squeezes her and lifts her up. "See? I can still pick up my little girl," he laughs. "It smells divine in here, Gabby, what ever did you make?" He takes off his coat, tosses it on an empty chair and gives his wife a smooch. "I'm so sorry I'm late, there was a glitch with the internet connection, and then Stan had a hard time getting a source to get back to him, so he was late with his last story, it was just one thing after another." He pours himself a glass of wine and sits back. "Lizzie, I am so sorry you got bitten by the journalism bug. I blame myself for that."

Lizzie refills her own wine glass and motions to Matt if he wants more, he shakes his head and points to Sophie sleeping on his lap.

"Dad, I love writing! The business could be a bit different, but you taught me to love telling stories. I'm grateful!"

Gabby brings him a plate of food. "Here you go, I knew you'd be late so when we sat down I'd already made you a plate to keep warm." She kisses the top of his head. "You work way too hard!"

He grabs her hand and kisses it. "Didn't that used to be me lecturing you about working too hard, Dr. Martin?"

"Well, now the worry is on the other shoe, or foot, or whatever...."

Lizzie and Matt laugh. "Shoe is on the other foot, Mom," Matt smiles at her. "You've both always worked way too hard." He points back and forth with Lizzie, "Trees, meet your apples."

Peter digs into his dinner, "Oh my gosh, Gabby, you've outdone yourself, this pot roast is amazing!"

The three of them look at each other with conspiratorial smiles.

"Seriously, this is I think the best pot roast you've ever made!" He's already almost done with his first serving and is looking for more.

"Who's going to tell him?" Lizzie teases.

"I will!" Matt jumps in. "It's not meat, Dad. It's a vegetarian dish."

"No," he shakes his head and wipes his mouth. "I know beef when I taste it."

Gabby comes in, bringing him a second serving. "No, honey, he's right."

Peter takes another bite. "Okay, then what is it?"

All three at the same time call out, "Jackfruit!"

"You're kidding me, well I'll be," he takes another mouthful. "You may need to write this up for the Gazette, darlin', I've been thinking about how we need a food column since Deborah retired."

"Mom, that could be great! A healthy cooking column!" Lizzie says.

Gabby isn't so sure. "Maybe, let me think about it. I've had fun since your Dad's cholesterol came back a little elevated working on ways to change our diet, but that could take all the fun out of it!"

"I'm betting a lot of people in Cranberry Harbor could use some help eating better," Matt adds.

"We'll see, let's get past Christmas and the festival first. Then we can think about what's next. In the meantime, who wants another slice of silken tofu cheesecake?"

After the table is cleared and the dishes mostly done, they all retire to the living room. Matt puts a sleepy Sophie on the couch and stokes the fire.

"This is so nice," says Gabby, curled up on the couch, and Peter joins her. "It's been way too long since we've all been together. I miss this."

Lizzie lies on her side, propped up on her elbow near the fireplace. "Okay, I promise, no more missed Christmases," she says smiling.

"And Easter, and Fourth of July, your birthday..." Peter teases her.

"You forgot Flag Day and Arbor Day, Dad," Matt teases. "She does the best she can getting back here, guys. Don't pressure her." He pokes the fire a bit for emphasis.

"Sorry, honey, we don't mean to bug you, we just miss you," says Gabby.

"And I miss all of you. I for one will be very happy when we finally solve this teleporting puzzle and I can just blink my eyes and be here. But until then, I will make an effort to do better, okay?" Ready to change the subject Lizzie sits up and turns to her dad. "So what are the lead stories in the Gazette this week?"

"Hmmm, well, the Christmas festival of course, that's coming up fast," he says, "and the wastewater committee is working on some new plans, and we're always talking about housing, jobs, and renovations at the high school. Those are the main stories."

"And it's still just you and Stan writing everything and taking all the photos, doing the layout, editing and getting it off to the printer?" Lizzie asks.

"Yup, it's a lot." He puts his feet up on the coffee table and stretches. "I don't want to join your mom in retirement because, well, I love it, and even if I am kind of tired sometimes, I can't leave. The Gazette is the last independent paper left on the Cape. If we close down, they win."

"The corporations? I hear you on that, Dad," Matt says.

"Yes, I'm just stubborn enough that I am not going to let them have this paper. This one, last independent voice in a sea of wire stories and executives who don't care about the communities they're covering. Or rather not covering," Peter is getting upset, and sits forward on the edge of the couch, elbows on knees. "When I started this paper it was an embarrassment to run stories from the AP wire, it meant you didn't have enough local news and were using filler." He sits back and puts his arm around Gabby. "I'm not giving up, not yet, anyway."

"It's hard everywhere, Dad, it's not just you," says Lizzie. "You wouldn't recognize the newsroom at the Sentinel since you came to visit last year. So many layoffs, and they're starting to furlough people too. I'm sure it's just a matter of time before it's my turn."

"And that's when you come back here!" says Matt cheerfully. "Sorry, too soon? Maybe I shouldn't be celebrating a potential layoff?" He begins to try to slip a sleeping Sophie into her jacket without waking her. "I need to get her home, everyone. This has been awesome." He picks up his sleepy daughter. "Shannon wants to have all of you over tomorrow night, if that's okay? Taco Tuesday?"

"Tomorrow is Thursday, Matt?" teases Lizzie.

"I know, I think she just wanted to make tacos, so go with it, okay?" He laughs and gives his sister a kiss on the cheek. "See you at 6?"

"Sounds good," says Peter. "I can't wait to see what kind of fruit you two use instead of meat!"

Gabby laughs, "We're just all trying to keep you around as long as possible." She kisses Sophie's head, and then Matt. "Thanks for coming, honey. I'll call tomorrow to see what we can bring."

Lizzie gathers up the rest of Sophie's belongings, "Here, I'll help you out to the car," she puts on her coat. "I'll be right back," she says to her parents.

Matt settles Sophie who is surprisingly still asleep into her car seat. He snaps the buckle, closes the door and turns to hug his sister. "It is so good to see you. I'm really glad you're going to be around for a little bit."

She sinks into her brother's embrace, closes her eyes and squeezes him right back. "Yeah, it's really good to be here. Maybe I can even help Dad a little while I'm here."

Matt opens his car door and smiles at her, "He could sure use it," he gets in the car and starts it up. "Who knows, maybe you could too."

And with that, he closes the door, drives off, and Lizzie stands there for a moment taking in the cold, salt-tinged air, looking back at her childhood home trying to ignore how much better she feels being there than alone in Boston. Nope, she shakes her head, there's nothing here for you, don't get sucked in. But as she stands there, some snowflakes begin to fall, and it's hard to not feel the magic and comfort of home.

CHAPTER 4

THERE IS ALWAYS something very surreal about being an adult and waking up in your childhood bedroom. It wasn't like it was covered with posters from her teen years, those were long put away, but it was a feeling. A feeling of being safe from the world out there, beyond this town, safe from the realities of the world.

Lizzie turns on her side toward the window and can see that it's starting to snow. She instinctively pulls up the covers and shivers. She then realizes that they'd been having such a mild stretch of weather she'd forgotten to bring any snow boots. Hopefully her mom hadn't Marie Kondo-ed the hall closet in retirement and had some old ones in there to use.

She stretches, relishing not having any deadlines or anything she has to do. She can't remember the last time that happened. She hears a scratch at the door, and a little whine.

"Come on in, Daisy," she calls. The closest anyone had come to decoding what breeds Daisy could be was a veterinarian who'd been vacationing in Cranberry Harbor and spotted Gabby walking her on Main Street one afternoon. She'd told her that Daisy appeared to have Havanese and poodle in her. Whatever she was made of, she was the snuggliest dog Lizzie had ever met. She immediately jumped on to the bed and got right under the covers. Lizzie thought back to her conversation with Matt about her breaking up with Ed partly based on his disdain for dogs. Though clearly it had been a long time coming. "How could anyone not love you?" she asks Daisy, hugging her.

"How indeed," Gabby says, coming into the room with a cup of hot coffee for Lizzie and placing it on the nightstand. She ruffles Daisy's fur. "I see our living alarm clock found you. Sorry about that."

"I was already awake, no worries." She sits up and takes a sip of the coffee. "Mom, you are totally going to spoil me. How will I ever go back to the real world when you treat me like a princess?" She takes another sip and leans back. "Good morning, by the way. So what's on the schedule for today? Do you need to bake eight thousand cookies for the festival or just four thousand?"

Gabby laughs. "I think it's only twenty dozen, but that's plenty." She picks up Lizzie's clothes laying on the floor, "I'm going to head to Bradford's to get some baking supplies pretty soon if you want to come with?"

"Did you just say 'come with,' Mom?" Lizzie laughs. "And you don't have to pick up after me!"

"Hey, I keep up!" She drops the clothes in a pile on the floor. "Old habits die hard," she says.

"I love it, and that you still don't shop at the chain supermarkets," Lizzie says, throwing back the covers.

"Never have, never will. I believe in shopping local, and Tim Bradford has been great about creating a whole section of organic items, and all the meat substitutes I keep slipping your dad without him knowing it."

"You are a sneaky one," Lizzie laughs. "Do I have time to take a quick shower first?"

"Of course, take your time." She grabs Daisy to walk out and turns back. "I loved waking up this morning knowing you were here."

Lizzie smiles at her mom. "Yeah, it made me feel good too. I've been running really hard in Boston, not always sure what I'm running for, or to. It feels nice to slow down for a minute and take a breath. Thanks for having me."

"Having you? Honey, this is and always will be your home. You can come here and take a break anytime."

"Thanks, Mom. I always know that, but I sometimes forget. It's good to hear. I promise I'll be right down!"

Lizzie pulls some jeans, a sweater, underwear and socks out of her suitcase and puts them on the unmade bed. She grabs an old terry cloth robe of her mom's out of the closet and heads to the bathroom and starts the shower. Her mother, always the consummate hostess, has a new toothbrush, toothpaste and two big fluffy towels on the counter waiting for her. It's been so long since she's had anyone do anything for her, to be taken care of feels nice.

She steps into the shower and sighs as the hot water hits her. She sees her mother has also gotten the organic shampoo and conditioner she likes - in reusable containers, and the amazing lavender and oat soap from her friends, Lindsey and Jason's farm. "You really went all in, Mom," she smiles as she lathers up her hair.

Twenty minutes later she's all dressed, hair still a little damp, standing in the kitchen. Gabby has assembled quite the baking workstation for them. Two standing mixers, a half-dozen cookie sheets, lots of wire racks and a Bluetooth speaker, "So we can listen to Christmas music while we bake!" she tells Lizzie.

Lizzie goes to the French doors in the kitchen, munching on a blueberry muffin from the plate Gabby left on the counter, and sees the snow beginning to accumulate on the deck. "So I didn't remember to bring any snow boots, of course, weather ignorer that I am. Do you have any of my old boots around?"

Gabby stops building her assembly line and walks to the hall closet. "I'm sure there have to be some in here. What size do you wear?" She's a bit muted with her head deep in the closet, on her knees trying to find something suitable. "Darn that 'Tidying Up' show! I always hate to part with things, but I got tired of asking myself if something 'sparked joy' and ended up donating a whole bunch of things. I'm sorry honey, I've got nothing. And your feet are a couple of sizes bigger than mine, so that won't do." She crawls out of the closet, stands up and smooths out her hair and clothes. "How about after Bradford's we run into the church thrift shop and see what they've got? When I brought a few things in last week I saw they had some boots. No need to spend a lot when you've got good ones at home. You know what they say - reduce, reuse and recycle!"

Lizzie laughs, "I'm so impressed Mom, You're really doing your part. The thrift shop sounds perfect. I'll just wear these shoes for now, it will be fine. I still can't believe what a poor New Englander I am. Who travels in December without boots?" She slips her ballet flats on.

"We're trying very hard in Cranberry Harbor to lead the way on the Cape, and in the state toward making the town carbon neutral by 2030," Gabby says, circling back to the topic of environmental friendliness. "I'm on the committee that reports to the selectboard, and we're really getting things done."

"I'm so proud of you, Mom, that's awesome. And that's how change happens, one person, one town at a time."

They each put on their coats, hats and gloves and head to the garage. "Come on, Daisy, wanna go in the car?" Daisy, who'd been sound asleep under the kitchen table suddenly awakens and runs to catch up. "We can't leave you behind, little one," she says as she opens the car door for her. Daisy jumps right in and snuggles into her waiting bed and cozy blanket.

"That girl has quite the life, Mom," Lizzie says and she gets in the car and fastens her seatbelt.

"Oh, you have no idea just how spoiled she is. But I love having her. She's a lot of company. Your dad works so much, and well, I guess I'm still kind of adjusting to not working sixty or so hours a week." She backs out of the garage. "I'm someone who needs someone or something to care for," she says as they carefully drive into town.

"Really? I had no idea," Lizzie teases. Her mother laughs as she glances at her daughter.

When it snows, there's simply no way around it. Cranberry Harbor looks like a postcard. Mostly people come and visit in the summer, but Lizzie had often thought, before settling in Boston, that she'd just as soon spend her summers elsewhere, but the rest of the year right here. Until she got bitten by the city bug. Though lately that wasn't feeling as wonderful. With so many of her colleagues either furloughed in shifts of a few weeks at a time, or laid off completely, the thrill of writing for a big city paper was fading.

Lizzie hadn't been a journalism major; she'd double majored in business and English. She'd always loved to write, something she got from her dad for sure. As they drove carefully along the snowy streets and she looked out the window at this picture-perfect town, she felt that flip in her stomach again. *Oh no, no way*, she thought to herself, *don't you go being seduced by Christmas. This is still the place where almost all young people have fled because they can't afford it, there aren't any jobs, you can't make a life here. Don't go falling in love with a fantasy. That's all this is, a Christmas fantasy. This is not real life.*

They pull into Bradford's and park right in front. Lizzie looks over to the side parking lot which is filled with snow covered Christmas trees for sale, and it couldn't look any prettier or more perfect. *Stop it, Cranberry Harbor and your seductive, magical powers. I will not fall in love with this place again, I will not.* She and Jack had plans to eventually settle here, but those plans were long gone.

After repeating that affirmation to herself as she opens her door to get out of the car, Lizzie stands up, slips on some ice and falls right on her bottom, all thanks to her stupid, weather-inappropriate shoes.

More embarrassed than hurt, she scrambles to get up, still sliding around, when a hand appears to help her up. When she's finally standing she turns to thank the good samaritan, who's still holding her hand. It's Jack. Again. She shakes her head, and thinks, *Darn you Cranberry Harbor, stop messing with me.*

CHAPTER 5

JACK CONTINUED to hold Lizzie's hand until they were safely in a shoveled area of the lot.

"So, we meet again. Are you okay? That was a hard fall, on your–"

Lizzie interrupts him, "Oh, that? Nah, I'm fine. No biggie." She's aware of how awkward she seems. *'No biggie?' What am I, twelve?* "Thank you for the assistance though, I really appreciate it." She doesn't want to think about it, she'd ignored it yesterday, but she can't help noticing how good he looks. California seems to have a way of making people look younger, less pale and wan. Must be all the avocados and sunshine.

Gabby, who hadn't seen the mishap as it happened because she'd been retrieving her reusable shopping bags from the back of the car, comes running over. "Honey, are you okay? Those dumb shoes! Right after this we are getting you some proper footwear."

"I'm fine Mom, really."

"Hey, Dr. Martin, I haven't seen you in forever." Jack gives her a hug, and Gabby looks to Lizzie to see if this is allowed or not.

The three of them stand there, rather awkwardly while it continues to snow, like figures in a really strange snow globe.

"So nice to see you, Jack, how are your folks?" she asks trying to get a read from Lizzie on whether she wants to scoot into the store or chat for a minute.

"They're very well, thank you. They sure miss you though, they say they like the doctor who took over your practice, but that there's no one like you. Heck, you saved my dad's life."

Gabby always gets embarrassed when she hears compliments. "It's what I do, or rather did. I'm so glad they're doing well. Please give them my best, will you?" Still not sure what to do, Gabby turns to head into the store. "I'm going to start shopping honey, I'll see you in there. No hurry. So nice to see you, Jack," she calls as she walks to the doors, glancing back at the two of them as she enters the store.

"You know you could probably sue Tim Bradford if you wanted to for not having shoveled and salted the lot," Jack jokes.

"Yeah, that would be perfect, I can see the headline in the Gazette now, 'Visiting Local Woman Falls in Bradford Parking Lot, Sues For Bruises...To Her Ego.'" There's a silence. The uncomfortable kind. "Well, I should go help my Mom, she's making cookies for I think every man, woman and child in this town. Thank you for helping me up, that was very kind of you–"

Jack interrupts her and steps closer, "Look, I know you probably hate me, and with good reason, but," he hesitates. "... but, you are and always have been one of my favorite people. I miss you."

Lizzie crosses her arms across her chest. If she wasn't so afraid of falling again she might have tapped her foot too. "You have a strange way of showing it, Jack."

"I know, I did not leave well."

"Wow, that's an understatement."

36

"I'd really like to be...friends? Maybe we could meet at Sea Coast while we're both here and talk? I owe you that."

"You owe me a latte?"

"You know what I mean," he smiles at her. "A latte is the very least that I owe you. What do you say? I've missed talking to you so much."

Lizzie didn't know what to do. In a perfect world, a couple breaks up, some time passes and they are able to be friends. Well, sometimes. Other times your heart is so crushed, your dreams for the future so dashed, it's impossible to be friends. But they hadn't talked since Jack had broken their engagement and moved to California, and she did have some things she wanted to say to him, and not in a parking lot having just fallen on her butt. She takes a deep breath, "Okay. I'll meet you, but you might not like what I have to say."

He nods. "I deserve to hear it, and you deserve to say whatever you need to." They stand there awkwardly for at least thirty seconds. "Your number still the same?"

"Yes it is," she says, wondering if this is a good idea. "I'm going to be pretty busy the next couple of days helping Mom bake cookies, but I'm sure I can fit you in somewhere. How long are you here?"

"I'm not sure. It's kind of open ended," he says. "You?"

"Two weeks. Can't wait to head back to Boston," she says, saying this to convince herself as much as she's telling him to cement her departure date with no wiggle room. Wanting him to get the message about the wonderful life she wasn't necessarily having.

"I'll text you in the next couple of days," he says, turning to head to his car. "Don't fall! Okay?" he calls out to her as he gets into his car.

Lizzie shakes her head, looks over to the picture-perfect snow-covered Christmas trees and walks towards the door to the store. "This is all your fault you know, if it wasn't for you I never would have let down my guard," she calls out quietly to the trees and goes to find her mom.

She finally finds her mom who is looking perplexed in the baking aisle.

"That is a very serious face, Dr. Martin, can I help you make a decision?" Lizzie stands next to her mom and stares at the bags of chocolate chip morsels along with her.

Gabby laughs. "I was planning on semi-sweet, but then I saw the dark chocolate, and well, dark chocolate is healthier, and in my opinion, tastier, but lots of people like semi-sweet, and what if people don't like the dark chocolate and–"

"Mom," Lizzie stops her mid-meltdown. "How many bags were you getting?"

"Ten."

Lizzie grabs five semi-sweet and five dark. "We will combine them and everyone will be happy. Okay?" She starts to push the cart. "Next?"

"I think I was preoccupied," Gabby says as they turn down another aisle. "The chocolate chip dilemma - I'm not losing my mind or anything."

Lizzie laughs. "I wasn't worried. I know you're fine."

"It was just so surprising to see you standing there talking to Jack. Are you alright?"

Lizzie throws a bag of cheddar Goldfish crackers into the basket and keeps moving. She turns around, goes back and picks up another one and puts that in too. "Yeah, it was just super embarrassing to fall on my butt and have him of all people see me. You always have a fantasy about when you run into your ex, you know? Now twice in less than 24 hours he's seen me being a total klutz and that's not the impression I want to give, you know?"

Gabby nods, placing dozens of eggs and several boxes of butter into the cart.

"I always imagined when I'd run into him, not that I think about it all the time or anything, but that I'd be in a perfect outfit, holding a book I'd written, and I'd be with Brad Pitt or something."

"No," says Gabby.

"No book? No perfect outfit?"

"No Brad Pitt, he's too old for you." Gabby pauses at the display of holiday cookie decorations at the end of an aisle.

"Fine, then just someone that good looking."

"Are you writing a book?" her mother asks as she puts several containers of red and green sprinkles into the cart.

Lizzie looks confused and then realizes her mom is responding to her fantasy. "Um, no, it's a dream, Mom, no I'm not writing a book."

"Why not? You're as good as anyone else out there."

As they traverse the store Lizzie is growing frustrated, and hungry. She tears open the bag of the Goldfish crackers and begins eating them."Mom," she says, her mouth full of tiny fish crackers, "It's a fantasy. And when would I have the time to write a book anyway? I work full time at the Sentinel." She shoves more crackers into her mouth and gives her mom the universal look for, "Duh!" You know, like a fully realized woman in her thirties does, in the middle of a store while shopping with her highly accomplished mother.

"Let me just look through my list one more time," Gabby says, ignoring Lizzie. "I think we have everything." She's quiet for a moment as she checks off all the items on her typed list. "Okay, I think we're good." She steers the cart to the checkout lane with the shortest line. "And as far as finding the time to write the book you've always wanted to write? Just remember that I had you and Matt, I also managed to run a solo family practice." She shrugs her shoulders. "When something is important to us we find the time one way or another," she says as she starts to unload the cart onto the belt. "Anything else you want, honey?"

Lizzie quietly shakes her head, puts the crackers back in the basket and realizes her mom just very nicely put her very whiny self in her place.

CHAPTER 6

LIZZIE WAS a little nervous about going anywhere else after her display both in and out of Bradfords, but there was no way she could go home without looking for some boots first. She prayed that the St. Sebastian Thrift Shop was not next on Jack's to-do list of errands.

It has been years since Lizzie has been in here, but time seems to have stood still. There were racks of coats, a mountain of handmade hats - the knitters in town had clearly been busy, and tables full of household items - everything from lamps to ladles.

"Good morning, Doc," the older gentleman sitting behind the counter said as they came in.

"Hello, Richard, how's that hip doing?" Gabby asked as she combed through the holiday pins on the counter.

"Good days and not so much. I'm headed to Boston in two-weeks for a replacement with that ortha-whatchamacallit you sent me to last year. Probably should have done it sooner, but whatcha gonna do?"

As Richard and her mom discuss his hip, Lizzie was having fun exploring the store. The boot search would happen eventually, but the table of old toys has pulled her in. She had several, probably too many presents for Sophie, but she loved seeing these old toys from the 1990s. Some millennial must have just come home and cleaned out their closet - there was a Furby, still in its box, a Tamagotchi, and even a Nintendo 64 that had Matt's name written all over it. She had planned to go shopping for him once she got here, and this would be perfect.

"Lizzie," her mom calls, "They've got some really nice L.L. Bean boots over here - size 9, will that work?"

Lizzie snaps out of her 1990s nostalgia and remembers the real reason they're there. "Be right there," she says. She gathers up the Furby, Tamagotchi and Nintendo, and lugs them all over to the counter. "Hi, can I leave these here while I try on some boots?"

"Of course, young lady. You Doc Martin's kid?" he asks as he starts a sales slip for her.

"I am," she says, smiling and extending her hand. "I'm Lizzie Martin, nice to meet you sir."

"I'm Richard Johnson. Nice to meet you too. I'm betting you might know my granddaughter, she's about your age, Alexis?"

"Oh my gosh, yes! We were super close all through school, and then kind of lost touch when she went to South Korea to teach English after college. Is she still there? I never see her on social media."

"She's been all over. She taught in Korea, Spain, and Dubai. She came back about six months ago. She doesn't really like all the Instakarma, Facespace stuff. I can't say I blame her," Richard says.

Lizzie chuckles. "Yeah, Facespace is kind of a timekiller," she says. "When you talk to her next please tell her Lizzie Martin says hi. As a matter of fact, can I give you my number to pass on to her?"

"Certainly, and I'll be seeing her as soon as I get out of here, she's living with Dorrie, my wife, and me."

"Really?! She's back in Cranberry Harbor?" He hands her a pen and paper. "I'm going to be here for a couple of weeks and would love to see her." She writes down her number along with a, 'I'd love to see you!' and hands the paper back to Richard, "Thank you so much."

Lizzie goes over to the shoe area, a mishmash of shoes and boots with no real sense or order.

"I found two pairs," Gabby holds them up - both variations on the classic duck-boot style.

Lizzie points to the navy and brown pair. She sits on the floor, takes off her shoes, slips the boots on and stands up, "Mom? Did you know that guy is Alexis Johnson's grandfather?" she asks as she walks around in the boots giving them a test drive.

"Of course."

Of course she did. After living in Boston it's easy to forget the one to two degrees of separation from everyone in Cranberry Harbor.

"I like these, I think I'll wear them home to be on the safe side," she announces. "These will be perfect." She leans down and looks at the price, five dollars. "How do they make any money here, with prices like this?" She picks up her shoes and tucks them under her arm. "They could charge four times that amount and it would still be a bargain," she says.

Gabby heads to the counter. "They keep the prices low so anyone can shop here, because everyone needs boots. And coats. And well, anything. Your dad and I donate money a few times a year, a lot of us do. It's a service to the community, a place where those who have too much, or more than they need can make sure those who don't are taken care of."

The thought of that gives Lizzie pause, and makes her see how cut off she is from life in a small town, her hometown.

All her items come to a grand total of $20.50, Lizzie gives

Richard $30 and tells him to keep the change. It's the very least she could do, she thinks.

Daisy is excited to see them when they return. Gabby had bought her the coziest of blankets so she was always warm and toasty. She didn't bring her along if she was ever going to be at a stop for more than twenty minutes or so, and never to do errands when it was higher than 75 degrees out. Gabby reaches into the glove compartment and grabs a little treat for the pup, who happily devours it.

"Anyplace else you want to go before we head back for the baking marathon? Gabby asks as she starts the car.

"I know we have to get baking, but do you mind if we take a quick peek at Sea Meadow Beach?"

"Of course not! I love seeing the ocean in the snow too!"

Gabby takes the next left and starts heading towards the beach. "So, is it okay to ask you how it went seeing Jack?" she asks, quickly glancing at her daughter, but not wanting to take her eyes off the snowy road.

Lizzie is quiet for a moment. "You can always ask me anything Mom, whether or not I answer is another thing," she teases. She sighs a deep sigh.

"Oh, it was that good, huh?" her mom teases back.

"No, not bad, not good either...weird. I have finally managed to stop thinking about him every single day. And when I did, I pretty much cast him as this total jerk who just picked up and left Cranberry Harbor, and left me. But the thing is, he's not a jerk. I wouldn't have planned on marrying him if he was. But he left me, and all our plans just died." She looks out the window at the snow falling on the ocean. "It wasn't going to be easy–I had my job in Boston, he was trying to start something here, but we could have made it work." She's quiet again. "It's always felt like he made the decision to completely upend our lives and did it without me. I don't know that I could ever trust him again. Even as a friend."

"I can understand that completely," Gabby says. "I was so angry at him when he broke your engagement, and then just suddenly moved. I always felt like he was part of our family and couldn't believe he'd do that."

"Me either." Lizzie says.

"So what did he say?" Gabby asks.

"He said he misses talking to me, and that he's hoping we could be friends, and he'd like to have coffee to talk to me," Lizzie says, watching a seagull gliding above the shuttered snack bar in the distance.

"Do you see yourself being able to forgive him and be friends?"

"I haven't, no. He ended up not being who I thought he was. The Jack I knew and loved would never have let me down like that, He never tried to reach out before, and that's unforgivable." she says.

Gabby looks at her, starts to say something and stops herself.

"What? What were you going to say? You can say anything to me, Mom," Lizzie says.

"Well, it's not really true that he didn't reach out, he called you again and again and you didn't answer. And then when he tried calling you through your dad and I, you told us to tell him to stop calling," Gabby looks very uncomfortable telling her daughter that her memories are wrong. "He also sent some letters, and you threw them in the fireplace."

"Oh my god, you're right!" Lizzie says. "It still doesn't excuse his leaving, but I guess I blocked that out the more I villainized him."

"You have every right to be angry and hurt, honey, but we all make mistakes, and we all look for forgiveness and hope we get it," Gabby says.

"So you think I should forgive him?"

"I would never tell you what to do, I'd just say think about it." Gabby says.

"They say staying angry at someone is worse for you than them," Lizzie says. "It's not good to hold onto resentments."

"So you think you'll meet up with him?"

"My first thought was no, I want nothing to do with him, but you're right, and I think that I need to tell him how I feel. I never got the chance to do that, I didn't take the opportunity to do that when I wouldn't talk to him. It would be good to clear the air, finally," Lizzie says.

There's only one other car in the lot. The sea is wild, and it looks beautiful as the snow blows all around them. The fences are up, trying their best to guard against the erosion that happens every winter. Cape Cod is such a beautiful and completely fragile place.

"In three years I've gained some perspective and am actually glad we didn't get married. I'm happy I'm not married right now," she says, not very convincingly.

"Good," Gabby says. "It's important to feel good about where your life is. And I'm happy you're good." Gabby turns in her seat to face her. "My and your father's loyalty was and always is to you, I hope you know that."

"I do. And I always know that."

"So how did you leave things?"

"He asked if my number was the same, so we'll see if he even reaches out, but I guess I kind of said I'd meet up. Do you think I'm being stupid?"

"Not at all. And it may make it easier to move on. Or not." Gabby shifts back to facing ahead, "You ready to go?" She puts the car in reverse, ready to back up.

"Whoa, whoa, whoa, you can't just say, 'move on or not,' and head home, Mom! You think I should get back with him? After he broke our engagement and moved across the country?" she says, raising her voice a bit. "Really?"

"I did not say that." Gabby decides this is not a moment to be driving in the snow and puts the car back in park. "I'm just saying life is not black and white, and you never know."

"What I do know is I was ready to spend the rest of my life with him and he bailed. End of story."

"I was only thinking about you moving on, that's all," Gabby says.

Lizzie is a little sullen. "I've moved on. Sort of. Moved on...ish." She hates it when her mom is right. Why is she always so calm and rational? The petulant teen in her who could apparently still be poked by her parents was calming down. "Fine," she says, the grumpy teen in her starting to retreat.

"Ha! I love that at your age I can still evoke an angry, 'Fine!' from you. Makes me feel young." They both laugh.

"I'll agree to meet with him, and I will listen and tell him how I feel. Okay?"

"Hey, I have no dog in this fight, no offense Miss Daisy, " Gabby says looking in the rearview mirror at her happy little dog. "Your happiness is all I care about."

"I know." As they head home to start baking a mountain of cookies, Lizzie looks out at the snowy landscape and wonders when *was* the last time she felt truly happy? It had been a while, that's for sure, but one thing she is sure of–Jack Cahoon was never, ever going to have the chance to make her unhappy again.

CHAPTER 7

THE FIRST TIME Lizzie had made Christmas cookies with her mom was when she was three. She didn't have any clear memory of it, but this tale was now the stuff of family lore. The story went that after insisting on breaking the eggs by herself, and being denied, she'd grabbed the carton and ran toward the dining room, tripping over Misty, their golden retriever, falling flat on the eggs, breaking them all covering herself and the dog with a sticky, gooey mess. Her mother sat down on the floor amongst the wreckage and explained to her that she would have done the eggs *with* her, but she ran off without listening, and well, look what happened. She had a little bit of history with impulsivity, never anything terrible, but she was passionate and strong-willed, something her parents always encouraged, and she'd learned how to rein in when needed.

"How do you want to do this, Mom?" Lizzie asks as she assembles the ingredients on the large kitchen island. Lizzie loved her parent's kitchen. They had redone it several years ago and it was everything Lizzie would have wanted in her own dream kitchen. For years it had been the original farmhouse design with too little storage and too little space. It had been a major renovation sparked, Gabby openly admitted, by watching Nancy Meyers' movies like *Something's Gotta Give* and *The Holiday*, with their sumptuous, open, dreamy spaces where families gathered and things always ended well. "Should I do the chocolate chip and you do the sugar cookies and then we can both frost and decorate those? Or did you have another idea? You've always been better at the rolling out than me, you're more patient!"

"That's fine, honey, I am happy to roll away."

Gabby takes her phone out of her pocket and syncs it up to the Bluetooth speakers and suddenly they are surrounded by Christmas music. Then, with a click of a remote, she turns on the gas fireplace in the corner of the kitchen, part of the renovation as well, setting a blissful stage.

"Okay, I want to know how you arranged all this, Mom. Cookies, snow, Christmas music...you must have put in an order for this day. I get it, Christmas in Cranberry Harbor is pretty perfect," she laughs as she carefully measures brown and white sugars, and expertly cracks the eggs.

"The snow really puts it over the top, doesn't it?" Gabby says, looking out the French doors that line the back wall of the kitchen as the snow accumulates on the patio. "Too much?" she laughs.

"No, it's perfect." Lizzie adds the butter to the mix, and while that's combining, grabs another bowl and mixes up the two kinds of chocolate. "I think this is kind of a genius idea," she says as she adds them to the batter. "This will be our new thing, the difference that sets the Martin's cookies apart from everyone else - semi-sweet, dark chocolate cookies will be our special brand."

Hours later they're making great progress with their trays and trays of cookies when Peter comes running in from outside, slipping a little with his snowy boots.

CHRISTMAS IN CRANBERRY HARBOR

"Honey, take your boots off, okay? You're getting snow and water all over the floor!" Gabby pleads, mid-cookie cutting.

"Oh, sorry!" He rushes back to the door and slips off his boots. "I left a notebook here I need, and Stan's off helping put up Christmas lights at town hall, and I have to get to the fire station to take photos for the story he wrote about the toy drive for the festival, then meet the chair of the festival committee to interview them and get the schedule of events double checked..."

"Dad, can you take a break for a minute? You look so stressed, let me make you some tea, maybe a sandwich or something," Lizzie says. "It's not healthy to run around like this every day." Without waiting for an answer she pulls out a stool at the island where they're working and points to it.

"Lizzie's right, honey, you need to take a break." She fills the electric kettle, gets out some tea and a mug. Peter goes to reach for a warm cookie and Gabby slaps his hand. "Uh huh, not until you have something healthy. I'm going to heat up some of last night's dinner for you, then you can have a cookie."

"Yes, ma'am," he jokes, saluting her.

The water is boiling in no time, "Mom, you want some tea, too?" Lizzie walks over and turns it off. "I'm going to have some." Gabby nods as she prepares Peter's lunch, and Lizzie takes out two more mugs and drops a tea bag in each.

"So Dad, is it like this every single day?" She slides a mug of tea over to him and he blows on it.

"Not always, I mean, it's always a lot, but the festival puts a lot of pressure on us. It's like summer, but it's only a few issues of the paper where it's this intense. The couple of issues leading up to it, doing all the press, and then the week of. The difference is we're doing it without the college interns we have in the summer."

Lizzie dunks a tea bag in her mug, Gabby continues to roll and cut her cookies while Lizzie waits for a batch in the oven.

"So you still get interns? You mean people still actually want to go into journalism? I'm shocked," she laughs.

"Believe it or not, yeah. Most have dreams of being famous authors, or writing for the Washington Post or New York Times, but no one wants to do what we're doing, covering a small town in an independent weekly. It's a dying newspaper model, that's for sure."

"I don't know of a model that isn't in crisis, Dad, it's not just you. We used to have one of the busiest newsrooms in the country, and the company that bought us just keeps laying off more and more people. We have a managing editor, no senior editor, and all but two copy editors are gone, along with three quarters of the sports department and one person in arts and lifestyle. It's so sad."

The microwave beeps, and Gabby takes out the yummy smelling plate and hands it to Peter along with a fork and napkin. "Eat this sweetie, relax for a minute. Doctor's orders."

"She may have retired, Lizzie, but she's in charge of me and my health. Yes, dear." he smiles and takes a bite.

"Good," Lizzie says, "We want you healthy and around for a really long time." She takes a sheet of cookies out of the oven, places them on the island, picks up a spatula and begins to place them on one of the wire cooling racks.

Lizzie is pensive as she finishes that task and begins filling up the sheet again with rounded spoonfuls of dough. "Dad?" she pauses nervously. "I know you get offers all the time for the paper, do you ever think-"

"No way!" he loudly interrupts her, holding up his hand for emphasis. "Sorry, I don't mean to snap at you. It's just you know as well as I do what will happen. They won't hire any reporters, they'll run stories from their other papers, not even the other papers around here, it could be a story from Kansas for goodness sake, stories that have nothing to do with the Cape, with Cranberry Harbor, with our community." He puts his fork down and takes a deep breath. "We have incredible things happening here, and we have really challenging things happening here, but you have to actually *be* here to see it. You have to know the community and care to tell the stories and help implement change."

"I hear you Dad, but I just can't help but wonder how much of this is tilting at windmills and fighting the inevitable."

"Your dad has been fighting for what he thinks is right ever since I met him, honey. He's not about to change now," Gabby says, knowing he won't ever give up.

"How is it going, financially?" Lizzie nervously asks.

"It's never been a big money maker. You know that, Lizzie. Your Mom is the one who really supported this family. Smart move on my part, marrying a doctor," he says smiling at his wife. "And she can make a mean fake pot roast to boot," he says, finishing the last of his lunch. "I really do have to get back." He stands up, takes his plate to the sink and runs some water on it.

"Just leave it, sweetheart, I'll get it, I know you have to go." Peter comes over and hugs her.

"How did I ever get so lucky?" he kisses her on the cheek, and then hugs Lizzie. "It is so damn good to see you here with your Mom, I almost can't stand how happy I feel," he beams.

"Me too, Dad," she says as she kisses him on the cheek.

He walks over to the bench where they keep their shoes and slips his boots on. "I will see you two later," he says and opens the door.

"Dad, I don't mean to–"

"Honey, I get it, you didn't say anything I don't think every single day, I know everything you say is said with love and care, and I appreciate that. I'm just a stubborn old coot who can't let the corporate world win and take over what I've worked at for over thirty years. Not yet anyway." His cell rings, he takes it out of his pocket. "How'd that happen? But he's okay?" Lizzie and Gabby look over at him as he's listening to whoever is calling.

"Okay, so Maggie's with him?" More silence. "Well thanks for letting me know, I'll go to the hospital later to see him. Thanks, John." He ends the call and puts his phone in his pocket.

"What happened? It must be Stan, you mentioned Maggie, is he okay?" asks a very worried Gabby.

"Yeah, he's fine, but he broke his arm. He was helping put up the Christmas lights at Town Hall, the ladder slipped in the snow and he fell. Luckily a couple of guys from the fire station were there too so they checked him out and got him to the ER." He's standing there looking stunned.

"I'm so glad he's okay," Lizzie says feeling relieved that it wasn't her brother falling off a roof or something.

"Yeah, apparently he might need surgery to set it," Lizzie and Gabby could see his wheels were turning. "He's going to be laid up for a while."

"Dad? What's going on? He's going to be okay, right?"

"Yeah, yeah, John was certain of it. He didn't hit his head, he fell on the soft snow, he just landed wrong on his arm."

"So what's going through your head?" she asks.

"I have no idea how I can run this paper by myself for the next two weeks through the festival. He had a bunch of stories due, it's going to set us back. He won't be able to type, or take notes, it's his right arm. I'm in big trouble."

Lizzie reflects for a minute, not sure about what she's going to offer, but knows she has to help.

"I'll step in, Dad. I can write some stories, I'd really like to help you," she says.

"Oh honey, I can't ask you to do that. It's your vacation."

"You didn't ask me Dad, I offered. There's nothing I'd rather be doing than helping you. I mean it."

"You're sure? You're really sure?" he says, quietly relieved.

"I'm really, really, sure." she says, taking off her apron. "Looks like I have got to go, Mom, are you good here? The last batch of the chocolate chip are in the bottom oven. I hate leaving you to wrap them and clean up, if you can wait until I get back - "

"Stop it! You two go. I've got this," Gabby says.

"I've got my laptop upstairs, Dad, and some reporter's note-books, I'll be right down."

Lizzie runs upstairs and Gabby walks over to give Peter a hug. "It's going to be okay. You've got an award winning journalist on the job now," she jokes. "I'm just relieved Stan is going to be okay."

"Me too," he says. "That really gave me a scare." He pauses for a moment. "Do you think–"

"Don't go hoping she's going to want to stay. Enjoy having her here right now, okay?"

"You're right. I know you're right, but a guy can dream. Maybe with her help I could keep this thing afloat, I'm not so sure otherwise." Lizzie comes running down the stairs. "You all set, honey?"

"Yup! I am good to go. Let's go tell some local stories!" she says, slipping on her coat.

CHAPTER 8

"Okay, so when we get back to the office we can divvy up the stories and I can figure out what Stan's already filed, and where we're at," Peter says as they drive toward town. He pauses, "I'm pretty sure he has his password written down on his desk blotter so I can get into his files."

"Desk blotter?" Lizzie laughs. "We're really going old-school, huh?"

"Stan is nothing but old-school. You have no idea what it was like getting him to switch from a typewriter to computer. Now he loves it, it's pretty funny." He grows quiet as they drive along a very snowy Main Street. "When I got that call, I couldn't help but think-"

Lizzie puts her hand on his arm. "I know Dad, you guys have been a team for a long time. But the good news is, he's fine. He may not be writing for a little bit, but he'll soon be back sitting across from you. Oh! Maybe he can dictate his stories, there's lots of tools for that, I can help you figure out what would be the most user friendly."

"Yeah, that would be great, thank you," he looks over at her,

"But for now I've got one of the best writers I know working for me, so I'm not complaining."

They pull into the little group of offices housed in a Cape-style building right on Main Street. Lizzie gets out and thinks back to practically growing up in this building. When she was in middle and high school, and college too, she wrote stories and columns for the paper. She hadn't had a byline in the Gazette since the last summer she'd lived there, right after graduating from college.

They quickly get themselves situated at the antique partners desk Peter and Stan have been using since they began the paper well over thirty years ago. When she was little, Lizzie often fantasized about growing up and working across from her dad, just like this. She'd never had any interest in medicine, and Gabby had never pressured her. She and Matt had been raised to find what they loved to do and create a career around that. Matt had been passionate about the environment and climate change since, well, forever. He was always charting weather patterns and temperature changes around the world. Everyone, including his teachers figured he'd head off to be a meteorologist, climate activist or scientist. He'd surprised everyone, even himself, by coming back home after college. He loved the Cape, and nothing meant more to him than trying to save it from climate change.

Lizzie on the other hand was never without a book, some paper and a pen, and later, a computer. She was so much like her dad. Infinitely curious about people, their stories and how to share them with others. After she received her Master's in journalism at Boston University, she stayed there. She liked Boston–not too big, not too small.

When she was hired at the Sentinel it was as a features writer, which is what she loved. But now with so many reporters gone, feature stories were often grabbed from the wire, and she was more often relegated to news, something she didn't feel competent at, nor was it her passion. Just reporting on the who, what, when, where and why didn't satisfy her desire to go deeper, to get to know people. The 'going deeper in' stories were why she had become a writer.

"Okay, so new to the festival is storytelling at Tall Tale Books, I don't think you've met the new owners, Anika and Jay Patel. They're wonderful, they had a great idea to have older kids telling stories to younger kids and I think it's going to be great."

Lizzie starts making a list. "How many words are you looking at for these stories? 500? 800?"

"These can be pretty quick hits, yeah, anywhere in that range. And if you could take a couple of pictures for each one that would be great. We lost the money for a photographer years ago. Thank goodness for smartphones."

"Got it. What else?"

Peter is looking through his notes. "Hmm, I see another story Stan didn't get to yet, he was going to talk to Leah Alden over at - "

"Sea Coast, yeah. Hope's granddaughter. What's the angle on that one?" she asks, writing down some notes.

"She's pretty much taken over running the business side of the shop, and she's really involved in climate change efforts," he says.

"So how does this tie in with the festival?" she asks, wanting to know what this story is about.

Peter laughs, "Yeah, that would be good to know, huh? She brought forth a proposal to make sure that nothing being used to decorate the town was single use. Everything could either be used again next year, turned into mulch, or would naturally biodegrade."

"Wow, that's very cool," Lizzie says, writing all this down. "I keep saying it's going to be this younger generation that's going to save the world."

"Ha! Listen to you, you're only 32 yourself!" her dad jokes. "It's not like you're old, honey."

"No, but this generation, they have people like Greta Thunberg blazing a trail. When I was 17, 18-years-old I certainly wasn't protesting climate change and doing anything to help change the world. I was worried about whether some boy liked me, or what college I was going to."

"Do not sell yourself short, you were writing about housing issues here all the way back in high school, remember?" Peter says, organizing some papers on his desk.

"I guess, but I wasn't doing anything big," she says.

"Every change that happens starts somewhere," he boots up his computer. "Anyway, if you could do those two stories today that would be a huge help.

"Got it. I'll start with these and then report back."

"Sounds good." He's a bit distracted looking at his screen.

"Dad?"

"Sorry, I'm just looking at where we've got other holes for this week's issue."

She stands up and gets ready to head out, "Well consider these two filled, and I can do as many more as you need."

Peter takes a relieved breath and sighs. "Thank you honey, you have no idea how much you're helping me."

"It's kind of helping me too," she says, putting on her coat. "I wasn't feeling too Christmasy before I came back here, but I think between making cookies and doing this I'm finally starting to feel like it's Christmas. So thank you!" She pulls on her hat and heads toward the door. "I'm going to walk over to Tall Tales and talk to the Patels, and then I'll go to Sea Coast and talk to Leah. Do you want me to grab you something when I come back?"

"I think I'm good, sweetie, thanks, but I'll text you if I change my mind."

"Okeedokey, love you!"

"Love you too."

The book store was just around the corner, and Lizzie was happy to get out and get some fresh air. Everything looked so beautiful covered in the freshly dropped snow that had finally stopped. It definitely gave everything an extra dose of holiday cheer. She was enjoying her new boots as she confidently strode the sidewalk. Best five dollars she'd spent in a while.

When she arrived at Tall Tales she put her notebook and pen down on the freshly shoveled steps, and moved back to take a photo. She'd invested in the phone with the best rated camera when the Sentinel started asking all the reporters to take their own photos. It was well worth the extra $10 a month on her bill.

She gathered up her things and walked into the store. It looked very different from the last time she'd been in, but still had the same cozy and inviting feel with lots of warm woods, and little white lights wrapped around the rafters, and there was even a real Christmas tree in the middle of the shop.

"Can I help you?" a man, who she assumes must be Jay. asks from behind the counter.

"Hi, I'm Lizzie Martin," she says, extending her hand. "I'm writing a story for the Gazette about your storytelling event for the festival? Is this a good time? I promise not to bother you for long."

"Hey, I'm Jay Patel," he pauses for a moment, "Wait, are you Peter's daughter? The one he's always talking about?"

"As hard as I try to break him of that habit," she shakes her head in embarrassment. "Yes, that would be me. Sorry about that."

"Stop, your dad is awesome. I'm a dad too. It comes with the territory, I'm afraid. My wife is the one who's the force behind the event. Let me get her from the back, hold on."

While Jay goes to find his wife, Lizzie takes the opportunity to browse around her former workplace. The shelves had all been upgraded, and she can see the children's section has expanded and is full of new and diverse titles. The section for local authors has also grown, carrying classics from the past and present. Cape Cod is very famous for its writers and artists of all types.

"Hi, I'm Anika Patel," she hears from behind her as she's thumbing through a book about cats she thinks Sophie might like.

"Hi!" Lizzie puts the book back on the shelf. She turns and shakes her hand. "I'm Lizzie Martin, are you sure you have a few minutes now? I could always come later if this isn't a good time."

"No, this is fine. Weirdly there seems to be a lull almost every day around 2. We have yet to figure out why, but you can practically set your watch to it." She motions Lizzie over to a cozy reading area with overstuffed chairs near the counter. "This okay?" Lizzie nods and sits down.

"This is perfect. I promise I'll be quick."

"No hurry! We love the Gazette, your dad and Stan have been so good to us. They've covered anything we've done since we took over, from our grand opening to signings, to the story slam we host once a month."

"Wow, that's so cool, you have a monthly story slam? How did my parents not tell me this?" She's taking notes.

"Your dad is actually a regular storyteller. He's got a lot of stories," Anika laughs.

"Well, this is news to me, I am going to have to find out more." Putting on her reporter hat, she switches gears. "When did you and Jay take over the store?"

"About a year and a half ago. It was completely by the seat of our pants, but we're learning!"

"What were you both doing before?"

Anika sits back. "Well, Jay is, or was, I guess, an attorney, we lived in D.C. He worked in government, and I worked for a nonprofit that was focused on supporting community efforts to bring awareness and problem solving around climate change."

"Wow, and you left all that to come here and run a bookstore?" Lizzie is intrigued.

"The thing was, we knew we were doing good things, but we had no quality of life. We hardly saw each other, and we had two kids who were growing up and we were missing it. We figured we'll have time to get involved with bigger projects when they are a little older, and we hope to do some things for the community here, now that we're more settled, but we wanted balance. Which probably sounds very hokey," she laughs.

"No, quite the contrary, it sounds very smart and well, conscious." She's quickly writing everything down. "How old are your kids, and were they okay with the move?"

"They're 9 and 12 now, and they were nervous about leaving their friends and school, but we'd vacationed here many times and they loved it, so it was a pretty easy sell," she smiles. "And even though we're busy, it's our business, so if there's a school event we close for an hour, and they come here after school when they don't have sports, band or theater. We're really happy."

"I don't blame you, it sounds like you've created a great life for all of you. So is this your first time participating in the festival?"

"Yeah, last year we were still so new, other than handing out cookies and discount coupons we didn't do much. This event was actually my daughter Neve's idea."

"Tell me more," Lizzie says.

"She comes sometimes to the story slam and she had the idea of doing one for kids telling stories to other kids, and we thought it was perfect. She came up with the theme of 'Your Biggest Christmas Surprise,' and recruited story tellers at school."

"She sounds very creative! How many storytellers will there be?"

"There are eight of them that will be taking turns telling stories to a new batch of little kids over a couple of hours. There is one very important rule that they all must adhere to though…"

"And what is that?"

"They can't say anything that would lead any child to doubt their belief in Santa Claus," Anika says very seriously.

Lizzie smiles as she writes that down. "Good rule, no spoilers."

"I don't want to be responsible for ruining a child believing in Santa!"

"No, never," Lizzie concurs. "Well this is perfect, you've given me plenty to work with. Just one last thing, why did you and Jay want to be part of the festival this year?"

Anika pauses for a moment. "We have grown to love this community so much, and they have supported our business and us as we started a new life here. I guess it's partly a way to say thank you, and to also give back when so much has been given to us."

"Perfect. After all these years I always know the perfect end quote when I hear it, and that was it." Lizzie stands up, "I can't thank you enough for your time, it's such a pleasure to talk to you. I will have to make it down for one of your story slams. I am extremely curious to hear my dad!" She puts her coat back on, and gets ready to leave.

"Well, if you're still here we're doing one on New Year's Eve for the folks who like a mellower event to go to."

Lizzie buttons her coat, "Darn! I will be back in Boston then, but maybe next time!"

"For sure, I hope you come in again while you're here," Anika says as she walks her toward the door.

Jay calls over, "Yes! Please come back, I'm sorry I got stuck over here with a cranky computer."

"Definitely, you have not seen the last of me. Oh! Can I just take a quick photo of you two?"

"Of course," Anika says. Jay comes over and puts his arm around his wife.

"Perfect," Lizzie says after clicking a few. "Thank you again, I'll see you soon."

She walks outside into the cold air and feels happy, that unfamiliar feeling, again. Being around good people doing good things has a special kind of magic that's contagious. Walking toward Sea Coast Coffee in her own little happy bubble, she wants to keep that feeling going. The best way she knew to do that was a Sea Coast latte. She texts her dad

Stopping at Sea Coast, want anything? Oh! I loved the Patels!

She sees the three dots lingering in the cloud on her phone.

Nope, thanks honey, I'm good. I knew you would! See you soon.

She puts her phone in her pocket, walks towards the coffee shop and sees Jack standing outside looking toward her smiling. Before she can think, she smiles back. Damn it.

CHAPTER 9

"FANCY RUNNING INTO YOU, HERE," Jack holds the door for her and motions for her to go in. He takes off his jacket and puts it on the back of a chair, "Do you have time to hang out for a few minutes?" he asks. "Whatever you want, I've got it."

Lizzie wonders if the next two weeks are going to be a sea of endless run-ins with Jack. She was suddenly missing the anonymity of living in Boston. She'd forgotten how small this place was. It was good in some ways–locals were always helping each other out–but the downside was there were no secrets and no privacy.

"Thanks, but I can't, I'm here for work," she says not wanting to stand here too long talking to him.

"Is the Boston Sentinel doing a story about Cranberry Harbor?" he asks, curious.

"Oh, no, I'm helping my dad," she wants to just get away but finds herself explaining the broken arm situation.

"That's so nice of you to help him, I'm sure he really appreciates it," he says. "Are you sure I can't get you a coffee or something? Even when you're working you need coffee, especially when you're working. I know you."

She's not taking the bait of him knowing her so well, and being charmed by it. "No, really, I'm good, thanks though," she turns to go find Leah.

"Okay, maybe another time, I'll text you," he says, getting in line to get his coffee, then turning to watch her go.

Lizzie pokes her head in the doorway to the back of the shop where all the baking magic happens. "Leah?" she calls out.

"Just a minute," a young voice calls back. "Be right there."

Lizzie leans against the doorframe thinking about how she can avoid seeing Jack for the rest of the time she's home and thinks it's pretty impossible unless she just stays at her parent's house and never leaves. Leah emerges, drying her hands on a towel.

"Oh my gosh, Lizzie! I didn't know it was you!" Leah gives her a big hug. "What are you doing here? I mean not in Cranberry Harbor, but here, now?"

"Well, you may have heard, since Sea Coast is the nerve center of the town, that Stan fell and broke his arm," she says.

"I did hear that. My grandma took some muffins and coffee to them. I was so sorry to hear that. So what can I do for you?"

"Well, I'm helping my dad out by doing some stories for the paper, and he said that you had been very involved in trying to make the festival more eco-friendly. Would you have a couple of minutes to give me the basics of what you're doing?"

Leah glances back at the kitchen, "Yeah, I don't have too long, but if we can be quick." They walk over to an empty table and sit down. "I don't mean to be difficult or anything, it's just with the holidays and people taking time off, it's a little crazy. I have a hard enough time getting enough help, never mind at Christmas."

Lizzie has taken out a notebook and pen. "My brother was

filling me in a bit about the lack of help, he's having a really hard time."

"It's all so interconnected - the lack of affordable housing, and I'm not even talking affordable with a big A, just housing normal, working people can afford is getting more and more rare. So, that means fewer families. This used to be a perfect after-school, first-time job but there are fewer and fewer teenagers around here," Leah says, sitting back and taking a deep breath. "If my family didn't live here I wouldn't be able to."

"I've been off-Cape since I graduated from college. I knew it was bad, but I didn't realize quite how bad," Lizzie says.

"It's really reaching a crisis point," Leah says. "Something has to change. Someone has to come up with some innovative ideas or no working people will be able to live here. Ugh, I'm so sorry, I didn't mean to go off on that. That's not what you came here to talk to me about!"

"Don't apologize! This is an important subject and after the festival I think I may want to talk to you again and get more into this. But yeah, for now, tell me what is happening with the festival," she says, pen poised to start writing.

"Well, first of all, all plastic is banned from drinking bottles to forks, spoons, decorations," she says.

"Was that a hard sell to the other businesses and vendors?" Lizzie asks.

"Not really, we've been edging more and more toward no plastic for a while. And most restaurants who do takeout switched to compostable containers, bamboo cutlery, things like that," Leah says.

"And what about decorations?"

"More businesses are decorating with living trees that will be planted after the holidays, and they are using decorations that will be able to be used year after year, and we're doing a big push to shop local and convince people to not shop online but to support local businesses."

"That seems like a lot to try to control!" Lizzie says, writing everything down.

"It is!" Leah laughs. "I'm very passionate about not throwing decorations away, wrapping paper too, and I especially want to encourage people to shop locally. It's hard. People love sitting at home in their jammies with their laptop clicking and putting all their gifts in their shopping cart. But we've got some tricks up our sleeves," she teases.

"Oh yeah?" Lizzie smiles back.

"Yes, we're having raffles, giveaways, contests, people can win gift certificates, and lots of businesses are offering free shipping for gifts you need to send. Oh! And everyone is using lights that use lots less energy and the lights used in the town square, thanks to your brother, are all solar, with battery backup in case we have a dark and stormy stretch."

"You seem to have thought of everything," Lizzie says.

"Hardly, I know we could do so much more, but it's baby steps, you know? Introducing people here to be thinking in terms of not throwing things away and being proactive about promoting ourselves in a conscious way is a lot. Too many people just think they can't compete with the big online options and don't even try. Getting more businesses to have a social media presence is a big part of getting people to know they're here and show them the amazing gifts they can find locally."

"Leah, I am so impressed at your commitment to Cranberry Harbor, and the planet. This town is very lucky to have you," Lizzie says, feeling very sentimental about her hometown. "With involved and committed people like you I actually have hope that things can get better here."

"Aw, you're too nice," Leah says, blushing. "I love it here, and it makes me so sad that there are so few people my age in town. This community can't survive without young adults to work, and who wants to live somewhere with no young families?"

"It wouldn't be the Cape I grew up on, that's for sure." She hesitates to ask her something personal, but decides to. "This isn't for the story, but I just wondered…" she pauses.

"You can ask me anything, Lizzie, I've known you my whole life," Leah says.

"Do you get lonely being here? Do you feel like you're missing out on having friends, a social life?" Lizzie shakes her head in embarrassment. "Ugh, I just made so many assumptions there, I'm sorry."

"No! Don't apologize, you're actually one of the few people who has asked me that and I honestly appreciate it. It's like you see me, and what it's like to live in a town where the median age is 65."

"Okay, I just didn't want to overstep and seem like I was prying. I guess I was partly asking because, I don't know, I've sometimes wondered what it would be like to live here. My parents certainly want me to!" They both laugh. "So I just wondered if the reality matched what I have always imagined."

"And what have you imagined?" Leah asks, raising a brow.

"That in the summer it would be lots of bros from off-Cape maybe looking to go out with a local girl or woman, and then they're gone. And in the off-season, it's desolate and all the guys my age are either married or single for a very good reason." Again, they both laugh.

"Yeah, that pretty well sums it up." She's quiet for a minute. "But, my Grandma Hope always says it only takes one special person. One might not be too hard to come by, right? At least that's what I tell myself."

"That's a very good point, Hope is very wise," Lizzie agrees.

"You live in Boston, has it been easy to find love there?" Leah asks, tilting her head inquisitively.

"Good point! The answer to that question would be no," Lizzie answers.

Leah shrugs her shoulders, "I think when it's supposed to

happen it does, and you just have to be smart enough to recognize it when it appears."

She may be very young, but she's pretty wise, Lizzie thinks. She wonders if she'd recognize love herself if it showed up. She's been pretty closed off these last three years. She shakes herself out of her thoughts, and aware that Leah has a lot to do, starts to gather up her things.

"Thank you so much for your time, and for all you're doing. I meant it that I said I want to talk to my dad about doing a story about the future of Cranberry Harbor. Something is going to have to change, people need to get involved or the town we love will be gone."

They both stand up. "I'd love that," says Leah, giving Lizzie a hug. "I'll be here! After the festival, come by. I can introduce you to some other people who are involved too. I've talked to Jack Cahoon a bit, he seems interested in helping too. You know him, right?"

There is truly no escaping him. "Yup, I do," Lizzie says, nodding.

"He's got all the tech knowledge and his getting involved could be a game changer," Leah says. "Like he wants to help create a unified app for all the restaurants so people have one user-friendly place to go to order take out in town. Amazing!"

"Good to know. I'll have to talk to him about that," Lizzie says, putting on her coat. "We will be in touch! I'm sure I will see you when I make my daily stop here while I'm home."

"I look forward to it!" Leah says, heading back to the kitchen.

Lizzie pushes open the door and starts walking back to the Gazette office. Looking around at the town as she walks she feels a sadness that the town she grew up in, where her family lives, is at risk. She has to admit that she hasn't given it much thought before and feels horrible that she's been blind. But maybe in a small way she can help by shining a light on what is going on. It might not be a lot, but it's a start.

It's getting dark as she starts walking back to the Gazette, hoping her dad is still there to give her a ride home. When she spies his car in his space she's relieved.

"Hey Dad," she says to him, still writing away. "Have you gotten up since I left two hours ago?" she asks. "You know they say sitting is the new smoking. Maybe you should get a standing desk?"

He waves her off. "No way, I need to sit and ponder, I could never write standing up."

"It was just a thought, I know better than to push," she says, walking around the desk to see what he's working on. "How are things coming?" she asks, looking at the screen.

"Good, I think? It might be a little light this week, but what we lack in editorial will be made up for in holiday ads, so it should look okay."

"I'll write these stories up tonight and email them to you so they're here in the morning." She's feeling hungry but doesn't want to push her dad to leave. "Um, so I was wondering how long you might be?"

"Oh gosh, I forgot completely that you don't have your car here," he stands up. "I have a bit more to do but I'll run you home and come back."

"I hate for you to do that, Dad, I could come back and get you when you're done," she says.

"No, see? I'm standing up! Consider this my exercise," he jokes as he slips on his jacket.

"Dad," Lizzie says, as they walk out the door, "driving a car three miles down the road is hardly a workout."

"I know, I know, but at least I am getting some fresh air," he says as they each get in the car.

"I won't push you today, but sometime this week we're going for a walk, okay?" Lizzie says, fastening her seatbelt.

"Deal," he says, starting the car and backing up. "Just don't give your mom any more ideas, okay? Jackfruit pot roast, veggie burgers and tofu are quite enough to be dealing with, thank you very much," he looks at her and smiles.

"Deal. My lips are sealed." As they drive this very familiar route Lizzie can't help but keep thinking about her conversation with Leah. "I really enjoyed talking to Leah, Dad, and I was thinking, after the festival I'd like to write something along with her about what's happening here with jobs, housing, the environment, would you be up for that?"

"Most definitely!" he says, turning onto their street. "Those are the kinds of in-depth stories I want to do more of, but with just Stan and me it never happens. I'd be thrilled to have you do it, thank you, honey."

"I miss writing stories that matter, they have me writing these news snippets, I hardly ever get more than 600 words which is not nearly enough space to write anything of any importance," she says.

Peter pulls into their driveway. "I know, it's horrible what's happening," he says, putting the car in park. "Okay, tell your mom I will be home a bit later," he leans over and gives her a kiss on the cheek. "I love getting to work with you," he says.

"It is fun, I will say that," she says getting out of the car. "See you soon," she says, closing the door and heading to the house, which she has to admit feels a lot more like home right now than Boston does.

CHAPTER 10

LIZZIE IS EXCITED when she steps in the front door to see that Sophie has come to visit. She hasn't even taken off her coat or put anything down when Sophie comes running over, crashing into Lizzie and grabbing her legs.

"Aunt Wiz! You're finally here!" she keeps squeezing Lizzie's legs, making it impossible to walk. Lizzie laughs and picks the toddler up and hugs her.

"Oh my gosh, this is the best surprise ever!" She spins the giggling little girl around and around, kissing her rosy cheeks over and over. "I thought we were coming to your house for dinner? Did you eat already?"

"Nope, Mommy and Daddy had work 'mergenices, so I came here. Grabby told me we were waiting for you. So now we can eat. I am so hungry." She squirms out of Lizzie's arms and runs into the kitchen.

If Lizzie thought she'd lost the Sophie-name lottery with being Aunt Wiz, her mother wasn't far behind with Grabby. Something Sophie had created herself combining Grandma and Gabby which she had heard so many people calling her.

"Mom, I'm home," she says, rounding the corner into the

kitchen. "Something smells very good." She's stopped in her tracks by the mountain of Christmas cookies all wrapped in eco-friendly bags and tied with festive, and reusable, ribbons. "How did you get all this done, babysit for this one, and make dinner? And why did I not get those genes from you?" she asks, lifting Sophie onto a stool at the counter.

"She's only been here an hour or so. I've developed a system wrapping the cookies over the years, and got into a rhythm with it, and I'd already prepped a soup to make in the instant pot for tomorrow night, and I had some bread I made last week in the freezer, so I think we're all good!" She goes over to the stool where Sophie is busy trying to count the bags of cookies, and squeezes her. "And Miss Sophie and I got to play out in the snow for a while and took Daisy for a little walk."

"I'm exhausted just hearing about it!" Lizzie says.

"How was your day?" Gabby asks as the instant pot begins to hiss, releasing steam. She goes over and makes sure the valve is clear. "Where'd you go? What'd you do?" Who'd you see?" Gabby is teasing her as she peppers her with questions while monitoring the noise as the instant pot decompresses.

"Well, I went to Tall Tales, and met the Patels, who were lovely, I love what they've done with the store–and then I went to Sea Coast and interviewed Leah Alden about the festival," she says, sitting down on a stool next to Sophie.

"So where are Matt and Shannon? And hey, wasn't this supposed to be Taco Tuesday on Thursday night at their house?" Lizzie asks.

"They both got stuck with work and festival projects, so I said I'd do it. It's not a big deal."

"Well they sure are lucky to have you."

"We sure are!" says Shannon, Sophie jumps down and runs to her mom.

"Mommy!"

Shannon swoops her up, and gives Lizzie a hug. "Group hug!" says Sophie.

Shannon puts her down and takes off her coat. "Gabby, I can't thank you enough."

"You know I'm always happy to spend time with this peanut," she says. "Did you get everything done you needed to?"

"Not exactly...I was wondering, Lizzie, if you'd like to help me with something after dinner? It shouldn't take too long."

"Sure, I have to write some stories for my dad, but if it's pretty quick I can help."

"I had this crazy idea for the kids to make little reindeers with candy canes, using pipe cleaners and little googly eyes, but the head librarian said there's not enough time and just wants us to read Christmas stories with them, and have Santa pass these out, so now I'm going to make them."

Shannon, who looks completely overwhelmed, shows Lizzie a picture of the project on her phone–very cute little reindeer, with pipe cleaner antlers, little googly eyes and a piece of red candy for a nose. "I've got all the supplies," she lifts up a big canvas tote.

"Okay, let's set up a little assembly line on the island," Lizzie says, moving the mountain of cookies aside. "How many do you need to make?"

"Well, I bought materials for 400?"

Lizzie is a little taken aback,"Okay, we'd better get started then!" she says plugging in the two hot glue guns she found in the bag.

"What about dinner?" Gabby asks. "Want to just have your soup while you work? I can keep Sophie busy."

"Sounds good, Gabby, and thank you both. Lizzie, I can't tell you how much I appreciate this. I was thinking I might be up all night. Matt got stuck at this job site because per usual he has no help. And he was setting up some solar thing at the town square." She's near tears. "Sometimes it's hard to do it all."

Lizzie hugs her. "You don't have to do it all, we're here to help you, that's what family's for. And, it's been a long time since I've done a craft project. This will be fun."

There's a commotion in the hall, voices, laughter and footsteps. Lizzie turns to see her brother Matt, and Jack walking in.

"What—" Lizzie stammers.

Jack is holding some type of tech device. "I was helping Matt set up a timer for the solar panel powered Christmas lights in the center of town, and he forgot this," he says, holding up something, though Lizzie has no idea what.

"I told him I was coming here, so he tracked me down," Matt says, giving his wife and daughter each a kiss.

"Jack, stay and have some soup with us, there's plenty," Gabby offers.

He looks at Lizzie for any type of signal. "Um, I'm—"

"He's staying," says Matt, taking control of the situation. "He helped me all morning and this afternoon, it's the least we can do."

"If it's not an imposition, sure, I'd love to." He takes off his coat and surveys the mountain of craft supplies Shannon is sorting. "What's going on here? A Santa workshop annex?"

"Hey, Jack," Shannon greets him. "Lizzie kindly offered to help me make 400 little reindeer for the library festival event." she looks at him and smiles, "We could always use more hands, if you'd care to join?"

"Well, how can I say no to helping a good cause?" he says, pulling up a stool.

"You know, upstairs in the hall closet, along with my abandoned knitting projects are two more glue guns and a bag of glue sticks. Matt, would you run up and get them?" Gabby asks. "That way all four of you can work on it, or I can do it and one of you can watch Sophie."

"I got it, Mom, thanks," Matt runs up the backstairs and

returns in under a minute. "I wish we could keep our closets organized like that, Mom."

"Ha! Well, it's amazing what one finds time to do when they retire! The soup and bowls are all here whenever you want to take a break and eat," she says. "Sophie, why don't you and I take our dinner and go eat by the Christmas tree?"

"Yay! Daddy! I'm going to have dinner with Grabby in the Christmas tree!"

He picks up his little girl, "Next to the tree, and that is great!" He puts her down and she scurries into the living room, trailed by Gabby carrying a tray for them, and Daisy hoping for some fallen treats.

"Okay, so what do these little guys look like," Jack asks, ready to get to work.

"You really don't have to do this," Lizzie says to him quietly. "I'm sure you've got better things to do."

"It's fine, I'd like to do it. All that was waiting for me at home was some leftover lasagna, and Netflix. My parents went to some board meeting, so it's all good," he says.

Lizzie isn't too sure about sitting with her ex-fiance' making candy cane reindeer, but it's for a good cause so she decides to make the best of it and not make anyone else uncomfortable.

In short order the four of them are moving right along and soon have a growing pile of mini-Rudolphs.

Matt, glue gun in hand, points to Lizzie and Jack, "Do you two remember, I was a sophomore, you two were seniors, when we decided to make a float for the festival?"

"Even though there was no parade?" Jack laughs.

"Yes! It was kind of, 'the sea meets the North Pole'. Jason Miller got a Santa suit and insisted on being Santa," Matt says laughing.

"Even though he was six-foot-four and maybe weighed 150,"

"Wait, I think I remember this, he was on a boat, being pulled on a trailer, and the kids didn't get permission or a permit to have this one-float parade and the police came?" Lizzie says.

"But they were nice and let us make it all the way down Main Street before they stopped us," says Jack.

"Did you like growing up here? I worry about Sophie sometimes, is there enough going on, things like that," asks Shannon. "I moved here later, when I was a junior, so I didn't have the childhood all of you did here."

"I liked it, most of the time," Lizzie says as she glues googly eyes and a red candy nose onto yet another candy cane. "But I was ready to leave when the time came."

"Getting away for a while is important," says Jack. "If you grow up here and never go anywhere else it is a pretty sheltered life. I'm grateful for having had all the experiences I've had, the small town, and moving away. But now that I'm older, I miss it."

"What about you, Lizzie?" Shannon asks, getting up to get the basket she brought to put finished reindeer in.

"Same, except I don't feel the pull to come back," though she's not sure how she feels honestly. After college and grad school, she'd thought she and Jack would eventually perhaps build a life there, but as a single person, she wasn't sure this sandbar was the best spot for her. "There's no perfect place," she shrugs. "I see kids growing up in Boston and think it's really cool that they get to go to museums, ride the T, and have so much diversity around them. But then I think of learning to sail as a really little kid, searching for hermit crabs, and toasting marshmallows on the Outer Beach as the sun goes down."

"I like the idea of having both," says Jack, precisely twisting a brown pipe cleaner into antlers. "Having this as a homebase, but also getting to Boston or New York often enough to be happy to come back here." He keeps looking over at Lizzie and she is trying to ignore him.

After an hour and a half of reminiscing, eating some soup and reindeer making, Lizzie stands up and stretches. "I hate to leave the party, but my editor is going to have my head if I don't write those stories for him." She pushes in her stool, and takes her bowl to the sink.

"I've heard he's impossible to deal with," says Peter, coming in at the end of a very long day.

"Hey, Dad," Matt says.

Jack goes to stand, "Mr. Martin."

"Jack, sit down, and for goodness sake, call me Peter." He claps his hands together and rubs them to warm them, "This looks like Santa's–"

"Workshop, yeah, Peter, we've already used that one," Shannon says. "These guys were wonderful enough to help me with this project for the library. Tell me again why we have this festival every year?" she laughs, completely exhausted, jokingly putting her head down on the counter.

"I'd say because it's fun, but it's also a ridiculous amount of work," Peter says. "I'm pretty festival-ed out myself." He goes over to the still-warm instant pot and gets himself some soup. "I feel terrible making you leave the party to write those stories, honey," he says to Lizzie and she picks up her notebooks.

"Dad, it's not a big deal," she says, kind of happy to have the excuse to leave. "See you all later, give me a shout before you go, Matt and Shannon," she turns to go upstairs, and stops to look back at Jack laughing with her brother as they have a battle with their reindeer. Jack looks up and sees her, and she hurries up the stairs.

CHAPTER 11

LIZZIE OPENS her laptop and her notebook. Sitting at her teenage desk, she squirms in the uncomfortable straight back chair. Why did she never ask her parents for a more comfortable chair when she was a kid, she wonders.

Looking at her notes from the bookstore she keeps feeling distracted by thoughts of Jack. "No, no, no, no," she says out loud to no one but herself. As a way to procrastinate she opens the desk drawer and finds a treasure trove of photos, tickets, cards, notes, and other memorabilia that Marie Kondo would immediately have her edit. She kept things. Concert and movie ticket stubs, shells found on walks, and a million other things. She couldn't think of one thing she had in Boston to remember her time with Ed, yet here was a history of her life laid bare in a drawer. Was it that there were too many things to keep track of now, or that there were too few?

She slams the drawer shut and starts typing:

"Something new to the festival this year, courtesy of Anika and Jay Patel of Tall Tale books, is a chance for children to attend their first Story Slam. Storytellers from Seaward Regional Middle School will be telling their real-life tales of

Christmas surprises to younger children who will most certainly have fun hearing stories from these older kids...."

Grabbing quotes from her chat with Anika, and filling in with some color, describing the cozy store and a little information on the Patels, she's done with that one in about 45 minutes. Since she'd been writing more news stories on tight deadlines she'd gotten faster.

"Hey, we're heading out!" She hears Matt call from downstairs. She gets up and runs down the stairs to say goodbye.

"Bye, Aunt Wiz!" she stoops down to give Sophie a hug.

"Night, Sophie-bug!" she says.

"I'm not a bug!" she laughs.

"Fine, night Sophie-cat,"

"I'm not a-"

Matt scoops her up, "Okay, this could go on for an hour," he kisses Lizzie on the cheek, "'Night, I'm sure I'll see you tomorrow."

Shannon is right behind them carrying the basket of reindeer. "We got them all done! I don't know what I'd do without this family, thank you for your help," she gives Lizzie a one-armed hug.

"I loved it, I haven't used a glue gun in years, I had a lot of fun. See you soon, I'm sure!"

They all leave, Lizzie looks around.

"He left about a half-hour ago," says Peter, scooping some frozen yogurt into a bowl. "After you left there wasn't much holding him here," he smiles. "How you doing up there?" He sits down with his treat. "Oh! I should have asked! Do you want some?" She shakes her head, no.

"I got the bookstore story done, and I'll whip out the interview with Leah Alden when I go back up." She sits down next to her Dad. "Did you get to see Stan?"

"Yeah, briefly, he's doing okay. It's going to take some time to heal." He puts his spoon down. "Having him out it's really making me think a lot about what to do with the paper. It's been crazy enough trying to do it with the two of us, but with just one person, it's not really workable. I may be having to think about some changes after the first of the year. I have always vowed I'd never sell to the corporate folks, but I may not have a choice," he says, looking so sad it breaks Lizzie's heart. "Money-wise, it's getting near impossible."

She hates seeing her dad like this. She knows he probably goes through this tug-of-war in his head often, but she's only rarely been privy to it. "Now isn't the time to make any big decisions, Dad. Wait until you know more about Stan, till after the holidays…you've got me for the next couple of weeks, and I can even help and do some pieces long-distance when I go back to Boston. There are always solutions, isn't that what you always told me?"

"I hate it when my parental words come back to haunt me," he laughs. "Okay, you're right. I won't decide anything right now. Other than, I'm deciding to have a second bowl of this frozen yogurt. Don't tell your Mom though."

She stands to go back upstairs. "My lips are sealed. I promise." She stops at the bottom of the stairs. "Dad?"

"Yes?"

"You also always told me you never know what unexpected thing might show up to turn everything around. Don't forget that."

"Boy, I really was full of advice, wasn't I? What a pain! I'm so sorry!"

She laughs. "Hardly, your words have gotten me through many tough times."

Peter smiles, "That's really nice to hear. I'm glad I did something right."

"You did a lot of things right. Oh! And don't let me forget that I want to run some ideas for a future story about what Leah and some of her friends are working on to make the town greener–in an environmental way, not more shrubs," she laughs.

"I'd love that, thanks honey. It's nice to have your enthusiasm around here, I could really use it."

Lizzie runs up the stairs back to her childhood room to begin her next story, and tries to not think about how to save the family business. She has always sworn she would not let herself get pulled into saving the Gazette. It was never her passion, she wanted more. But now she's finding herself wondering what that even means.

The story about the more environmentally friendly Christmas festival was a cinch to write. She had great quotes from Leah, and she was excited about it, something that felt a bit foreign to her. She couldn't remember the last time she wrote something she truly cared about. Since Greylock Media had taken over the Sentinel, and hundreds of other local papers across the country, all that mattered was meeting the nightly deadline with as little fuss as possible. Less and less of features pages had anything to do with Boston. Writing something in real time that was happening and was not just fun but important felt so good.

In less than an hour she had that story done too, emailed to the Gazette, and was not ready to go to sleep. She was too wound up.

Instead of crawling into bed she finds herself opening that desk drawer and looking through those old photos again. She gathers them up, and brings them over to her bed where she sits cross-legged and starts going through them. There were several from prom she cringes looking at. Why had she ever decided that prom was the perfect time to dye her hair purple? She shakes her head and puts those aside. There were lots and lots of photos of her and Matt–on the beach, on their little Sunfish learning to sail, sitting at their Dad and Stan's desks pretending to be working. There were also many just of the town, the beaches, the shops. She recalls having taken a bunch of these for a school project, "Know Your Town", where she'd gone and talked to several business owners, Reverend Harold, who'd long-since retired, and members of the selectboard. Cranberry Harbor was such a beautiful and special place to have grown up. Maybe being away for some time had given her the distance she needed to appreciate it. She can't stand the thought of everyone her age leaving, of it being stuck in some postcard version of itself with no real sustainable future. Suddenly, she gets up and grabs her laptop, brings it back to the bed and starts writing.

She hasn't written anything personal in so long, and it feels good. She finds herself writing about the importance of having grown up in this town, how it has shaped who she became. She writes about community, about growing the town thoughtfully, being inclusive and welcoming, and leaning into a future that provides opportunities to young people - both those who'd grown up there, and new residents who want to create a future in Cranberry Harbor. She also touched on the fragile environment and how it's not like other places, and climate change is already hitting it hard. The thoughts and words are coming faster than she can type.

Eight-hundred words later she sits back and wonders where that came from. Two days back in town and here she is, waxing poetic about the place she couldn't run from fast enough. After a quick edit, and before she loses her nerve, she sends it to her Dad and wonders what prompted all that to tumble out. Whatever it was, she liked it. It felt good to voice an opinion. Especially about something that mattered so much to her.

CHAPTER 12

BY THE TIME Lizzie woke up, a little after 9, both her parents and Daisy were gone. There's a note on the coffeemaker–her Mom knows her so well, she knew that would be her first stop upon waking.

"Gone to drop off the cookies at Town Hall, and then taking Daisy to the groomer for a quick trim. Dad's at the paper, of course. Love you, Mom."

Lizzie sets the note aside, grinds some beans, and makes herself some coffee. As she waits for it to drip through, she checks her phone for messages, emails, missed calls and of course, Instagram. It bothers her that it is so hard to just sit and look out at the sun shining on the snow. It has been forever since she'd unplugged, forever as in never. She toasts a bagel and once both the coffee and it are done she takes them to a cozy chair by the Christmas tree and curls up.

While she's sitting there contemplating turning off her phone for the day it rings. "Hey Dad," she said with a mouth full of bagel.

"That column you wrote? You did that last night?"

She's quiet for a second, she'd actually forgotten about it until just now. "Yeah. You don't have to run it, it's really not festival related-"

"Are you kidding? I love it, I might save it though for the next issue. I think it's a perfect, 'what do we want our New Year to look like?' piece for that issue."

"Like I said, I was just rambling, it's not anything I am feeling all that precious about, you won't hurt my feelings if you just scrap it."

"Lizzie, this is beautiful. I haven't seen anything like this from you in a long time. I mean, your Sentinel stories are obviously not personal. This really choked me up."

"Aw, Dad, that's so sweet of you."

"What I wouldn't give to have that voice in this paper all the time," he teases. "But I can't afford you. I just had to call and say I loved it, and your other stories too."

"Thanks, Dad, that means a lot. How's it going? What else can I do? I've got a whole lot of nothing on my plate today."

"Well, since you offered, could you go by the Marshview Inn and talk to Ben Knowles about his wreath making class?"

"Sure, it would be fun to see him, is he expecting me?" she asks, finishing up her bagel.

"Yes, I told them I'd be sending you over. I felt very official, like I had a staff again," he laughs.

"Okay, I'll get myself together and head over."

"Thanks, darlin', I would be sunk without you."

They hang up, Lizzie quickly puts her dishes in the dishwasher and runs upstairs to get dressed. This is not the vacation she had planned… it's actually so much better! As she slips on some jeans, t-shirt and sweater she feels excited. A quick brush of her teeth, and a little makeup and she's ready to go. She's excited to have been able to connect with so many great people in town. The Patels, Leah, and now Ben, she'd forgotten what community can be like. It was warm and comforting.

In less than twenty minutes she's on the road to the inn. The Marshview Inn had one of the most beautiful long, winding driveways Lizzie had ever seen. Growing up in Cranberry Harbor it was always fun to have a reason to go there. It was cinematic in its beauty. When she arrives at the top of the hill she's greeted by a stunning 19th century mansion with a porch that wraps all the way around the front, perfectly decorated for the holidays of course, with greens with thick red ribbon woven through. It must be gorgeous at night, she thinks.

She's starting to ascend the stairs when the door opens, "This can't be real, Lizzie Martin, as I live and breathe, please tell me you're staying forever," Ben jokes.

"Not exactly, sorry," Lizzie says, smiling at him. "I think my Dad told you I'd be coming by?"

Ben reaches out to hug her. "He did! It's so nice to see you, I haven't seen you in way too long." He turns and opens the door, "Come on in, it's freezing out here."

The entry way is just as beautiful as the exterior. It's all so perfectly done. The perfect combination of festive and fun. Lizzie hasn't been to the inn since high school when they hosted a breakfast for seniors. Ben and Sean have updated it, but still kept its historical charm.

"Ben, this place is amazing, you have done an incredible job," says Lizzie, putting her coat over her arm. "When I drove up I felt like I was in a Bing Crosby movie, it's stunning."

"Let me take that for you," Ben says, taking her coat. "Would you like some cocoa? Coffee? Tea? We've got it all!"

"I'd love some coffee, if it's not a pain," she says. She's still taking in the surroundings, the art, which is exquisite, though not of the period. Still, it all works.

"No problem at all, we have this fantastic coffee from this local couple who've created this great roasting company with coffee beans they import from Colombia. How do you take it?"

"Just some milk, please, thanks so much." She's still taking in her surroundings. The place is just incredible.

Ben directs her to a living room with a fire that's snapping and crackling. "This should be a good place to sit. Sean will be here in a minute, he was just finishing something up in the studio."

He's back in a flash with her coffee. "Here you go, take a sip. I think you'll be impressed."

"Wow, you did not oversell, this is incredible. It's rich, yet mild, it's delicious." She puts her cup down on the table near her. "So he's an artist? Sean, I mean," Lizzie asks.

"Yeah, lots of these paintings are his. Not all, some are from friends he went to school with at RISD. It's been interesting to meld all our interests and passions together in this one place."

"Last I knew you were a chef in Portland, right?" asks Lizzie, taking out her pen and pad.

"Yeah, I went to Johnson and Wales in Providence. I met Sean when he was at RISD, and then came back here and worked for my parents for a while, then decided I needed an experience off Cape, and we ended up in Maine."

Sean, a tall man with bright blue eyes comes in, wiping his hands on a towel. "Hey, I'm sorry to have kept you waiting. I assume Ben offered you something?"

"Yes! I have this amazing local coffee right here," she says, picking up her cup and taking another sip.

"I'm Lizzie Martin, by the way," she stands and reaches out to shake Sean's hand. "It's so nice to meet you."

"Sean," he says, smiling at her. "I love meeting people Ben grew up with, it's so fun. There are so few of you around."

"Yeah, there's not a lot of us for sure," she says, sitting back down. "We had a lot of fun together, it was an interesting place to grow up," she says. "We had to make our own fun a lot of the time, but we had a great childhood."

"We did," Ben agrees, "and only got into trouble a few times," he laughs.

"Yes" Lizzie says, remembering a few incidents, like TP'ing the principal's house one Halloween, and letting all the frogs loose from the biology department in Seymour Pond. Which had definitely been Jack's idea.

"I don't want to take up your whole morning, so let me get to it." She takes out her notebook and pen. "So my Dad said that you are going to be hosting sessions on creating wreaths from items found locally?"

Ben laughs, "That sounds like it could really be terrible, doesn't it? Like we're going to be hanging some old sticks and brown leaves on your door?"

"I wouldn't say that–" Lizzie demurs.

"But hey, stick a bow on it and it will be gorgeous!" Sean jokes. "I'll admit when Ben told me what he wanted to do I thought it was a little iffy, but I think it's going to be very cool, even more so if we call it 'Earth Art,' he laughs.

"Hey, it's going to be great," he gives Sean a gentle nudge. "I know it sounds a little hokey, but the thing is, it's so much better for the environment if you don't buy balsam wreaths and swags, and make your own decorations from locally sourced vegetation. Our brand here is farm to table and we've created pretty extensive gardens, and I source lots of items from other local farms too."

"So when people come to your workshop they will leave with a swag or wreath made up of...what?" Lizzie asks, writing everything down.

"We have an abundance of spruce on the Cape so there will be lots of that for a strong base, and I have a lot of dried lavender bundles, winterberry, rose hips, juniper, and various berries and other dried herbs which will make them smell really nice," Ben says. "Oh, and one day at the post office, I randomly ran into Jill Mayo whose parents owned–"

"The old fabric store," Lizzie says.

"Yeah! And she'd heard I was doing this and she told me she had a ton of vintage ribbons in her garage leftover from the shop and said we could have them. They are super retro and really cool. I can guarantee no one will have a wreath like yours when you're done."

"This is sounding very cool and creative," Lizzie says as she's quickly writing everything down. I may have to come by and make one myself."

"You definitely should, it's going to be a lot of fun and I'm worried no one will come, so we need some ringers," Sean teases.

There's a knock on the door, "I'll get it," Ben says, jumping to his feet, "It's probably the firewood delivery."

He returns in a minute accompanied by Jack.

"I'm sorry, I feel like I'm interrupting something, I can come back later," Jack says as soon as he enters, looking at Lizzie. "I just wanted to return your notebook," he says, handing an over-stuffed, worn binder to Sean.

"Actually, I'm about done, anyway," she says, putting her things in her bag. "Oh, I need a few photos," she says, getting ready to stand.

"Please don't go yet," Ben says. "It's been way too long since we've all hung out, please? Just for a little while? And I can send you photos. We have plenty."

Lizzie isn't sure how long she wants to stay, but puts her things down. "Sure, I can visit for a minute."

"Coffee, Jack?"

"Uh, yeah, sure," he says, sitting down across from Lizzie. "So, thanks for the notes. They gave me some ideas for what we might be able to do," Jack says to Sean.

"Jack was over the other day and we were talking about how many artists, farmers, fisherfolk, food creators and stuff, and how nothing is at all coordinated on how to find people and their products." says Sean.

Lizzie is impressed that Jack is trying to help all these people in Cranberry Harbor. "Are there that many entrepreneur types here? I'm really out of the loop."

"Yeah, looking at the list Sean and Ben have there's easily a couple of dozen right here, and I think if people had assurance that there was a way to actually get the word out, and it wasn't all up to them, probably more would jump in," says Jack.

"I want to set up a time to talk with some of the people who want to be involved, but right now I want to catch up with you two," Ben says, putting another log on the fire."So how are things in both your lives going?"

Lizzie and Jack look at each other.

"Wow, way to start with something light, Ben!" Jack laughs.

"You go," Jack says, nodding at Lizzie. "I think I need a minute to think about this."

"Uh, hmmm," she offers, not exactly sure herself of what to say.

"That good?" Ben laughs sitting back down. An 'uh hmm' doesn't sound great."

"It's complicated?" she finally lands on. "I always loved the idea of living in Boston, and getting to write for a paper like the Sentinel that's been around for over 150 years, but it's not the same. I mean, of course it's not the same as it was 150 years ago, but it's not the same as it was 20 years ago, or even ten. And the thing is, it's not that people don't want good writing and good stories, it's just that big corporations come in, buy good news-papers, and it's basically death by a thousand papercuts - liter-ally and figuratively. Like what my Dad is doing here? It's not sustainable as it is, and it makes me so sad. Sorry, that's prob-ably way more than you wanted or needed to know!"

"Your Dad is amazing, how he and Stan turn that paper out

every week, just the two of them? It's incredible, and it really is the lifeblood of this community, I look forward to it every Thursday," Ben says.

"And what's your story, Jack? The tech world has to be pretty interesting in Cali?" Ben asks.

Jack takes a sip of his coffee and sits back in his chair. "I'm torn, let me just say that."

"Oh man, you can't leave it at that! That's just cruel!" presses Sean.

Jack laughs. "I'm not being vague to be interesting, I'm being vague because I literally don't have a clue as to what I'm doing right now."

Everyone is quiet.

"I think you're saying the thing so many of us feel and think we're not supposed to say," Lizzie says. "I'm not so sure about what I'm doing. It's hard to say that. To be in your early 30s when so many people our age are married, happy, and seem to be living the dream, like you two, and lots of us seem aeons away from that, and it feels like you're not doing it right."

"Do you ever think of coming back here and starting something up?" Ben asks Jack.

"Maybe?" Jack says completely unsure. "It's so damn hard to get anything off the ground here, and we need a way to retain, or bring back more young working adults here. Retirees? We've got plenty. Young adults who want to help build a startup? Not so much. I ran into that four years ago, and it was not good."

"It's really hard to find balance," says Ben. "We're really lucky that my parents pretty much handed us this business, though that said, in the high season it's 100 hour work weeks, but we really like meeting people. Most of the people," they look at each other and laugh.

"Yeah, there's always a few challenging ones every summer, but for the most part it's good. And when it's quiet I get lots of time to paint and sculpt, and that's really nice."

"This coffee is so good," Lizzie says, relaxing into the couch. "It's pretty incredible that something this good is roasted right here."

"That's the thing, there are so many of us here who are building businesses and creating locally, but there's nothing that really connects it all."

"That's why I'm leaning toward an app," Jack says, "something that connects all the locally sourced and produced products and in turn connects the creators with businesses and people to buy their products? That's what I'm thinking about anyway. All those notes you gave me? That's what kept coming back to me. An app that could connect it all."

"You know a couple of us have talked about that but none of us has the expertise, that's something you'd know how to do?" Sean asks, sounding hopeful.

"Yeah, heck, yeah,"says Jack. "Are you sure people would be into doing that? I know entrepreneurs can get very territorial."

"I'm positive. There's tons of people making soaps, lotions, cheeses, herbal tinctures, bread, wine, kombucha, there's so much happening and it's all sort of underground and not coordinated in any meaningful way, I totally think they'd be all in," says Sean.

"Are we witnessing the birth of a business idea, here, gentleman?" Lizzie jokes.

"It could be," says Jack. "I mean it's not like it's going to make anyone rich, but it could be the start of something."

Lizzie knows Jack well enough to see the wheels turning and it's fun to watch his creative and technical brain at work.

"Well, I should get going. Goodness knows what else my dad has up his sleeve for me today," Lizzie says.

Ben stands up and gives Lizzie a hug. "It was so good to see you, I hope it's not the only time while you're here."

"Absolutely, I'm sure we have lots more chances to meet up." Ben helps her on with her coat. "Sean, it was lovely to meet you," she hugs him. Jack, who is not leaving right away, gives her a small wave. "I seem to see you everywhere, so I will just be expecting to run into you probably later today," she says and waves back.

She gets in her car, waving goodbye to Ben and Sean, and wonders if she will ever feel that settled and happy.

CHAPTER 13

"HEY DAD," Lizzie says, taking her coat off as she walks, the sleeve getting caught on the things in her hand. *One thing at a time, one thing at a time...* she reminds herself, putting her bag and notebook down on the desk, and throwing her coat over the back of her chair. "So I had a great time with Ben and Sean Knowles, I can write that up really fast, Ben said he'd send photos." She boots up Stan's ancient computer and makes a mental note to travel with her laptop.

"Already got 'em," he says. "They're beautiful. So glad it went well."

He seems oddly quiet, like there's something he wants to say but isn't.

"What's up Dad?"

Peter clears his throat, "Well, after you went upstairs to write last night I got talking to Jack before he took off."

Lizzie's worried about where this is going. What was her Dad up to?

"And he was saying how he'd like to figure out some housing and job solutions."

"Wouldn't we all," she says, nodding her head and opening her notebook to her quotes from Ben.

"No, he's actually been working on some ideas, and I'd love for you to see what he has in mind, pick his brain a little, and see if any of it is viable. And maybe also write something about skating on Thacher's cranberry bog? Today?"

Lizzie laughs. "What? I'm starting to think that Stan threw himself off the ladder to get away from working for you! Jeez, Dad, you want me to make a pie and solve global warming today too?" she teases. "I just got here and now you want me to go skating, and interview Jack about some idea that isn't even a thing, and write it up?"

"I know, it sounds like a lot, but I just want to see if he's planning to do anything, and I figured if he'd talk to anyone it would be you." There's a pause. "Would that be uncomfortable for you?

She sighs. "Fine. I'll see what I can find out."

"You sure you don't mind? Your mother would probably kick me for asking you to do this, but I think it's important."

"Oh now you're all,'only if you want to,'" she laughs. "No, it's fine. Except as far as me writing the skating story goes I have no skates and I don't know if Jack is free to talk to me today. He had stopped by Ben and Sean's and was there when I left. But besides that I can do the Marshview story and the skating."

"He's going to pick you up here at 1, and there are skates in my car for you both, all ready to go."

"What? Now I'm interviewing him and going skating with him? Dad..."

"Oops, my cell is vibrating, I have to take this, it's Town Hall," he says, getting up from his desk.

"Likely story, Peter Martin. Likely story." She shakes her head, and can't believe once again she's being thrown in with Jack.

Her phone dings, alerting her to a text. It's from Jack

So your father has been busy this morning...apparently we're going skating and discussing the future of Cranberry Harbor? You okay with that?

Honestly, she doesn't know how she feels.

I am so sorry he twisted your arm into doing this. We don't have to. He was just...excited.

She hits send. The gray bubble and dots appear, then disappear.

No! I want to go. Just don't make fun of me okay?

Lizzie laughs out loud, and then catches herself, looking to see if her dad is watching her, but he's not there. No, Jack is not charming her, not this time.

I am not exactly Olympic material myself so no worries.

More dots...

Deal. See you at 1.

Lizzie did not get dressed that morning to go skating, so she quickly texts Jack back.

I need to go home and change. Could you meet me there instead?

Yup.

Peter comes in the door from outside. "Dad, I'm going home, I did not dress for ice skating. I can't believe what you're getting me to do."

He shrugs and smiles. "I put the skates next to your car, it was locked."

"You will pay, sir, that's for sure," she says, heading to her car and home to change.

As she rummages through her suitcase- she had never bothered to actually unpack - she has a weird feeling of deja-vu. Getting ready for a date with Jack. There is something very early-aughts about this situation. Finally she settles on some fleece-lined leggings, a long-sleeved T-shirt, a flannel shirt and an old sweater of Matt's she'd confiscated long ago and left in her closet. And two pairs of socks. She lays them all on her bed, like she's dressing a very chilly scarecrow to see if it all works. It does.

She knew there was an assortment of hats, scarves and gloves in the downstairs closet, and she'd find something suitable in that department on her way out.

After she changes she goes into the bathroom and fusses a bit with her makeup, something certainly not required for an outside skating expedition, she puts down her brow brush and picks up her phone to text Sarah.

Okay, so Jack and I are going skating. And I ran into him AGAIN while interviewing a guy we went to school with.

She goes back to trying to create the perfect brow, her phone dings. Sarah is on it.

Aw, what an old fashioned DATE!

Lizzie sighs.

Not.A.Date. It's actually for another story for my dad.

She waits for a reply.

Are you putting on makeup? Did you spend more than ten minutes figuring out what to wear? If so, that's a date.

Did she have Lizzie on surveillance somehow?

Only a little makeup, and I don't want to freeze, so the outfit took some time. And I have to say that I kind of hate it that you know me so well.

She pictures Sarah laughing in her cubicle.

I do know you and I want you to stop overthinking this and go have fun. And don't break an ankle or anything.

She shakes her head and smiles.

Thanks, I'll try not to. Hope all is well there.

Sarah doesn't text right back. She's probably on deadline. As she starts layering up she hears her phone.

Yeah, it's okay. Looking forward to a few days away from here. It's been more stressful than usual. Love you, have fun!

Lizzie was always wondering when and who the next person

to be laid off would be. It was a lot of stress, but she just sends a heart and hugs emojis and finishes getting ready.

Jack arrives promptly at 12:59, and Lizzie is ready to go. She has retrieved both pairs of skates from her car and is as ready as she will ever be to spend time alone with the man who broke her heart. What was she even doing? Why did she let her dad orchestrate this? She takes a deep breath. She's doing this for him, and is going to make the best of it. Being pleasant for a couple of hours won't be the end of the world.

"Hey, you're being a very good sport to let my dad plan your afternoon," Lizzie says, trying to appear cool in control and breezy while wrapping a scarf around her neck. She pulls on a knit cap with flower appliques and glances in the hall mirror. She turns to Jack. "This kind of looks like something Mom bought at a rummage sale that had been living in someone's closet since the '70s."

He laughs, "No, I like it. It's original, very...you."

She squints at her reflection. "I'm not sure if that's a good thing, but it feels warm, so no matter how silly I look I'm wearing it. Should we stop and get some cocoa on the way to make sure we don't freeze?" she asks as she zips her coat.

"Actually, Sea Coast has a little food truck down there selling hot drinks and snacks–it was Leah's idea, and Hope ok'd it for the next couple of weeks."

"Of course it was. Boy, that girl thinks of everything, she's incredible" She picks up the skates, and her bag. "Well I'm as ready as I'll ever be, should we go?"

Jack takes the skates from her and opens the door. "So we're in agreement on the no laughing thing, right?" he says, leading the way to his car.

"I make no promises sir," she looks over the car roof at him. "Of course. You think I've been on skates, in the last decade and a half? This could get really ugly, really fast."

They both fasten their seatbelts. "We could always just go

down there, and say we went skating and not..." he floats this idea like it's the most genius thing ever. This coming from a guy who never, ever cheated on a test or skipped school is the equivalent of selling state secrets.

"I am shocked that you would suggest lying to my father, Jack."

"No, of course that would be wrong, and I don't want to betray him, or your journalistic integrity–"

"Actually, the same thought went through my head. I don't have to write this in first person, we could say we did and not. How about we feel it out when we get there? If it's a bunch of hot shots doing triple salchows and spins or whatever, we just watch, I can get some quotes, and we drink some cocoa. Sound good?

"Sounds good."

But the thing was, when they got there there was only a couple with their two little kids on the ice, none of them Olympic champion material, and it actually looked...fun.

"What do you think?" Jack looks a little excited to try it.

It was a picture perfect day, the sky was that rich, deep blue it turned on the Cape in the cooler months. It wasn't even as cold as Lizzie had worried it would be, so she agrees. She can do this. She can get up on skates and she can spend time with Jack and be civil.

"Okay, you jump I jump, Jack," she pauses, "that little 'Titanic' quote works particularly well when you're actually with someone named Jack," she says, still not completely sold on the skating or being with him.

"Yeah, not the first time I've heard it," he says as they head to the bench on the edge of the bog to put on their skates.

"Sorry. Must get old." As she laces up her skates she suddenly starts to feel very nervous. Not only does she not want to look like an idiot, she also doesn't want to get hurt. The last thing she wants is to need Jack in any way, but she'd rather wound her pride than break her ankle, so she decides to be honest. "Uh, I'm a little nervous. You okay if I kind of hold on to you for a little bit? 'Til I get my bearings?" She stands and wobbles in the snow on the two thin blades. Before getting on the ice she pulls her phone out of her pocket and grabs a few photos for her story.

"I was just going to ask you the same thing, I think I need to hold on to you too. I am suddenly feeling a lot older than the last time I did this," Jack says, looking a little panicked.

"That's because we are," Lizzie says, haltingly working her way to the flooded bog. And just when they set foot on the ice a school bus pulls up and at least thirty middle-schoolers pour out and head to the ice all at once. Kids go whizzing by as Lizzie and Jack cling to each other for dear life.

"Once around and then we're good?" Lizzie pleads.

"Oh yeah, that sounds good to me."

They're quiet as they inch their way along, and Lizzie feels uncomfortable about that.

"So, it was really nice seeing Ben and meeting Sean this morning, they seem like they've really made it work here," she says, still keeping a tight grip on Jack's arm.

"Yeah, I've gotten together with them a few times since I've been back, I really enjoy their company." They are still moving at a snail's pace. "It's really great when you grow up and find you still really like people you hung out with. It doesn't always happen." They quickly exchange a knowing glance about a few classmates they did not feel similarly about.

Apparently Lizzie's father was unaware that the middle school had been bringing groups there daily for gym class as a way to let the kids get outside and have some fun so the ice is now teeming with tweens.

"Were we ever that fearless?" Lizzie asks as she and Jack slowly begin to make their way around the edge of the bog. "Because I don't remember going that fast or hurling myself down on the ice so I could glide through someone's legs."

"It's hard to remember," Jack says, not looking at her, only his feet which are inching along at a slow crawl. "I don't remember feeling scared, but I probably was?"

"I was more scared of looking stupid than getting hurt. I'm sure even now, if I were to fall, the embarrassment of falling would be far worse than the pain of it. I need look no further than the other day outside Bradford's for verification of that theory."

Despite themselves after ten minutes or so they start to loosen up a little and gain some confidence. They're still not ready to let go of each other, but they've picked up some speed.

"Do I dare say this is feeling a little fun?" Jack says.

"I was just thinking the same thing. The bit of joy I'm feeling is distracting nicely from the dull, constant ache in my ankles, but this is feeling kind of okay." They're both still only looking down at their feet. "Want to try letting go and fly solo for a minute?"

"I don't know, you think we're okay?" Jack looks concerned.

"Yeah, I think we're good. On three, okay?" She braces herself. "One, two, two and a half, and three!" And with that she pushes off and glides forward, with Jack following closely behind. They are both so buoyed by their amazing skills, they fail to notice a kid hurtling toward them in hot pursuit of a ball, and they all collide, sending Lizzie and Jack into each other, and taking them down like two dominos.

"Oh, sorry, lady, sorry mister," the kid says, retrieving his ball and skating off.

There's an awkward moment of being so close, and they quickly sit up. Lizzie feels very strange being in such proximity to him.

"I don't know which is worse, falling or being called, 'lady,' my Mom is a 'lady.'" Lizzie says, shaking off the self-consciousness of being closer to him than she's been in three years.

Jack laughs, "I'm not crazy about 'mister' either. All kidding

CHRISTMAS IN CRANBERRY HARBOR

aside, are you okay?" He gets up on his knees and manages to stand up. "Here, let me help you, lady."

"Ha, thank you. I don't know about you, but I could kind of use a break, Want to get some cocoa?" Lizzie says.

"You read my mind." They slowly make their way back to the bench. "Well that will teach me to not get too confident while on skates. I think any later-in-life plans I may have had to become a hockey player have been thoroughly dashed now," Jack says, sitting down.

"Really? You're going to give up that easily?" Lizzie teases as she unlaces her skates. "I was so looking forward to finally going to a Bruins game and cheering for you, the oldest player on the team." Humor has always been her deflection method of choice.

"You know, I could easily leave you here to find your way back to town," he jokes as he slips his feet into his now freezing boots. "Oh wow, that's cold!" he exclaims. "You know, other than those nice couple of minutes I am failing to see what is so great about this. Don't quote me, I'm sure your dad wants this to sound like super fun for the whole family."

"No worries, that was completely off the record. "I'm going to throw this stuff in your car and meet you at the coffee truck?" she says.

When Lizzie heads back to the coffee truck she sees Jack happily chatting with whoever is inside.

"Here she is!" he says to the person in the food truck, "Lizzie, look who's here!"

"Oh my god! Alexis?!" she yells.

"Lizzie!"

Alexis comes running out from the truck and they embrace.

"I saw your grandfather at the thrift shop and he said you were back but I had no idea - "

Alexis laughs, "Yeah, this is just something I'm doing for now while I'm on break from school."

"Teaching or studying?" Jack asks.

"I'm finishing my Master's in community planning, so I'm off for a while. Working on my thesis."

"The last I knew you were teaching in Spain," says Lizzie.

"Oh you're way behind," Alexis says, laughing. "That was five years ago. I was there for two years, came back for a bit, and then got hired to teach in South Korea, and stayed there for a year and a half."

"I feel so boring!" Lizzie says.

"Stop! I heard you're a writer in Boston, that's hardly boring."

Kids are starting to line up and want some cocoa. Alexis gives Lizzie her phone and gets back in the truck. "Put in your number and we'll make a plan while you're here, okay? My grandpa gave me your note, but I haven't had a chance to put your number in yet "

"I'd love that, it is so good to see you," she hands Alexis back her phone after texting herself so she has her number as well.

"So you two want some cocoa or something else?" she asks.

"Cocoa," they both say.

"Yeah, this is definitely a cocoa day," Alexis says, handing them two cups of cocoa and a bag.

There's a long line behind them, so they say their goodbyes to Alexis, and head to the car with their cocoas and the two cookies that Alexis threw in as a treat.

"Wow, I forget that about living here," Lizzie says.

"You mean her giving us some cookies and not charging us, which was totally not necessary but very much appreciated?" Jack says, smiling.

She shakes her head, "No, how just how out of the blue you can run into someone you haven't seen in the longest time, and it's perfectly, almost expected."

"It's a small community, that's for sure," says Jack.

"It's more than that, it's the connection we all have that's so special. It's like a special badge we all have having grown up here. Lots of people summer here, but a whole lot less are born and grow up here."

"The bond of locals," he jokes.

"Yeah, it sort of is." She is quiet for a moment, "Do you have a dog? I heard you have a dog." In her head she yells at herself for going there. Even if he had a pack of dogs he is not ever, ever going to be the guy for her. We are never, ever getting back together. Thank you very much Taylor Swift for giving me an anthem to cling to.

He laughs. "Wow, that's random. Uh, no, my life feels too transient right now, but someday I'd like one, maybe two so they'd have a buddy, Why do you ask?"

"No reason, I thought I'd heard something from somewhere. Good to know. You know, that you like them. Dogs."

"Okay, glad to be of assistance," he looks at her quizzically.

Lizzie sits back and looks out at the bog. It starts to flurry a bit and she watches the kids having their cocoa and skating, and doesn't think she's seen anything quite that wonderful in a very long time.

CHAPTER 14

"Just so we're clear, no one ever finds out that we were knocked down by a sixth grader, right?" Jack asks as they head toward town.

Lizzie nods. "Yes, nowhere in what I'm going to submit to my dad will there be anything about two millennials being taken down by a 12-year-old."

"Good, I may not have much of a reputation around here, but I don't want to be the lead story at our next reunion," he says.

"Me either!" She doesn't really want to spend more time with him, but she has to talk to him about ideas he may have for the future of Cranberry Harbor. "So my Dad told me you had some ideas you were talking to him about, are they anything you're ready to share, or are you still figuring things out? He thought it would be a good story, but I completely respect that you may feel it's too early to share anything."

"Would I sound like an evasive jerk if I said I wasn't quite ready?" He looks straight ahead on the road. "Where are we going, by the way? Are you ready to head home, or could I take you someplace else? To further evade your question."

"I don't have anything immediate to do," she says, feeling like this might not be the best idea. But she's curious about what he has in mind for the town, and thinks perhaps he'll open up if she spends a little more time with him. As much as she's tried to distance herself from the town she does care about its future and wants it to be a vital community. "So, sure."

"Let's see, we've had cocoa and cookies, so we don't need more sugar. We've gotten some fresh air. Oh! I've got an idea, you trust me?"

"Yeah. Yeah-ish?" She's a little skeptical and thinks, let's not open that can of worms, but doesn't say that.

"I'm not sensing a lot of enthusiasm here," he jokes, taking a right at the traffic light and heading into a more rural part of town.

"Well you didn't exactly keep me safe ice skating, so, can I trust you? That remains to be seen."

"You can trust me," he keeps driving and they come to an area of town Lizzie hasn't been to in years. No I can't, she thinks, not with my heart at least.

"This is the spot they were going to develop and it got shot down, right?" Lizzie asks, opening her window and looking out. "It's so beautiful."

Jack pulls over. "Yeah, this company was going to basically clear cut it and build a bunch of huge, expensive houses." He's a little nervous, he turns toward Lizzie. "Okay, so this is what I've been thinking about. Please don't tell anyone, not yet." He takes a deep breath. "I am looking into creating an eco-friendly community out here that is as low-impact as possible. We could build some tiny houses, amongst some regular-sized houses, and promote farming and encourage young locals to live here. It could be a mix of people who want to create a life with the land, be it with animals or growing fruits and vegetables, artisans, and people who telecommute, or have other local jobs, and artists and entrepreneurs who are making products from local sourced materials, like soaps, oils, various food items. I'd even want a commercial kitchen on-site that could be used to make and sell food items, like there's a guy making awesome veggie burgers, and he could make them here to sell to local stores and restaurants. We'd make it affordable and doable for locals with investors, grants and subsidies. I'm thinking there could even be crossover between the two - the tech savvy folks helping the people who aren't so much, and the people creating products and growing things teaching others about that. And I want it to be completely self-sufficient energy-wise, so we'd need your brother in on it too. It would be a combination of solar, state-of-the-art-batteries, and wind."

"Wow, you've really put a lot of thought into this. Would the town ever go for it?" Lizzie asks, taking in the space, intrigued by the idea.

"That's the thing, I don't know. There's always been a contingent here who laments that all the young, viable working people are leaving, but who don't want anything to change. They want it to be like a postcard, but my feeling is that by thinking outside the box you can have both. You can keep the integrity of the town, but make it a more progressive, and forward-thinking community where small business, technology, farming and entrepreneurship can thrive."

"You've been thinking about this for a while, haven't you?" Lizzie asks.

He nods. "Yeah, every time I come home I keep thinking about how I had hoped to create this startup that would employ all sorts of young tech people, but I failed to take into account that they wouldn't be able to afford to live here and relying on tech alone left out a whole lot of people who aren't tech-centric, who want to be more creative, who want to maybe work with their hands, the land, the ocean, with animals, who want to nurture the land here, not just look at it. What do you think?" He's so excited it takes Lizzie by surprise.

"I think it's a really amazing idea. The problem will be wresting the land out of the hands of the town, they own it now, right?"

"They do, but it's not registered wetlands or anything, so I know it's buildable. We just have to convince them that while this is gorgeous, it can still be gorgeous and support a lot of the people and businesses we really need here."

"We?" She furrows her brow. "You're drafting me?"

"Well, I am good with technology, and I know people who would be interested in investing, you're the one who's good with words."

Lizzie opens the car door and gets out. She shivers a little, it's windy and flurrying a bit. It is absolutely beautiful. Jack gets out of the car too, and walks over to her side and leans against the door. She feels torn about doing anything to change this property, but also knows that Jack is correct about so many things, and if it could be developed in the right way it could be an example to other rural communities on how to develop thoughtfully and graciously with the environment, and bring jobs and housing.

"You know I'm only here for a short time, right? I can help you while I'm here, but I'm not planning to move back." She feels her back stiffen. She will not be convinced to come back here, especially for him, even if this is the most exciting idea for the town she's ever heard of.

He looks a bit disappointed, but Lizzie has never been anything but clear about not staying in Cranberry Harbor. "Yeah, I know. If you could just help me draft a proposal to the town, and maybe even the county, that would be great. I'm good with the numbers, and the projections, it's making it flow thoughtfully I'm not so good at."

She nods. "Of course I can help you with that." She leans against the car too. "It is pretty amazing to think of what could be here. To have people raising goats and chickens next to the house where the next big technology breakthrough is happening is pretty incredible."

He smiles a huge smile and starts pacing in the new snow. "I know! It could be a total game changer!" He stops. "It would be like taking everything I love and putting it all together into one project."

"You mentioned investors, you've got people who are seriously interested?"

"I do, nothing set in stone yet, because I don't even know if it can happen, but I know a lot of people in California with a lot of money who are interested in projects just like this. Ways that we can thoughtfully grow communities and not ruin what already exists both in terms of the environment and the people who live there. And we need good, local journalism telling people what's going on, and getting them on board."

"Yeah, because all too often big tech moves in, real estate prices soar and the people who actually live there can't find any place to live because these monster companies take over everything, I'd never want that to happen to Cranberry Harbor, or for some corporation to come in and take over the Gazette," Lizzie says.

"Me either. That's why I'd want a board with people like your Dad, your Mom, and other locals who would always keep things in balance."

"So this would be a nonprofit?" she asks.

"Yes, some type of nonprofit, or maybe a B corp, not sure what yet," he says. "I need to do more research. But a B corp would be a way to have public transparency, and make sure we're held accountable to fulfill our mission. There's someone I know in California who's really good with that stuff so I'd ask them for guidance. Sorry, this is probably really boring."

"No, not at all, I'm just getting cold," Lizzie says, starting to shiver and gets back in the car. Jack comes around and gets back in too.

"Thank you for trusting me with this," says Lizzie fastening her seatbelt. "I won't tell anyone. I'll give my dad a little idea, but not everything. Just to calm him down until you're ready to talk more."

"Thank you for not thinking I'm crazy for thinking about this." He starts the car and the heat comes on, warming them both up.

"I think the world needs more windmill tilters." She looks out the window as they drive along. She's really impressed by the thought and expertise Jack has put into this idea. It's just the kind of future-building the town needs. What she's not so sure about is spending time with him, about letting her guard down. She's still angry and hurt, but he is a good guy. How does one reconcile that?

"Would you mind if I stopped at Sea Coast and grabbed a coffee? I can be fast, I just need a caffeine boost before I start in on some work," Jack says.

"Not at all, I could use some too," Lizzie says as he pulls into a parking spot. "I'll come in with you."

"Should we get it to go, or do you want to grab a table?" Jack asks.

Lizzie looks up at the menu on the wall and realizes she's really hungry, it's well past lunchtime. "Would you mind if I got something to eat really quick? I've got a bunch of writing to do and am suddenly feeling famished."

"I could eat too, what do you want?" he asks, turning to look at the menu as well.

"Uh, maybe the mac and cheese? And a latte," she takes out her wallet.

Jack pushes her money away, "Stop, I've got this."

"You sure?" She says, still holding out a ten dollar bill.

"I'm sure, I can handle this. You can go sit down if you want, and I'll bring it over," he says.

Lizzie barely had time to sit down and check her email before Jack was there with a tray.

"Thank you, for this," she says as she takes her cup of very warm mac and cheese off the tray. "Sure I can't pay you back?"

He smiles, "No, I can handle it, it's a pleasure to buy you some lunch." He picks up his panini sandwich and takes a bite. "Hmmm, this is amazing, I always ask for extra pesto and it's incredible. I'd offer you a bite but I know you don't like pesto." He closes his eyes and chews.

Lizzie had forgotten this detail. Jack loved food, Actually he loved anything that he was doing. She had never known someone who so enjoyed everything from a walk on the beach, to skateboarding to, well, a sandwich. Jack savored life, and when they were together he helped slow her down enough to do so too. She had a way of speeding through things, not always noticing everything she could have, Jack was good for her in that way. She often thought about his thoughtful approach to math problems, coding and everything tech, while she was always on deadline and rushing to get to the next item on her list. She'd always thought that was what made them a good match. Until he shocked her and everyone in town by bailing on her and Cranberry Harbor.

"I really like that they're not using plastic utensils anymore," she notes, unsure of what to talk about.

"Yeah, Leah has really helped Hope get up to speed with more eco-friendly practices. Everything is either reusable, or biodegradable now, and there's a guy who has a local farm who picks up waste from all the restaurants and composts it. These cups, your bowl, my plate? They all turn into compost."

"I know, I actually interviewed her about the festival and making it greener. I wish more places in Boston were doing that. I'd love to talk to the farmer who's doing the composting,"

Jack laughs, "Look at you, already all-in about telling local stories."

"You're right, I'm going to do some festival stories, and that's it. I am not getting invested." She sits back and drinks her coffee. She doesn't want to let down her guard or let him in too much, so she once again deflects. "So besides thinking about this project, what else are you doing while you're here?"

"No, no no, you can't change the subject that easily," he says. "You're already invested, Lizzie, because whether you want to admit it or not, you care about this town. Just like I do. Just because we move away doesn't mean we don't care what goes on here."

"Fine, so I care. What are you doing?" she asks again, determined to not give up, always the reporter, she will just keep asking and Jack knows it.

"Honestly? I'm not sure. I'm doing some work remotely, but I'm mostly trying to figure some things out."

"Like?"

"You're determined to get a story, aren't you?" he laughs. "I meant it when I said I don't know. There's a lot I like about California, but I know deep down I'm an East Coaster. I miss the seasons, I miss the people." He's quiet for a moment. "There's something about the intensity of working in the atmosphere of the place where it's all happening that is exciting, but pretty exhausting as well. It's work 24/7 and I miss having balance. Going for a walk on the beach, taking my sailboat out, working in a garden."

Lizzie crinkles her forehead, "You never had a garden."

"Well, I *could* have a garden if I didn't work all the time." he says. "I mean, don't you find that too? Isn't working in journalism at that level intense?"

She nods her head. "Oh, you have no idea. It's always speed and quantity over quality now, and I feel like a writing bot sometimes, not a person. I swear if Greylock, the company that now owns the Sentinel, could find a way to run a newspaper without writers they would. We're just a necessary nuisance to them at this point. All creativity is gone, it's just how fast can you spit this story out and get it up on the website."

Jack is quiet. "So what are we both doing?"

"I don't know. Getting better at what we do? Learning? Advancing our careers?" She's quiet for a moment. "It wasn't supposed to be like this. We did have a different plan, remember?" Her pulse quickens and she picks up her napkin and begins twisting it. She's been holding all this in for so long. "We could have made it work, but you decided we couldn't."

Jack sits back and takes a deep breath. "You're right." He looks at her directly, he's not hiding from her honesty. "There isn't a day that goes by that I don't think about you, about the life we had planned and how I blew it. I am so, so sorry, Lizzie."

"Yeah, you did blow it," she says, not giving him an inch. "But the good news is I got to see that now rather than ten years from now."

"I'm not sure what you mean," Jack says, now leaning forward on the table, his hands tightly gripped together.

"That when we got hit with a crisis—your venture not working out– "

"Completely failing, and losing hundreds of thousands, actually millions, of dollars," he corrects her.

"Fine, however you choose to describe it, when things got hard, really hard, instead of working with me, treating me like a partner, you turned away from me. I'm just glad I found that out before I'd invested more years of my life, before we had a couple of kids, and owned a home. It was good for me to see how things would go," she says cooly.

It's getting tense at this tiny round table.

Jack leans back again in his seat. Lizzie can't tell what he's thinking, his expression is giving nothing away.

"I have to admit, I never thought of it like that," he says, running his hands through his hair and sighing. "I failed you, I failed us." He looks out the window at the snow that's started falling again. "I was so ashamed of how wrong things had gone, at how all my planning and calculations and predictors had been wrong. All I could think was I didn't want to burden you with my failure. I didn't want you tied to a failure. You deserve the best of everything and I didn't want to take you down with me. I was completely wrong, and I will spend the rest of my life regretting how I handled it."

"I had thought we were a team, that we'd face whatever life threw at us together. I wasn't judging you, I wanted to help you," Lizzie says, choking up. "We just didn't end up having the same idea of what a marriage and partnership is, like I said, better to have found out sooner than later."

Lizzie wants to end this discussion and move on. She's said what she needed to, no need to keep going over it.

"So you don't know when you're going back to California?" Lizzie asks, shifting the conversation away from the past.

"I don't know," he looks like he's reeling from all Lizzie has laid on him. "I may take a break to work off-site for a bit to figure some things out."

"They let you do that?" Lizzie asks enviously. "You can go on a kind of walkabout?"

"We're all given time for sabbaticals every three years. They say it's a way to encourage people to get creative, but I think it's because after three years people are burned out and need a break. It's a sneaky way of getting people not to quit. And what often happens is as people buy houses, have kids etcetera, they're sewed in, they can't leave, so lots don't."

"Are you?"

"Am I leaving?"

"Yeah, I have to say it's hard to picture you living back here," she says. "You seem like you've outgrown Cranberry Harbor. But you talk about these plans that seem like they would be impossible to implement remotely."

"That is very true. I need to figure out what there would be

CHRISTMAS IN CRANBERRY HARBOR

to come back to, though," he says as he plays with his coffee cup, swirling the contents around. "I burned a lot of bridges, clearly. I'm trying to figure out if a return would be welcome, or a bad idea for all involved."

She's quiet. "I don't think all your bridges are burned, maybe just singed." Despite everything she does care what happens to him. "I'm sure your family would love to have you back."

He laughs, "Oh, you have no idea, my mom keeps leaving real estate ads on my bed and circling stories in the Gazette about the need for more young people here to create opportunities and move the town toward the future. I'm just not sure where I fit into the grand scheme of things. My last venture was such a flop, I worry about letting people down again with this new idea. Who would trust me?"

"I don't think you were a flop. If anything I think you came with your ideas before people were ready to listen. A lot has changed, people are more attuned to having their job look different than it may have even just three years ago."

"You're probably right, but I don't know...I don't even know that many people here anymore, do you? I mean, other than family?"

"Not really, most everyone I knew left. Ben, and now Alexis are the only ones of my close friends here."

"Yeah, me too. A couple of guys I played soccer with are here doing construction," he says.

It's hard to return to easy chit-chat after the conversation they just had, so Lizzie decides to cut and run. "Thanks so much for the lunch, the skating," she cocks her head about the skating, which wasn't the greatest, "and for taking me out to see the property and hear about your plans." She stands up. "I am going to head over to the Gazette and get that story done and see how my dad is doing."

Jack stands too. "Lizzie, I meant it when I said I was sorry. I know sorry hardly covers it, but I–"

She puts up her hand. "We're okay, Jack, really. I appreciate the apology. I really do. I'm fine."

"Could we maybe be...friends? I know it's a lot to ask," he says.

She looks at him and he looks so sad. "A couple of days ago I would have said absolutely not, but maybe."

"Well, a maybe is a lot better than absolutely not, so I will take that," he says.

Lizzie gathers her things, puts her mother's funky hat on and turns to go. "Thanks for a good day. And for listening to me."

"Any time," he says. "I'm sorry it took so long for us to have that conversation, and for me to apologize."

"It's good, we're good," she says. She turns to leave and turns back. "Can I just ask you one thing?"

"Of course, I owe you that," he says, shifting his weight from foot to foot nervously.

"You just gave up, you stopped calling, you never came to see me, you didn't fight for me at all," she says.

"I did call, Lizzie, for weeks, and then you told me not to. I didn't want to foist myself on you. I was respecting your wishes," he says. He looks down at the floor. "And I did make the big, bold move. Months after you told me not to call I spontaneously got on a plane and flew to Boston. I went to your building and sat outside. I sat on a curb for a couple of hours. It got dark and you came home with a guy. You were laughing and having fun. It looked like you'd moved on, so I left."

"I don't remember that night, or who that was," she says. "I had no idea you came to see me."

"After that I decided I needed to let you go, so I stopped thinking I could ever fix things."

Lizzie feels really sad, and realizes she has jumped to a lot of conclusions. "This doesn't erase all the hurt, but it helps explain things. Thanks." She starts to leave.

"So maybe I'll see you at Santa and Mrs. Claus's arrival at the cove tomorrow, and pancakes? Jack asks.

"I will be there, wearing stretchy pants." she jokes.

"It's a date, er, a plan, I'll see you there."

Apropos of nothing, Lizzie high-fives him, "I have no idea why I did that," she says, shaking her head.

"It's cool, I like a nice high-five once in a while," and they both laugh.

As she heads to the Gazette she hopes she hasn't made a huge mistake taking down that wall by a few, well, it seems maybe by many bricks. But as she walks she feels lighter than she has in what feels like forever. A smile spontaneously crosses her face. She feels happy for the first time in a long time, and it feels good.

CHAPTER 15

AFTER TOUCHING base with her dad she borrows his car to go home and finish her work from there. It's been a long day and she needs to get cozy.

"You look awfully cheery," her Mom says as Lizzie comes into the kitchen, setting down her things and peeling off several clothing layers, leaving them on the bench in a big, wooly pile.

"Duh, it's Christmas time, Mom! We're supposed to be cheery!"

Her mom glances at her, "Did you, an accomplished journalist, just 'duh' me?" she smiles. "Well, I'm glad to see you so happy." She continues to place the pie crusts she's working on into quiche dishes. "How was skating? Your Dad said you and Jack were going."

Lizzie pulls up a stool and is picking at the grated cheese and chopped vegetables her mother has assembled, Gabby playfully slaps her hand.

"Elizabeth Leland Martin, stop eating all my quiche ingredients!"

Lizzie knew she was in big trouble when her full name was used. Leland, her mother's maiden name, always stopped her in her tracks as a kid. She pulls back and sits up straight. "Yes, ma'am, it won't happen again," and as soon as her mother's back is turned she steals another cherry tomato.

"I saw what you did, there's going to be nothing left!" Gabby laughs.

"I'm sorry, I'm just hungry, must have been all that fresh air." She pauses and looks at her mom, "Somehow being back here I have time-traveled to my childhood and it's been kind of nice." She gets up, and opens the fridge, looking for something to nibble on.

"You still didn't tell me how the skating was," asks Gabby, as she cracks eggs into a bowl, adds milk and begins to whisk them together.

"Oh, it was fine," she shrugs. "We did get knocked down by an overzealous middle schooler, but only our pride was hurt." She finds a bowl of some cut up fruit to nibble on and sits down again. "Oh! You'll never guess who I saw there!"

"Who?"

"Alexis! She was working the food truck for Hope. We're going to try to get together while I'm here. She's so incredible. She was teaching in South Korea, and now she's getting her Master's in town or community planning or something."

"I always loved her, she was always so passionate about everything she did, and was so good at everything." She begins assembling the quiches, spreading cheese on the crusts, then layering in the vegetables. "Did Jack have fun too?"

"I love how you're trying so hard to not ask me what you want to ask me. Mom, you can ask me anything, you know."

She pours the egg and milk mixture onto the cheese and vegetables. "I don't want to be THAT mom," she says, looking uncomfortable. "You know, the mom who is pressuring you to settle down already, and how'd that date go, and is he the one…"

"You've never been that mom and never could be, so don't worry." She picks at the fruit in her bowl. "The answer is, I don't know. It's very confusing. I've spent three years moving on from Jack, and done okay with that, or so I thought."

"Do you feel like you've moved on?"

"Kind of? I mean, I dated other people, like Ed," she says, a little unsure of if that really means she's moved on.

Gabby rolls her eyes, not so Lizzie can see, but still, it's a big roll. "He wasn't right for you. Even before the big, 'he doesn't like dogs,' revelation, I knew that."

"Yeah, he wasn't. I'm not really worried about it. I've honestly got enough on my plate right now, week to week wondering if I'll still have a job the next day. A relationship right now would just add more stress to my life. And actually, Jack and I had a really good talk today. I got to say some things I never had. And he apologized. Very sincerely."

"Wow, that's a very big deal. You two hadn't really talked since he left. Do you feel better? Like you got some closure?" her mom asks.

"There's that word again," she eats another piece of cantaloupe. "Yeah, I feel better, less angry and resentful. I don't think I ever thought about how upset he was, how he felt like he'd failed so many people, including me, and he just wanted to run away from it all."

"He said that?" Gabby says, sprinkling some more low-fat cheese on the quiches.

"He did. I think enough time has passed that maybe I can see his pain now. I couldn't before."

"Oh, and what you said earlier about a relationship adding stress to your life? I kind of think if it's the right relationship it doesn't add stress, it actually reduces it, but hey, what do I know, I've been married for 800 years."

Lizzie laughs. "Yeah, at least!"

"Is Jack thinking of moving back to Cranberry Harbor? He sounded like he'd kind of like to the other night when he was here."

Lizzie is quiet, "I think if the right opportunity came along, he might. He seems to miss it a lot."

"And you, do you miss it?" Gabby asks after she puts the two quiches in the oven and sets the timer.

"Sometimes yes and sometimes no, I'm not sure."

"I can understand that." She's thoughtfully cleaning up the quiche-making mess. "You've built a really great life in Boston. You've got a great job, friends, a cute apartment, there's lots to do, not like here in the winter where the sidewalks roll up at five, and the nearest movie theater is a half hour away."

"Yeah, there's a lot to be said for being in the city, but there's a lot that's very special about being here. And being near you, Dad, Matt, Shannon and Sophie."

Her mother isn't sure how much to push, so she doesn't. "Well we're always here, you know that."

"I do, and believe me, that gets me through a lot of not-so-great times." She goes to put the now-empty fruit bowl in the sink and Gabby takes it.

"I got it." She rinses it out and turns to Lizzie, "I'm just glad for this, right now, it's wonderful having you here for however long that is."

"Me too," says Lizzie, gathering up her phone and purse. "Do I have time before dinner to quickly write up a couple of little blurbs about skating at Thacher's Bog and wreath making at the Marshview to send off to Dad?"

"Yeah, and if you're not done, they can sit for a bit, no hurry."

She heads for the stairs, "This won't take me long, they're just brief little what, when, where with some color pieces, I'll be down in a little bit. And I have to go back and get Dad too," she says reminding herself that she left him stranded at the office.

Back at her desk she looks through the photos she took before she and Jack were taken down by that kid. She'd caught one of him looking at her like she was crazy and it makes her laugh. Before she dares get sentimental she swipes through and finds three to send to her dad to go with the story, and sends those off.

Even though the writing she was doing for the Gazette wasn't Earth-shattering in its content, she couldn't help but notice how it just felt better than what she'd been doing for the Sentinel. There was a lot to be said about sharing the small stories of a close-knit community, rather than making sure to write headlines that would get the most clicks. Peter Martin did not give a hoot about clicks, he cared about the people at the coffee shop or the market feeling like their lives and the stories about them and their community mattered.

In short order she had written a 500 word ode to skating on a flooded cranberry bog, quickly followed by locally sourced wreath making. In under an hour they are both sent off to her dad.

She still hadn't heard from her dad to come get him, but before heading down for dinner she pulls up Alexis's number from her text, and sends her a quick message.

Hey friend, super last minute, but you want to meet up for some coffee and dessert later at Sea Coast? I understand if being in the truck all day it's the last thing you want to do...

She puts her phone on the nightstand and lies down on her bed, suddenly feeling very tired. She can feel her eyes getting heavy when her phone dings.

Hi! Yes! I'd love to see you. Especially since you are not a middle school kid who will dump a pile of sticky coins in front of me and ask me if that's enough for three cocoas and three chocolate covered pretzel rods. Ha ha.

Lizzie checks the time.

Would 7:30 be too late? Mom is making dinner and I don't want to bail on her.

As she waits to hear back she gets up and starts taking off some of the skating layers and puts on something less North-

Pole-explorer looking and more coffee shop hang with a friend. Her phone dings again.

That's perfect! I'll see you then! Can't wait!

Lizzie sends her back a heart emoji, and suddenly feels much less tired. Alexis was her best friend all through middle and high school. Neither were ever the most popular girls, but they managed to be themselves and also kind of under the radar socially. Alexis was always very creative, spent a lot of time in the art room, participated in Mock Trial, and also student government. By junior year Lizzie was editor of the student paper, working part-time for her father, the bookstore and Sea Coast, and was spending a lot of time with Jack, another slightly nerdy kid. They don't have student teaching assistants in high school generally, but Jack was so good at math and computer science, that by junior year they'd run out of classes for him and he was taking college classes online, and helping other kids who were struggling. He was always a great teacher. Lizzie had sometimes thought if Silicon Valley hadn't come calling he would have made a fantastic high school teacher, but the pay and perks certainly couldn't compete.

Once she had put together an outfit that felt comfortable and looked decently pulled together, she went into the bathroom and refreshed her makeup a little. How many times had she looked at herself in this very mirror she wondered? Turning left and right, studying her outfit–a flippy short skirt, leggings and a sweater– she felt like she looked pretty good. She paused for a moment while she was looking at herself and wondered what her teen self would think of her life. Being back in her parents house, writing for her dad, spending time with Jack were all taking her back to another time. For so long a city paper had been the big goal, and now that she had it, it wasn't really all she thought it would be. Granted, in the fifteen or so years since she'd graduated from high school, the world of newspapers had changed a lot. When she was in graduate school, things weren't as bad as they were now. As she brushed her hair, twisting it up into a messy bun, she felt a pang of worry in her gut. Would she soon be one of those unemployed millennials moving in with her parents?

She decided to save the lipgloss application until after the quiche, gives herself one final look, turns off the light and heads downstairs.

"Oh my gosh, Mom, that smells amazing!" She arrives in the kitchen to find both quiches and her Dad, who she'd been waiting to pick up, since she had his car."Dad! This is a nice surprise! How'd you get here? I've been waiting for you to let me know I needed to come get you." She walks over and hugs him.

"Matt came by so I bummed a ride so you wouldn't have to come back. I still have some editing to do - not your pieces, thank goodness They are clean as can be and don't need anything, thank you very much. I thought I would do the rest of my work here, and spend some time with my girls."

Suddenly Lizzie felt terrible. "Oh no," she says, helping her mom set the table. "I feel awful, I reached out to Alexis and we're meeting at Sea Coast in an hour. I'm sorry. I can cancel and hang out with you two, it's no problem."

"No," both her parents said at the same time. "You haven't gotten to spend time with her in years, you go," says her mom, carrying a quiche to the table with oven mitts. "Your dad can edit and I can do some wrapping, and we can be together by the tree and the fire. It will be lovely."

"Well, if you're sure you don't mind, I really would love to see her." Lizzie pulls out a chair and sits down. "Mom, you've done it again, this smells amazing." She lifts her plate and Gabby puts a warm slice on it. "You are spoiling me. I am never going to want to go back to grabbing some ramen from down the street, or reheating some mac and cheese from the night before."

"I worry about you not taking good care of yourself, honey,"

Gabby says, serving herself a slice. "You're not 17 anymore, you need to eat better, get enough sleep, exercise...do you take time for any of that?"

Lizzie is quiet. "Kind of? I go to a yoga class once in a while, but it doesn't always work with my schedule, and when it's nice I go running. But it's not consistent."

"Listen to your Mom, Lizzie," Peter interjects between bites of salad and quiche. "I never would have thought she'd get me to go vegetarian, join the gym or start meditating, but after listening to her I have to say I've never felt better."

Lizzie puts her hands up in surrender. "Okay, you two have got me, I promise. It will be my New Year's goal to start taking better care of myself. You're right. I look at you two and you are great role models."

When she's done, she takes her dishes to the sink.

"Just leave them, honey, I know you need to get going to meet Alexis, it's fine."

"I hate leaving you to clean up after having made this amazing dinner." She gives her mom, still sitting at the table, a hug. "Dinner and dishes are on me tomorrow night, okay? I'll think of something to make for all of us. Maybe Matt and family can come too. I'll text him." She runs upstairs to put on her lip gloss, grab her purse and phone, and she's down the stairs in a flash.

"Bye, guys! I'm sure I won't be late!"

"Give Alexis our love," Gabby calls, as Lizze is quickly out the door and headed to her car.

She beats Alexis there, so she grabs a table, not near the door, it's really windy, and it's a very cold spot every time someone comes in, a memory that is forever etched in her brain. She takes off her coat, puts it on the back of her chair, and just as she's sitting down, Alexis comes blowing in.

"Hey, sorry I'm late!" She rushes over and gives Lizzie a big hug.

"You're not late at all. I just got here myself." Lizzie pulls out her card, "What do you want? My treat."

"No, I can't let you do that," she goes to take out her wallet and Lizzie stops her.

"No, my invite, my treat." She starts walking toward the order counter. "I am going to have a decaf latte, because if I don't do decaf I will be up all night."

"Wow, look how you have changed, I'm so disappointed," Alexis laughs. "You used to drink coffee into the wee hours and never had any trouble sleeping. We're getting old!"

"No! We're not old, we're more...refined," Lizzie demurs.

"Uh huh, we're old," Alexis laughs.

"Fine, but don't tell anyone! What do you want for dessert? All these pieces of cake and pie look so huge! I shouldn't have had a second piece of my mom's quiche. Oh! My parents send their love by the way."

Alexis is staring into the case like it's Narnia. "Give mine to them too, I love your folks. Hey, how about we split something? I'm pretty full too."

"Perfect! Chocolate cake? Or something else?"

"No, that would be wonderful."

They're next in line. "And what do you want to drink?"

"How about a decaf green tea?"

"Ha! You can't do caffeine late anymore either!"

Alexis laughs, "Busted. I haven't slept great in months, I'm always stressing about something. Caffeine certainly doesn't help."

Lizzie places their order, pays, and they step aside to wait.

"I'm sorry, what are you stressing about?" Lizzie asks, concerned.

"Ugh, all the 'what am I doing with my life' angst." She shakes her head. "School is good and everything, but I don't know what I'll do with a Master's in Community Development. Especially if I decide to stay here. I can't imagine any town here being willing to hire me, the town boards like everything just the way it is."

They hear Lizzie's name called, pick up their drinks and the cake and head back to the table.

"It's funny, you remind me of Jack," Lizzie says.

They sit down and each pick up a fork and take a bite of cake.

"Hmmm, oh my gosh, this is so good," Alexis says. "What do you mean? Is he having an early mid-life crisis too?" she says, taking another bite.

Lizzie laughs, "Not exactly, and I concur on the cake by the way," she takes another bite, waits a minute and continues her thought. "He's just trying to figure out if there's a way he could create something here too. It seems we're all kind of in-between things."

"Not you, you've got the big-city job of your dreams, an apartment in Somerville, the cool place everyone wants to be, you even know the mayor of Boston."

"Ha, she knows my face and name which happens if you show up to every single press conference, ribbon cutting and hockey game, she can't help but recognize you," Lizzie smiles and takes another forkful of cake. "It's not at all personal, like here. I haven't been home for more than a day or two in a long time, I had forgotten what it's like to be seen, be known by people, and to know them. It's kind of nice." There's one bite left of the cake and she gestures for Alexis to take it.

"Okay, if you insist," she says and happily takes the final piece. She sits back and sighs a contented sigh. "Thank you, that was wonderful."

"You are so welcome, let's hope it's not another five years in between seeing each other." She sits back too. "I can't imagine having lived in all the places you have, teaching so many kids, was it hard to adjust to being back here? I mean, this is a bit different than Spain, or South Korea."

"I was ready, but I'm so glad I did it. Culturally it was incredible to not just visit, but actually live in all these different places, to become a part of a neighborhood in another country. And I loved expanding the world of kids. Like in Korea, for lots of them I was the first Black woman they'd ever known. I think that in the twenty-first century, it's important for kids to be global. But now I want to make where I come from a better place, and I missed the ocean, and my grandparents."

"I'm sure they missed you too." Lizzie suddenly gets quiet.

"You okay?" Alexis asks, looking worried.

"Yeah, I'm just thinking." She swirls her latte in its cup. "Truth be told, I'm a little between things too."

"Have you been seeing anyone in Boston?"

Lizzie shrugs. "I was, Ed."

"You don't look enthused."

"Eh, we dated for almost a year, but it was just kind of..."

"Boring? Convenient?" Alexis says.

"Yes and yes," she laughs. "He works in government, and has lots of plans for his future, wants to run for office and all that. He was a perfectly nice guy, but I just never felt–"

"Butterflies?"

"Yeah, no, never." she says, shaking her head. "It was like he was a good fit from a catalog, you know? But there were no surprises, no excitement. I could see if I didn't end things we would have had a perfectly serviceable life in a Boston suburb with 2.5 children, a Volvo and a golden retriever. What's sad is in that scenario the only thing that got me excited was the–"

"Let me guess, the Golden Retriever?" Alexis says laughing.

"Exactly! So, I broke it off. He said how sorry he was, but I saw him at an event I was covering about a week later and he was with someone else. He just wanted somebody, he didn't necessarily want me." Lizzie says, swirling her coffee in its cup.

"I hear you. Between school and working when I can for

Hope, I don't have any interest or time." She shifts in her chair. "Okay, so now I have to ask the obvious question, what about–"

"Nope, we're just friends now. He broke off our engagement and moved away. No, no way, no how."

"So that's a hard no, then?" Alexis asks, smiling at her.

"Yes," Lizzie laughs. "We had a good talk today, and I think we could be friends. That's a big step from despising him."

"Okay, because when I saw you two together, you looked like you were having an awful lot of fun, and things change, people change. You're not the same people in lots of ways that you were three years ago."

"It's been a big step for me to hang out with him again. We've had a lot of fun, but I can't count on him."

"I get it, but–"

Just as Alexis is about to finish her thought the high school chorus comes pouring in, there must have been thirty of them, all dressed up in long black skirts, white blouses and red capes on the girls, and dress black pants, white shirts, red ties and black blazers on the boys. They fan out around the tables and begin singing, *Deck the Halls.*

Lizzie leans into Alexis so she can hear her. "I'd forgotten all about this! I remember doing this once, before I quit chorus!"

Alexis laughs, and gestures for Lizzie to lean in. "Yeah, it felt so not cool to do this at 16, but now, I really like it. I would totally be into doing this now!"

"Me too, it's sweet," says Lizzie. She actually likes this a lot, she thinks, as she drinks the last of her latte.

The kids sang a half-dozen or so carols, got some cocoa and left. Lizzie managed to get a few photos that she sent to her dad, thinking they could be a nice last minute addition to the paper. Always a journalist, she can't help herself. This was a quintessential Cranberry Harbor at Christmas moment and she was so glad for the paper, and for herself that she was there.

"Anyway, all I was going to say was, promise me you'll keep

136

an open mind? We all grow up and learn from what we've been through," Alexis says as they put their coats on and get ready to leave. "I've known you for a long, long time. Jack too. I just have a feeling. And my feelings are rarely wrong." They head to the door and outside.

"Oh, I remember your gut feelings being right a whole lot of the time. Sadly I didn't ask you what your gut felt before I dyed my hair for prom." They both laugh. "Okay, I promise to keep an open mind. And I will do that all the way from my apartment in Somerville." She smiles, and gives Alexis a big hug. "We will have to do this again soon, okay? I'm here for a while longer. And when I'm back in Boston, you know you always have a place to stay, even if it is a lumpy couch."

"Sounds good, I would love a place to get away to, especially during February and March!" Alexis says as she heads to her car, "I'll text you soon!"

Lizzie gets in her car and heads back to her parents and wonders if she'll ever be able to keep an open mind about Jack. Is it really possible to forgive and forget? Or even really let him in again? Of that she was much less sure.

CHAPTER 16

LIZZIE ARRIVED home to find her dad asleep in his chair, laptop still glowing, and her mom quietly wrapping presents for Sophie on the floor while little Daisy was sound asleep under the Christmas tree.

She quietly sat down next to her mom, and put her head on shoulder.

"Aw, well that's sure nice," she says quietly, not wanting to disturb Peter. "Did you have fun?" she asks as she makes some ribbon curls with an open pair of scissors.

"I did. I forgot what it's like to have a friend who's known you forever." She picks up some art supplies for Sophie and doesn't say anything else. "Alexis says hi back, by the way."

"Aw, that's nice. There's a comfort and unspoken understanding with old friends that's special, but you can make close friends later in life too. Like your friend Sarah at the paper, you two seem close."

Lizzie shrugs, "Yeah, sort of. I mean, I really like her, she's awesome, but she's also married, has a kid and a fulltime job, there's not a lot of room in there for friends. Which I completely understand. If I do see her outside of work she usually has her son, who is adorable, but it's not like I have a movie friend, or coffee date friend."

Her mom looks at her. "That sounds kind of lonely, honey."

Not wanting to worry her mom she quickly perks up. "Oh, it's not bad, and there's lots of things that I go to on my own that are great, right in my neighborhood. Two weeks ago I went to a book signing and the author spoke, and it ended up being a really fun evening. She was really inspiring."

"What was the book?" her mom asks, starting on another gift.

"The author was Callie Simmons, and she had kind of done her own, millennial version of an *Eat, Pray, Love* year. She lived in Brooklyn, Boston and the Berkshires, and it was about community, friendship, and making peace with yourself. Not constantly comparing your successes or lack thereof, with anyone else. It was about coming to terms with being an actual adult and realizing that doesn't mean you have all the answers."

Her mom laughs. "Did you think that's what being an adult meant? Having all the answers?"

"Kind of?" She looks over at her sleeping dad. "I never saw you or dad falter, or seem to question what you were doing or the path you were on. You never seemed to skip a beat."

"Oh honey, we faltered and flailed all the time! Maybe we should have let you and Matt see that more!" She gets up and puts another log on the fire and pokes it a bit. She comes back and sits down. "Adulthood isn't about having all the answers, no one does, sweetheart. It's more learning to be sort of okay with some uncertainty and realizing for the most part, unless you do something really stupid, things generally turn out okay."

"How do you not do something really stupid? Asking for a friend," Lizzie smiles, but is seriously concerned.

"I think you kind of just know? That's why we listen to our gut, and ask others if we need to, but I think in general, we know what we're supposed to do. But also? You're not really living your life if you don't do a few stupid things along the way. I've often learned the most from the things that didn't go well."

Lizzie sits and thinks, looking at the little gifts for Sophie, and starts to cry.

"Oh honey, what's the matter?" Gabby says, pulling her into her.

"I don't know, I have no idea why I'm crying. It's just," she wipes her nose on her sleeve and takes a deep breath. "I feel like I walk around all the time looking over my shoulder wondering when I'll be discovered."

"Discovered as what?" her mom gently asks.

"A fraud. Someone who has no idea what they're doing."

"At work?"

"At work, at life," she takes a deep breath. "You saved people's lives, you did something really valuable. I write about parking tickets and bridge closures."

"Journalism is incredibly valuable, you respect what your dad has done, right?"

"Of course," Lizzie says. "But that's different. He's never compromised himself the way we have to now. He never sold out." Lizzie lets out a deep sigh and takes a sip from her mom's glass of red wine sitting on the coffee table. "Hope you don't mind," she smiles. Gabby shakes her head.

Gabby gets up and goes into the kitchen and brings back an open bottle of wine and another glass. "Here," she says, pouring a glass for Lizzie and handing it to her. "Life is full of compromises, my dear, we all do it, we just try to also do the things that count and matter to us."

Lizzie takes a sip of wine. "You're right, I can find other ways than just my work to feel like I'm contributing. Jack asked me to help him write up a proposal for the town, that's something I can do to help out."

"What kind of proposal?" Gabby asks, reaching the end of the pile of gifts.

"I'm not really free to say, but it is something that could be good for the community."

Gabby smiles and nods, "I like it. And he would be lucky to have you helping him. You have an excellent way with words."

"I second that," says Peter, suddenly awake from his nap. "How long was I out?" He puts his hands through his hair and tries to rouse himself. "I cannot pull 16 hour days like I used to, that's for sure."

"Dad, no one should be working 16 hour days. Especially-"

"If you say, 'at your age' so help me," he says laughing.

Lizzie puts up her hands, "Oh, I know way better than that!" She stands up, and picks up her wine. "I'm going to head upstairs. Oh, Dad, I don't know if you saw them, but I sent you a couple of shots of the Seaward High School chorus at Sea Coast tonight, thought they'd be nice to have in the paper."

"I did! Thank you honey. I forget how nice it is to have someone doing things like that, it's a big help," he stretches and tries to rouse himself.

"No problem," she gives both her parents a kiss goodnight and heads out of the room. "G'night, love you guys," she says as she heads upstairs.

"Love you too," they both call after her.

As soon as he thinks she's out of ear shot, Peter sits back in his chair, and sighs, "Boy, what I wouldn't give to have her-"

Lizzie pauses on the stairs, feeling a little guilty eavesdropping, but curious about what her parents are saying about her.

Gabby gets up off the floor and moves to the couch. "I know, I know, but don't pressure her, I've got a feeling she's doing a lot of thinking on her own, but if she feels like we're pushing her it may have the opposite effect."

"Okay, I'll stand down, I promise. It's just so hard when Greylock Media is breathing down my neck. They call me every single week to see if I want to sell. Some weeks it's tempting, but damn it, they own every other paper on the Cape now, and for no other reason than being the one holdout, I'm going to do my best to not ever let them have it. Having Lizzie here could make it a lot more possible to keep afloat. She could help grow the paper. I know it. But I'll keep my mouth shut for now."

"I'm going to hold you to that, because there is nothing I'd love more than to have her back here, and I know she could help you. I miss her so much, and I don't think she's really happy in Boston," Gabby says.

Lizzie is now leaning on the banister, not wanting to miss a word of her mom's assessment of her life.

"No?" Peter perks up, concerned.

"I think she's fine, we don't worry about her, it just doesn't seem like things are all she hoped they'd be."

"And you think they could be here?" Peter asks.

"I don't know, we both know there's no perfect life, but I just think maybe she could find more of what she's looking for here, that's all."

"And let me guess, you think part of what she's looking for is Jack."

"Maybe, maybe not, but I've got a feeling," her mom says.

Lizzie's face feels hot, what her mom thinks matters to her, she can't possibly think she belongs with Jack.

Peter smiles at her. "I would never bet against you and your intuition, that's for sure."

Gabby smiles back at him, "Oh, you would lose every time." She swings her legs around and curls up, "Sometimes I look at friends who are pushier with their kids and wonder if our mutual promise to never tell our adult children what to do is a good thing," she says half-joking.

Peter laughs, "I hear you, but the good news is, because we don't ever tell them what to do, they trust us and know we respect their autonomy. But I admit," he says stretching out and yawning, "things did seem a lot simpler when they were little."

"Big kids, big problems, little kids, little problems," Gabby says. She takes a last sip of her wine. "Well my love, I am going to head upstairs too. Tomorrow is the big kickoff to the festival week and I need to be ready for anything." She gets up and leans over to kiss Peter.

"I love you, Gabby," Peter says, taking her face gently in his hands. "Oh! Before you go, listen to what she wrote."

Gabby sits back down, and Lizzie is still listening, feeling like she's 14.

"Okay, I'm all ears," Gabby says.

"Listen to this, *"A community without young people is a community without a future,"* she writes. *"We need to find a way to marry progress with protecting what we all love about Cranberry Harbor. In this twenty-first century we are lucky to know more than ever before about how to protect our precious environment, and how to use the technology we have not just for jobs, but to make our community and our planet, a better, safer place for all. I believe with the right people, the right ideas, and a consensus, we can create a community that is diverse, welcoming, has room for all who love it here, and will help it become an example for other communities across the state, across the country, and around the world."*

"Wow, that is incredible, she is definitely your daughter," Gabby says.

"Our daughter, I can tell she still loves this town," Peter says.

"She needs to figure that out herself, honey, we can't force it on her," Gabby says. "I am now off to bed. Don't stay up too late." She gives him a kiss.

"I love you, sweetie," he says.

"I love you too," she neatly piles up all her wrapping tools and equipment. "I'll put all this away tomorrow," she says. "Now that you had your nap you're probably going to be up for a while," she says. "I'm going to take Daisy out one last time for the night before I head up. Can you make sure the doors are closed on the fireplace, and that you turn off the tree?"

Lizzie quietly hurries up the stairs before her mom turns the corner.

Peter nods, "Yes, dear, I promise. Go get some sleep. I'll be up before too long."

Lizzie goes into her room and closes the door. Alexis, her mom, her dad, why does everyone think she's going to end up back with Jack? Are they all seeing something she's too stubborn to? Or is she actually the only one who is not being blinded by history, romance and Christmas?

CHAPTER 17

LIZZIE WAS SHOCKED to find herself up before either of her parents and especially Daisy. She was even more surprised at how excited she was for the pancake breakfast and the Clauses arrival at the pier. She feels like she is eight again, and it feels good. She hasn't been to the pancake breakfast in at least three years, but it's more likely at least five. The older she gets the more self-conscious she has felt going, wondering if everyone is thinking, 'what the heck is that woman doing here? Again!'"

Padding down to the kitchen, not wanting to wake anyone, she takes the coffee beans and grinder out to the freezing cold garage so she doesn't wake her parents. Since when did they get so fancy? When she was growing up it was Folgers in a can all the way. This new-found passion for locally roasted beans continues to surprise her. It was one-hundred percent better though, that's for sure.

Once the coffee has brewed she takes her cup and curls up in a corner of the couch by the tree. She hops up to plug it in to get the full effect and snuggles back down. As she sips her coffee she scrolls mindlessly through her Instagram, she sees Ed with someone who appears to be his new girlfriend, if that kiss until the mistletoe is any indication. She doesn't feel jealous, more just kind of sad that she'd stayed as long as she had with him even though she knew she didn't love him. She decides to unfollow him, not because she's jealous, but because she's done. She wishes him all the best, but she doesn't need to be a witness to his life. It feels good to let him go.

She then wanders over to Jack's account. She'd long stopped connecting with him on social media in any way, but things are a bit different now. His Instagram page is pretty sparse, he never was much for putting his life online for all to see, kind of ironic for a tech guy living in Palo Alto. Lizzie was never much of a social media person either, which worked for her job. Journalists were supposed to keep their opinions and political leanings to themselves, so she'd never really gotten into sharing much of her life online. She always considered herself more of a lurker than an active participant on social media. There were some photos on his page from California, a few from many months ago with a very pretty woman who he looked pretty cozy with. She sees her name, @penelopej and, even though no one else is up, she looks around to see if anyone is watching as she goes to her page. She is beautiful, and if the white coat and stethoscope draped around her neck are any indication, a doctor too. Lizzie can feel some jealousy rising in her out of the blue, along with some insecurity. She looks to see if there are more photos of her with Jack, and if so, how recent. Jack is a free agent, he's free to date anyone he wants, but still, she's curious. Heck, she was seeing Ed until a few weeks ago, so she assumes he's been dating as well. Just as she is about to click away from Penelope's page her phone dings, it's Jack. Oh God, he knows, she irrationally thinks, he knows I'm stalking him and @PenelopeJ online.

Hey, hope I'm not texting too early, I wanted to make sure we were still on for Santa, a boat and pancakes. Do you think anyplace else does this? As I typed that sentence I suddenly realized how weird it sounds.

Lizzie chuckles. Having grown up with Santa and Mrs. Claus arriving on a boat every year, it didn't feel weird to her, but the more she thinks about it, it is the kind of thing that would probably only happen in a seaside town. Or a movie.

No worries, I'm up. Having coffee and trying to figure out what to wear - probably something stretchy. And yeah, it is a little weird.

She chuckles to herself and awaits his reply, and catches herself. Remember - you are never, ever getting back together, and he has a girlfriend.

Maybe I'll borrow some of my dad's sweatpants, we will make quite the couple...I mean, team. #teampancake

She looks at the copy of the Gazette sitting on the table, the page conveniently turned to the opening day schedule. She quickly skims the page and finds what she's looking for.

Santa and Mrs. Claus arrive at 9, we can just meet there a little before that?

Taking a last sip of her coffee she waits for his reply. There's no dots, nothing. Maybe Penelope was calling! Okay, you are officially losing your mind. Besides, it's like 4:30 in the morning in California. Finally she sees him writing.

I'll be there 8:45-ish?

Sounds good. I'll see you then-ish, she writes back.

As she gets up from the couch she hears Daisy clicking her way down the wooden stairs, she runs over to Lizzie.

"Good morning, you little cutie," she says petting the dog's wriggling, fuzzy body. She walks to the foyer and sees it's her mom who's up. "And good morning to you, you're a little cutie too," she smiles, patting her mom's head.

'You're sure up early," Gabby says, shaking her head as she heads into the kitchen. "You sleep okay?"

"Yeah, I just woke up and decided instead of trying to go

back to sleep to just get up. I'm meeting Jack at the pier, 8:45-ish. That's his ish, not mine."

"Just like old times, huh?" Gabby says, pouring herself some coffee. "Thanks so much for this, I didn't even hear the grinder."

"Oh, I did it in the garage."

"The gift of adult children," Gabby says laughing.

"What? I wasn't always a perfectly behaved and thoughtful angel when I was growing up?" she asks, laughing.

"No, thank goodness, you were not. That would have been scary."

"Are you going to the pier? Or do you have other things you have to do?" Lizzie asks. She mindlessly gets a bowl out of the cupboard, and starts looking through the very healthy selection of cereal and settles on some organic raisin bran.

Gabby reflexively goes to the fridge and pulls out some oat milk. "Try it with this, it's a fantastic combo."

"I will take that recommendation," she says, pouring it on over the flakes dotted with plump raisins. She takes a bite, Gabby waits... "Wow, that is good! It adds this whole other layer of flavor." She takes another spoonful, and chews. After she swallows she nods, "nice work Mom, you are definitely the queen of healthy deliciousness."

Lizzie looks at the clock on the oven and quickly finishes the cereal, rinses her bowl and puts it in the dishwasher. "I hate to eat and run, oh dear lord, why did I do that?! I'm going to eat pancakes!" She slaps her forehead.

"Oh, gosh, I wasn't thinking either! I'm sure you can still get one or two down."

"I'm just not very focused these days. I think it's the lack of routine."

"Want me to give you a routine? A list of things to do every day?" her mother jokes.

"No, I do not. Thank you very much. I just need to stop being so distracted."

"Distracted by what?" her mom slyly asks.

"Oh no, you are not going to get me to say anything! It's work, Christmas, trying to help dad–"

"Jack..."

"I'm going to go take a shower. Bye, Mom!" and with that Lizzie runs up the stairs.

She twists her long hair up and secures it with an old scrunchie she found in a drawer, and hops into the shower. While soaping up with the natural loofah, she keeps thinking about Penelope J. Jack never mentioned being in a relationship, she wondered how serious it was. If it was serious wouldn't she be here for Christmas with him? Or he would be with her family? "Ugh, stop it!" she says out loud. She rinses off, uses the exfoliating face scrub her mom has put in the shower, and after one final rinse, she turns off the water and hops out.

As she slips on the cozy robe, and has a stern talk with herself in the mirror. "You are going back to Boston soon, and you need to stop this, whatever *this* is, right now." Her reflection doesn't look particularly impressed or convinced. "He is the same guy who broke your heart, don't be wooed by how nice he is, or how much fun you have with him, no, you need to stop it right now. Nip this in the bud, Young Lady." She thought a stern, 'young lady,' might make more of an impression.

Twenty minutes later she's applied some minimal makeup, gotten dressed, taken down her bun and brushed out her hair. And she's put on a well-curated outfit of cozy olive green leggings, warm socks and an oversized cream-colored slouchy sweater.

She bolts down the stairs, Peter is now up too.

"Morning Sunshine," he calls out to her. "You headed to the pier?"

"Yes, sir, I am, you need me to do something?" she asks as she sits down on the bench and puts on her boots. Her now very favorite boots.

"If you could just grab a few photos with your phone it would save me a stop. I can save them for the preview for next year."

"No problem, I'm happy to, Dad." She puts on her coat, zips it up, puts her phone in her pocket and grabs her purse. "Okay, I will catch up with you two later!"

"Have fun, honey," Gabby calls from her perch at the counter.

"Don't eat too many pancakes like that time-"

"I will not throw up off the end of the pier, I promise, Dad," she says, laughing as she closes the door behind her.

She trudges through the snow that must have fallen after she got home last night, opens her car door and starts it up. While it's getting warm she does a cursory clean off with a brush she has in the back, then hops in and heads to see Santa arrive on a boat

CHAPTER 18

WHEN LIZZIE ARRIVED the parking lot was already filling up, and there were excited children everywhere.

Glancing at the clock on the dashboard, it is 8:44, or 8:45-ish. She pulls on her hat, gets out of the car and looks around for Jack. As she starts walking toward the pier, decorated with a red carpet, the railing is covered with greens and red bows and she sees him walking toward her.

"You're not wearing sweatpants," she says as they get closer to each other. "I'm so disappointed."

He smiles and throws his hands in the air. "Sorry to disappoint, I just couldn't do it. I do still have some pride."

"Fine, I hope my outfit isn't an embarrassment for your sartorial sensibilities, I wanted to be warm."

"You look great, as always." He turns toward the pier, "Shall we, madam? I believe there is an arrival happening very soon that we need to be there for."

"Yeah, I've got to take a few photos for my dad, so I have to be there when they pull in."

The two of them hurry across the parking lot and run down the pier and join all the others anxiously waiting for Santa.

"Oh my gosh it's cold!" Lizzie says, "I did not really factor in the being right on the water part of this activity!" She gently bobs up and down trying to warm herself.

Jack pulls her in and rubs her arms briskly, she feels both happy and unsure about the gesture. "It shouldn't be long. I saw Brady, Jess and Tom getting into Tom's lobster boat as I was driving here. They were about to head off."

"Ah, so they roped Brady into being Santa this year? I'm glad they'll be here soon," she says, still shivering.

And just then the kids all start yelling, "It's Santa! It's Santa!" As the boat gets closer to the pier.

A little girl standing next to Lizzie is so excited she starts crying. "He's really here! I've been waiting for Santa for my whole entire life!" she exclaims.

Jack and Lizzie look at each other and smile.

"I can't imagine being that excited about anything, it's so sweet." Lizzie says to him.

"I might get that excited if someone gave me season tickets for the Red Sox," Jack says. "Or the Pats."

"If I am ever in the position of seeing you get that gift I am going to hold you to that," Lizzie says. She has her phone out and quickly takes a handful of photos. The look of happiness and excitement on the children's faces is priceless, and she hopes she's doing it justice.

As the lobster boat pulls up, Santa, aka Brady Simms, one year ahead of them in high school, begins "Ho,ho,ho" ing very convincingly. There truly is nothing like seeing Santa Claus, and Mrs. Claus of course, surrounded by fishing gear and lobster traps on a boat. Lizzie hoped her photos captured it all well.

"Look at all of you who came out to greet me on this cold, cold morning!" he says. "Thank you! Are all of you ready to go inside and have some pancakes and cocoa?"

"Yes!!!" they all yell.

"Well, let's get inside, and then you can all tell me what you want for Christmas!"

And another yell of excitement.

"It doesn't take much to get this crowd excited does it?" Jack laughs as they head to the club house.

"Yeah, I think it's a safe bet that cocoa, pancakes and presents are kind of a slam dunk."

"Well, he had me at cocoa," says Jack.

"Me too!" They follow the running children to the door, which Jack holds open for the littler stragglers, and then gestures for Lizzie to go in ahead of him.

"Thank you sir," she says, giving him a curtsy, "You are so very kind."

The inside of the town clubhouse is decorated within an inch of its life. There is garland hanging from every possible fixture, two Christmas trees, a faux fireplace that is lit up, and little lights twinkling everywhere.

"Wow, is it just me or have they really upped their decorating game since we were kids?" Lizzie asks Jack as they both drink in all the Christmas.

"No, it's not just you. I remember one very Charlie Brown Christmas tree, some of those large Christmas light bulbs strung around the windows, and the pancakes on a very plain table. I also remember the crankiest Santas one year–"

At the same time they both blurt out, "Ernie Payne!" and laugh.

"Oh my gosh, he told me that dolls were dumb and he'd bring me something more useful, like a tool kit," Lizzie says laughing.

"Well, he told me I had a terrible arm and it was useless to bring me a new glove, that he'd be better off giving it to someone who could actually play the game."

"Clearly they did not vet the people they strong-armed into the role back then."

The kids were all lining up to sit on Santa's knee, so Lizzie and Jack took the opportunity to grab some plates and pile on some pancakes before they started clamoring for breakfast. Lizzie puts two on her plate, and a moderate amount of butter and syrup.

"I have to say I am incredibly disappointed in that poor showing, Ms. Martin. I would have taken you for at least four, maybe a five pancake stack."

Lizzie looks at him and narrows her eyes. "I don't know whether to take that as a compliment or an insult?" she says laughing.

"Oh, it's totally a complement," Jack says. "You just kept talking about how much you love these pancakes." He points to an empty table a bit removed from the crowd.

She puts her plate down, "Be right back," she says as she runs over to get a few more photos of the kids and Santa.

She rushes back and plunks herself into the seat. "Anyway...I made a stupid mistake at home and had a bowl of cereal completely not thinking about eating pancakes." She picks up her fork, cuts into the little stack and takes a bite. "Hmmm, these are just as good as I remember."

Jack takes a bite, chews and nods in solidarity. "You are quite right." He takes a knife and cuts through his much larger stack of about six pancakes. "I can't believe you wasted valuable stomach space on something as pedestrian as cereal."

She holds up a finger as she chews, then swallows and says, "Oh, this wasn't the least bit ordinary, it was organic raisin bran covered in organic oatmilk" She gestures to their plates, "As yummy as this is, I'm thinking, not organic, and I hate to break it to you, not even real maple syrup."

"Fine, you have me there, but maple flavored corn syrup can be quite delicious," he says, having put a big dent in his stack.

Lizzie looks around the room, half the kids are done with

Santa and have moved over to the pancake area, and are being delighted by Mrs. Claus.

"Jess makes a lovely Mrs. Claus," Lizzie says. "It's so weird to think back to when we were the little kids coming to this, and now we're old enough to be Santa and Mrs. Claus!" She takes a couple of more bites, but she's full even before finishing her paltry two pancakes.

"The sad thing is though, there's so few of us around anymore who remember these traditions, who are here to make sure they continue. I hate to think of a bunch of people who didn't grow up here doing these things. It just doesn't feel right."

Lizzie looks around at the mostly older retired folks who are volunteering. That is often the case since younger people are working, or have little kids, but she knows Jack is right. The median age of Cranberry Harbor is 65, and if something doesn't change in the next few years they are going to find themselves living in a retirement community, not a thriving small town.

As the children all sit down to eat, the adult volunteers start singing *Jingle Bells*. Never one who liked to sing, Jack finds himself swept into it too. The two of them get up and join the other adults as they serenade the kids. Normally Lizzie and Jack would have felt very self-conscious, but somehow singing along with Santa and Mrs. Claus has given them a big shot of Christmas spirit. *Jingle Bells* leads seamlessly into *We Wish You a Merry Christmas*, then *Rudolph the Red Nosed Reindeer*, and before they know it an hour has passed.

Jack and Lizzie are laughing as they head back to their table. "Oh my goodness," Lizzie says, "I do not remember the last time I sang one Christmas carol, nevermind an hour's worth! That was actually really fun. Somewhere my teen self is rolling her eyes. But I don't care, I liked it, darn it."

"Oh, we're hiding this from young Jack as well. He would be appalled that this is now what passes for fun on a Saturday morning." He sits back and takes a sip of his now-cold cocoa. "But you know? I don't care if it's hokey, it was fun. Really fun."

Lizzie nods and smiles. "Yeah, I'd kind of forgotten how much fun simple things can be. Why is it when we get to be adults we think happiness has to be elaborate, or expensive?" She sits back and sighs. "Bring back simple, is what I say."

"I like it. Let's make it happen–hashtag–bringbacksimple. It's going to go viral!" he laughs.

"No!" she scolds him. "You're thinking like a tech guy. Simple means unplugged, no hashtags allowed!"

"Yes, ma'am!" he laughs. "No, I hear you. In my world it's always all about scaling things up, making things bigger, and bigger isn't always better." They're both quiet. "I've got some notes in my car that I worked on last night that I wanted to show you, are you doing anything after this? Would you be free to get some coffee?"

"Yeah, no, I've got a bunch of nothing on my plate. Let's go."

Both of them offer to help clean up, but are shooed away by a trio of older ladies dressed like elves. Both Lizzie and Jack decide they did not want to mess with those elves, and head into town in their cars, meeting up minutes later at Sea Coast.

They walk in together, Jack once again holding the door for her. She had to give him points for never having lost his manners in all the years she'd known him. Even as a teenager he was always respectful and just, nice. And funny, and smart...The kind of guy it wouldn't be bad to spend the rest of your life with, she'd thought.

They snag a table, and put their things down, and head to the counter.

"What are you having?" Jack says, getting out his wallet.

"No, you treated last time, let me get this," Lizzie says, getting out her wallet.

"Lizzie, in all the unfairness in the world, one is that I make a ridiculous amount of money doing something I'd do for free–don't tell anyone that–while people in professions like journalism, which is incredibly important to our society, don't. So let me assuage some of my guilt by treating you to tea, or whatever you want."

"So it's a pity tea, huh?" she says, smiling at him. "Fine, you can work out your income guilt on me, I'm down with it." She looks up at the tea menu. "Now that you mentioned tea, that is sounding really good. I think I will have some Earl Grey, thank you very much."

"Earl Grey it is, and yeah, now I think I want tea too," he pauses for a moment and then says to the barista, "Two large teas, please, one Earl Grey, and one English breakfast. Thank you."

They step aside and as they wait for their order. Alexis spies them from the back and comes around.

"Hey you two, fancy meeting you here! Jack, nice to see you again," she gives him a hug. "And you lady, I just saw you last night!" she jokes giving Lizzie a hug.

"Are you working?" Jack asks. "If you're not, you're welcome to join us, we'd love to hang out."

"You sure? I wouldn't be crashing? I am due for a break."

"Absolutely not crashing. Grab something and come sit down," Lizzie says.

Jack's name is called, they get their teas and head back to the table.

"I think Alexis might be someone good to run some of my ideas by, what do you think?" Jack asks her as he blows on his tea. "You said she was getting a Master's in community development, right?"

"Yeah, I think that could be perfect, she's really interested in trying to find a way to build a career and make a life here. Let's see what she has to say."

Within a few minutes Alexis is back and pulls up a chair. "You two look like you're up to something," she says, looking back and forth between them. "Spill!"

Lizzie and Jack both laugh, "Boy, you are nothing if not perceptive," Jack says. He clears his throat, and pulls out his notebooks. "Okay, so you know that I tried to create this software start up here that went belly up-"

"Ancient history," says Lizzie. "Sorry, go on."

He smiles at her and continues. "But the thing is, nothing has changed here in terms of people needing jobs and housing." Jack sees Alexis looking at him like *tell me something I don't know*. "So I've been working on some ideas, a couple I ran by Lizzie, and I have some new ones as well. Could I bore you both for a few minutes?"

Both of them nod, "This is far from boring, Jack, you had me at having some ideas," says Alexis.

He pulls out a sketchpad. "Okay, so the first thing I talked to Lizzie about was that land on the outskirts of town-"

"The one that developer was going to put McMansions on, right?" Alexis asks.

"Yeah, it was not at all what Cranberry Harbor needed— more wealthy people and nothing for locals. So the town did the right thing, nixed that idea and took back the land." He flips open the pad. "So I've been working on this idea of melding the tech world with the growing farming and local business population here. It's completely self-sustaining energetically, between a couple of well-placed, discrete turbines, solar panels, and state-of-the-art battery technology. Farmers can lease out some of their property for solar panels, providing them with a passive income year-round, and we can build ecologically sustainable tiny houses, and regular-sized houses. The tiny houses would be perfect for college students who may come here for an internship, or single people who don't need the space or expense of a whole house." He takes a deep breath. "You bored yet?" he laughs.

"No, not at all. I feel like we're witnessing the future of the town right here," says Lizzie.

"Okay, so I've been thinking about this, and talking to some friends and colleagues out in California, and one company has been talking with the Cape Cod Marine Studies Center on a project they'd like to bring here, there's actually two things. These ideas are farther down the road, but good things to be thinking about. So these friends of mine, Max and Marnie, have a system for removing nitrogen from wastewater, a huge problem on this sandbar. I know, not exactly a glamorous business, but—"

"Could help save the Cape," says Alexis. "It's good for the environment and would provide good jobs too. That's amazing, Jack."

"But wait, there's more," he says, joking. "When I was in California I was working on some side projects, and there's an angel investor who wants to help us get this other project going."

"Okay, what's that?" asks Lizzie.

"I just talked to my friend and he said that they'd like to find a spot on the East Coast to coincide with the building of their Northern California facility for carbon capture, to help with global warming. And I was thinking of—"

"That old abandoned base down-Cape?" says Alexis.

"Exactly! We are at the forefront of climate change here on the Cape, and we need to do something, and this would bring really good jobs, and hopefully help the planet."

"Wow," Lizzie sits back. "This is amazing. And you really think you could get the money to actually do these things?"

"Yes, there are lots of people out there with lots of money who truly want to do good things with it. This is of course a one step at a time thing, we won't try to do everything at once."

"Well I'm interested, that's for sure," says Alexis. "Sign me up!"

"Be careful what you say, I could come knocking and want to hire you. We're going to need someone with community planning skills. What I really want to work on first is the project right here. I want to start with housing, energy and working with local farmers and artisans, introducing the tech world to the local one."

"Well, I'd be very interested. Not that I don't love Hope, but I'm almost done with my Master's and I'd like to be doing something in my field, and hang up my barista apron for good."

"We will definitely talk," says Jack, sitting back and taking a big sip of his tea.

Alexis's alarm on her phone chimes. "Ugh, I hate to, but I have to run," she says. "I told my granddad I'd help him pick out a Christmas tree," she stands up and pushes her chair in. "I am definitely very interested in this, please keep me in the loop. And thank you so much for thinking of me! I'll see you both soon, I hope," she says, gives them each a hug, and then heads off.

"I will certainly be in touch," Jack says. "Thanks for listening!"

"See you soon!" Lizzie calls after her. "Jack, this is amazing. I cannot believe what you've pulled together in such a short time. It's incredible."

"I want to make up for the last time. The promises I didn't keep," he says looking at her.

Lizzie isn't sure what he means. Personal promises? Business? Both? Suddenly she feels very nervous. "I hate to, but I should go too," she says, getting up and putting on her coat. "When you're ready, talk to my dad, he'll be able to tell you all the right people to reach out to. He'd love to help I'm sure."

"Okay," he says, unhappy that she's leaving. "Will I see you later? The scavenger hunt starts soon."

"Maybe? I'll shoot you a text, thanks so much for the tea," she says as she exits quickly. She doesn't know why, but she just couldn't stay one more minute. If she was part of his grand plan she honestly didn't know what she'd say. How could she ever trust him again, and what if he did in fact have a girlfriend back in California? There were just too many questions.

CHAPTER 19

LIZZIE WENT OUT and sat in her car for a few minutes to try to figure out what the heck freaked her out so much. There had been so much talk–with everyone she knew it seemed– about wanting to come back to Cranberry Harbor. She didn't get it. She and all of her friends had wanted nothing more than to get away from this sandbar when they graduated. To go and have adventures, and not live the roller coaster life that comes with living in a summer tourist destination. They all talked about wanting to live someplace that was affordable, and provided diversity, steadier incomes and didn't get invaded every summer. Was she the odd person out now? Was she not seeing the potential? As a journalist it was hard to make an argument for coming back to a place that had one daily paper owned by a terrible corporation that wasn't doing well, some weeklies owned by the same huge company, and her dad, god love him, who owned the last independent newspaper standing on Cape Cod. She didn't like feeling confused. She liked her life, mostly. While it was not always what she thought it would be, it was good. Okay, good-ish. She had her apartment, her favorite coffee spots, multiple coffee spots, thank you very much, not like here. But, yes, there was a but. It was also ridiculously expensive, her rent was over $2500 a month, and her family, whom she adored, is here. "Gah!" she says out loud, putting her head on the steering wheel.

She decides to call Sarah, she needs a reminder of her real life. She pulls her phone out of her pocket and waits for her to pick up.

"Hey, how's it going in Christmas fantasy land?" Sarah says instead of just hello.

"Oh I'm living the dream," she laughs. "It's fine–"

"Uh oh, anytime you say 'fine' I know something is up. Come on, out with it, and be quick because I am driving to pick up Wyatt from a birthday party."

"It's just, some people I grew up with have come back, or want to come back and it's like, I don't know, we all had an unspoken deal to move and declare the Cape unlivable except for visits."

"Like, how dare they go back on that unspoken deal you had in high school and want to return to the Cape, leaving you to be the odd girl out of their small town club!" Sarah nails it. How does she do that, every single time?

"Maybe?" Lizzie sits back in the car seat and looks around. "I mean, yeah, it's pretty, the people are really nice, the ocean is beautiful–"

"Wow, you make it sound like a nightmare," Sarah says laughing. "Does this have anything to do with the ex-fiancee'?"

Sarah doesn't pull any punches, which most of the time is one of the things Lizzie loves most about her. Unless she's the target. "No, yes, I don't know."

"So that's a yes," Sarah says. "I'm pulling into the party, so I can't talk much longer, but, what I'd say is, maybe it's time to think about what you want to do, and not what you think you should do."

"Succinct and to the point. You are always the best in life crisis moments, thank you."

"Well, you might want to wait on that opinion until you see me when I pick up a kid hopped up on sugar and Christmas before you render your verdict," she says laughing. "You are many things that are so wonderful, and also, an overthinker and over-analyzer. Just enjoy this time at home, keep an open mind, and see what feels right."

"Will do. Thank you my friend, I love you, and I hope Wyatt isn't too out of control!"

"I love you too, go have some fun, damn it. If not for you, do it for me, because I am so not having any fun right now."

Lizzie laughs. "Okay, I will do as you say. Thanks friend, talk soon!"

She's still sitting in her car when Jack comes out. He walks over to her car.

"Hey, I thought you were long gone," he says as she lowers the window. "Everything okay?"

"Yes," she shakes her head. "Sorry about, before…"

"No apology needed. We're always cool, no worries."

She nods and smiles at him. "I appreciate that. So where you headed?"

He pulls out what looks like a handwritten list and unfolds it. "I am going to meet up with Sean and Ben and wander around and do some of the scavenger hunt.They texted me that they're on their way. Wanna join us?"

"You sure?"

"Yes I'm sure, I was actually hoping you'd join us," he says.

Lizzie decides to heed Sarah's advice and just have some fun, something she clearly needs to work on. "Okay, I'm in." She gets out of her car. "Are we playing as a team, or is this an individual competition?" she says with a glint in her eye.

"Oh, I know better than to go up against you. You won this three years in a row in middle school."

Lizzie smiles, tosses her hair back and nods. "Oh, yeah. I was totally the queen of the Cranberry Harbor Christmas Festival scavenger hunt. I found things they'd even forgotten to put on the list!" She laughs. "There are times when being a compulsive overachiever comes in very handy."

"There's Ben and Sean," Jack says. "Guys, we're over here," he calls to them. Main Street is getting more crowded, but the pair spies Lizzie and Jack, as they cross the street, and join them.

There are hugs all around. "Lizzie, I'm so glad you're here, Jack wasn't sure you'd be able to come," says Ben, giving her a hug. "Thank you by the way, so much for the beautiful piece in the Gazette, thanks to you we are completely at capacity for our classes."

"Yes, thanks so much," echoes Sean. "Just about every single person who called to sign up said they'd seen it in the paper."

"You're so welcome.I forgot the paper came out this morning. I'm so glad it helped. I loved writing it! I'm probably way too late to sign up myself, damn it!" she laughs.

"No!" they both say at the same time and laugh. "Are you kidding? Of course you can come. You have to, actually," says Ben.

"Well, if I HAVE to, I'd better then," Lizzie says.

"And bring this guy," Sean says, fake-punching Jack in the arm. "You look like someone who could use a nice artisanal, locally sourced wreath."

"It sounds like something I could eat," jokes Jack. "An 'artisanal wreath' sounds like something made of organic crudité. I'm definitely in!"

"Ha ha, very funny," Ben says. "Your mom will love it, I promise."

"I'd love to come. I haven't made anything with my hands in years. Rebuilding a motherboard probably doesn't count," he says.

"Come to think of it, I never do anything crafty either," says Lizzie. "This will be good for me. Too much of what I do is all in my head, not at all hands-on. So Jack here has the list, should we start looking for some items?"

They all agree it's time to get started. Jack pulls out the list. "Okay, we are going to need a basket or something to put all these things in," he says, looking at the long list. "This first group of things looks like items for your wreaths, we need to find ten pinecones, preferably of different sizes, four feathers, a dried hydrangea flower, a sprig of holly, six clam shells and some seaweed."

"That's just the first group on the list?" asks Lizzie, taking it from Jack's hands. "Wow, this one alone could take us a while."

"That's why it goes on for the whole week," says Ben. "People kind of peck away at it." He looks over Lizzie's shoulder. "How about Sean and Jack go down to the pier to look for seaweed and clam shells, and Lizzie, you and me can take the path out toward Hanson's meadow and see what kind of foliage and pine cones we can find?"

"Sounds good to me," says Lizzie. "Hey, I saw over at Tall Tales they've got a bunch of baskets outside for the taking for this, I'll go grab two." She runs over and picks up two baskets from the stack. Anika spies her from inside and comes out to say hi.

"Hi!" she says, wrapping her arms around herself to try to stay warm. "Thank you so much for the wonderful article! Jay and I loved it! I don't know what we'd do without the Gazette to get the word out about events. Social media is good, but we love the old-school method."

"I loved writing it, it was completely my pleasure." She picks up two baskets. "Thank you for providing these, a few of us are going to do a bit of the scavenger hunt. I haven't done it in years."

"I heard that not long ago they used to give out plastic bags, which is so not a good thing, so we found these great baskets, and the town got them and we put them all over. Every little bit helps."

"You're freezing," Lizzie says, "You go get inside. I'll come by before Christmas. I need some last minute gifts for my parents."

"I'll look forward to that," Anika says, heading back inside.

"Say hi to Jay," Lizzie calls, and Anika gives her a thumb's up.

She hands a basket to Jack, and slings the other over her arm. "Okay, Ben, you ready?"

"So, ready!" he says. "Want to plan to meet up back here in say, an hour?" he says to Jack and Sean. "That should give us all enough time."

"Sounds good," Sean says as he and Jack head off.

"Alright Miss Lizzie, you feeling lucky? I'm a little worried about the feathers, how often do you see feathers on the ground this time of year?"

"Yeah, that could be a sticking point," she says as they start walking. "But, no matter what, at least it's not too cold, it's sunny, and I'm getting to spend some time with you," she says, putting her arm through his.

"Yes! This is a total treat."

They almost immediately come upon a hydrangea bush with a handful of dried blooms on it, and Lizzie goes to break one off. "Wait," Ben says, taking a small knife out of his pocket. "This will be better." He cuts the flower off and puts it in the basket. "One thing down, 500 to go!" he jokes.

"I think there's a holly bush near my Dad's office," Lizzie says, "Why don't we stop by there and snip a branch."

It's a gorgeous December day. One of those rare times when it's not windy, there's no clouds and the sky is a blue so deep and bright that it almost doesn't look real. The weather on the Cape can turn on a dime, so these gorgeous winter days are never to be taken for granted. The climate has changed though, even in Lizzie's lifetime. The warming of the planet has meant hotter, more humid summers, which has brought more seals coming to enjoy the warmer waters, which in turn has brought sharks. Something Lizzie never thought about when she was a kid boogie boarding at Sea Meadow beach. Now the life guards were always on the lookout, there were drones, boats with spotters, and all the beaches had shark warning flags. Winters were different too. It could be mild, then suddenly a powerful Nor'Easter could come up the coast, and there had even been dangerous microbursts, a weather event that creates damage similar to a tornado. Locals worried a lot about the effects of climate change, rising tides and storms that have been eroding much of the coastline. Cape Cod is a special and precious piece of land, and is also incredibly fragile.

"So you're happy being back here?" Lizzie asks, sounding almost reporter-like, not meaning to.

Ben looks at her and smiles. "Is this for a story, or is it just you asking?" he queries, watching where he's walking on the sidewalk that was only slightly shoveled after the last storm.

She laughs, "God, even when I don't mean to, I come off like I'm interviewing people. I sometimes feel like I've forgotten what it's like to just talk to someone. Sorry about that. No, this is just me asking you. Friend to friend."

"Okay, friend. Yes. I am happy being back here. No place is perfect, that's for sure. There are things that need work, housing, jobs, climate change…but I think if there were more of us here, more people our age I mean, we could create a lot of positive change."

"You sound like Jack, he's got a lot of ideas." She stops and points to a holly bush ahead. "Yay, there's some holly!"

Ben cuts off a sprig and puts it in the basket. "Yay, two items!" They keep walking, and head toward a little park on the outskirts of town. "Yeah, he's been talking to Sean and me about it a bit. He hasn't tipped his hand too much, but I'd love it if we could keep the integrity of the environment, and so much of what makes Cranberry Harbor special, but also grow and become an example of how to make it all work." He's quiet for a moment. "What about you? Where do you see your future? In Boston? It's a pretty great city. Do you have a good community there? Now who's interviewing who?" he jokes.

Lizzie thinks for a minute. Does she? She has familiar faces she sees, but she doesn't even really know her neighbors in her building. They're a mix of graduate students, a few families, and other young professionals. Everyone is working hard to make their own thing happen, they're not chatting in the halls or having pot luck dinners. And for the most part that has felt okay, until everyone here started talking about having more.

"Kind of? Eh, not really. You've lived in cities, you know what it's like. I mean I know the folks at the bodega on my block, and they're really nice to me at the neighborhood coffee shops, but there's been so much turnover at the paper I've lost a lot of colleagues. It's different than here."

"Yeah, it's really different. When my parents asked if we wanted to take over the inn I wasn't really sure. Sean was on board right away, but he didn't grow up here, he'd never spent a dreary winter wondering when the sun was going to shine, or if there was ever going to be people around again."

Lizzie laughs. "Yeah, a lot of people really romanticize a Cranberry Harbor winter."

"It may have its romantic moments, but it can be very long and gray."

"So what finally convinced you to come back?"

They continue to walk in silence for a little bit. "It's probably going to sound silly, but one day I was home and doing some errands for my parents, and everywhere I went there were people I knew. And they cared about how I was, and asked about my parents. When I was younger I admit I found it annoying, now I think it's really nice. It feels good to have people who know me and care about my family." He shakes his head. "That probably sounds really hokey."

"No it doesn't. Not in the least. It actually sounds really nice."

"It is." Ben stops and points, "Well look at that..."

"What?" Lizzie doesn't see what he's pointing at.

"I see two big turkey feathers up ahead." He quickly walks ahead, and leaning against a felled oak tree are two perfect turkey feathers. "Ta da!" he says, raising them in the air. "Two down and two to go," he says, placing them in the basket.

"Nicely done!" Lizzie says, "Now we only need two more, the 10 pinecones and we've done our part of the first part of the list."

"Pinecones should be everywhere in here, that will be easy. Oh, look, there's a bunch right here," he bends down and picks up five.

"I am definitely not pulling my weight," Lizzie says as she scans the area for feathers and pinecones. "Oh!" she exclaims, "Here's another feather, this looks like a blue jay." Into the basket it goes. "You know, the best thing about this, besides spending time with you of course–"

"Well, yeah, of course!"

She laughs, "No, the *other* best thing is it makes you look around and notice things. I feel like my face is buried in my phone about 90 percent of the time and I miss so much."

"That is one very good thing about running the inn, and especially the kitchen. I can't be looking at my phone all the time. I've noticed a big difference since I moved here. Of course I'm not always sure the trade-off of working round the clock in the summer is such a healthy thing, but I have seen a difference from when I lived in Providence and Portland."

They keep walking. It's a bit more wooded and the light is streaming through the branches, making the path look magical with the sun-dappled ground.

"Can I ask you a personal question?" Ben asks. "I don't want to pry."

"Oh, pry away. I've given up on having any secrets in this town!" she laughs.

"Wait, there's a pinecone," he scoops it up and tosses it in with the other treasures. "You and Jack, you seem so good together. I know you were going to get married, and then he moved, and..."

"And that was the end of that story." Lizzie says, kicking the mixture of snow and leaves with her toe as she walks. She shrugs, "He moved to California, and that was that."

"I'm sorry, I don't want to bring up anything that's uncomfortable. I shouldn't have said anything. But I can't help but see how he looks at you, and you have this level of comfort with each other that honestly, you don't see a lot. And we get a lot of honeymooners!" he jokes.

"Jack is a really good guy. That's why I planned on marrying him," she says, smiling with a trace of sadness. "I tried not liking him, being mad and staying mad, but it's hard since he's not a bad person. Maybe we were just too young?"

"So are you thinking it could work now that you're both a little older?" Ben asks, looking very hopeful.

"Are you and Sean desperate to have people to hang out with? Do you need people for bridge?" she jokes, they both laugh. "And I'm not so sure he doesn't have a girlfriend back in California. Penelope? I think she might be a doctor." She shrugs her shoulders.

"He hasn't said anything to me, I don't think he's seriously involved with anyone. I really don't. I'm sure by now he would have said something to one of us if he was. And nope, not looking for bridge partners," he laughs. "And I wouldn't say we're desperate for people to hang with, but yeah, we could use some good friends like you two, and honestly, the town could use you both as well. I have a feeling you could both do a lot to help grow the year-round economy and help those of us here to improve things." He stops walking and looks at Lizzie. "Honestly, I'm worried that if we don't make some big changes environmentally the Cape won't be here for our kids to enjoy, and if we don't find a way to keep younger people here, it's going to be like a retirement village in Florida, but with snow."

"I hear you, I know that's what Jack, Alexis and I have been talking about too. About finding a way to make it viable to live and work here." They keep walking slowly, keeping their eyes peeled for a few more pinecones and one final feather. Lizzie suddenly stops and puts her hand on Ben's arm. "Wait, did you say 'our kids'? Are you and Sean having a baby?"

Ben blushes and looks nervous. "He's going to kill me, we're not telling anyone yet-"

Lizzie raises her hand, "My lips are sealed!" she says.

"We've started the process to become foster parents. We're doing the home study, and having interviews, and have started the series of classes they have you take."

"That is the best thing I've heard in... forever. You two will be the best parents!" She hugs Ben. "I am so excited for you! And I won't say anything to anyone. Not even Jack. I promise."

"Thanks, yeah, we're excited, and terrified."

"That sounds completely right. It's a big step."

Ben takes a deep breath. "We told them we'd be open to siblings, and not necessarily a baby. So it could be a lot."

"You will have your family, friends, and the whole Cranberry Harbor community around to help. You won't be doing this alone."

"Exactly. I never could have thought of doing this anywhere else. My parents are over the moon about becoming grandparents, so I'm sure they'll be wanting to help a lot."

"Oh look," she bends down and picks up a cluster of four pinecones on a branch, and next to that one lone gray feather. "It's a sign! I think this is it, we're done." She puts them all in the basket. They turn around and start heading back to town. "I'm really glad we had this time together. It's been really nice," she says.

Ben puts his arm around her as they walk. "It really has been fun. Move back!" he whispers in her ear.

She smiles and puts her head on his shoulder, and for the first time, the idea of moving back is feeling a little tempting.

CHAPTER 20

JUST AS THEY return to the town center, Sean and Jack are walking back from the cove.

"How'd you two do?" Jack asks, swinging his and Sean's basket from hand to hand. "We got everything on our half of the list."

"And got dive-bombed by some very annoyed seagulls," says Sean laughing. "I thought Jack might actually fall off the pier, I was all ready to jump in if need be."

"Thankfully, I was able to keep my balance while those french-fry seeking marauders kept coming at me," Jack says dramatically.

"Marauders, huh?" Lizzie laughs. "I'm very glad to see you survived intact."

"Hey, those birds are big, and they are relentless!" he says, laughing at how funny it sounds.

"No, man, those guys are fierce and when they have their little hearts set on finding some fries, there is no getting them to stop," Ben says, piling on.

"You two are mean," says Sean. "They are no fun when there's a bunch around you and they want something. Be nice!"

Lizzie calms down and stops laughing. "Oh, I know. Seriously, I remember being a little kid and having one steal a sandwich right out of my hand. Freaked me out for the longest time." She playfully hits Jack on the shoulder. "We're just teasing, I know how pushy they can be, I'm very glad you did not end up in the freezing cold water." She looks into their basket and sees the shells and seaweed they needed to find. "There's a table over there in front of Sea Coast, let's put all our things on it and take a picture and text it in."

"I know I'm going to sound like I'm 90, but when I was a kid you had to go and track someone down and show them all your finds, and they'd check it off on an old clipboard. Now you just send a photo and that's it," says Ben. "Okay, I am now officially the grumpy, 'they didn't do things like that in my day.' old guy."

"You are hardly an old guy, and I agree, it loses some of its old-school flavor doing it this way. But I have to say, it is a lot quicker," says Lizzie.

They take a picture of all their findings, and for good measure, a selfie of the four of them.

"Okay, next on the list is, 'One thing that makes Christmas special,'" Lizzie reads. "Should we track down Santa and bring him in?" she suggests, smiling..

Jack takes the list from Lizzie and looks at it. "Yeah, this one leaves a lot up for interpretation, doesn't it?"

"I actually kind of like that," says Sean. "Christmas means something different to everyone, so this is a way for all of us to share what makes it special to us."

"You're right," Jack says, and thinks for a minute. "How about each of us chooses something that means Christmas to us, and then we put them all together?"

"I love that," Ben says. "Yeah, let's do it."

Lizzie looks around trying to think about what her one item could be. "Wow, that's not easy, to break it down to just one thing."

CHRISTMAS IN CRANBERRY HARBOR

"I know," Jack says, feeling just as perplexed. "Should we split up so we can focus? Say meet back here in a half-hour? And just take a photo - so you're not dragging back the huge tree from the square or something!" Jack looks to the trio for consensus.

They all nod in agreement. "Yeah, let's meet at Sea Coast for cocoa in a half hour?" suggests Ben, "Sound good?"

They all agree and head off in different directions. Lizzie doesn't have a clue as to where to even begin to look. A snow globe? Candy canes? Without thinking she starts walking toward the Gazette office at the other end of town. While she's walking down Main Street it starts to snow, not a lot, but just that perfect, like you're inside a snow-globe kind of snow. It was funny, when she was in Boston the snow just seemed like a pain that made parking harder - her neighborhood was filled with the folks who dig out a spot and put a beach chair in it while they're gone, the Boston signal for 'don't even think about parking here!' But here, now, this snow feels well, kind of magical. Oh boy, there you go again Cranberry Harbor, sinking your sweetness and homespun claws into me, she thinks.

It was truly impossible, looking all around her to find just one thing that made Christmas, Christmas to her. It was a million little things. Things she had managed to kind of block out of her mind in all the years she'd skipped coming home because so many of them were connected to Jack. She didn't even want to think about Jack making Christmas special, because he'd proposed to her at Christmas, and then left a year later for California, you guessed it, at Christmas.

Before she knows it she's at the Gazette office, so she decides to stop in and check on her dad. She climbs the stairs to the second floor office, opens the door and sees her father, mom, Matt and Sophie gathered around a little Christmas tree in the corner of the room.

"Well hey guys, did I miss the memo that we were having a

party today?" Lizzie asks as she walks over and scoops up Sophie.

"Hi, honey," her parents say.

"We texted you many, many times," Sophie says, wriggling out of her arms and going back to decorating the tiny tree. "You didn't come but then you did."

Matt laughs. "We texted you twice, I figured you were busy with Jack," he teases. "Was I right?" He continues to help Sophie with the little tree, keeping her from overloading it with so many ornaments on one side that it will fall over.

"Yeah, kind of, we…" she finds herself inadvertently blushing. "We were doing some of the scavenger hunt with Sean and Ben, and we just split up to go find something that represents Christmas to us."

"That sounds fun, and kind of challenging," Gabby says, wrapping a soft, plaid blanket around the base of the tree.

"So what's up with this little tree?" Lizzie asks, slipping off her coat.

"It was my idea, Aunt Wiz," says Sophie. "Grandpa spends all his time here so I thought he needed a Christmas tree so he wouldn't be lonely."

"And I thought it was a fabulous idea," says Peter, giving Sophie a kiss on the head.

Lizzie stands there, looking at this little Charlie Brown-esque tree, and realizes that this is what makes Christmas for her. It's not presents, or cookies, though cookies are nice, or a tree even, it's these people, the people she loves. Her eyes well up as she watches them bring this little girl's thoughtful vision to life. A scraggly tree decorated with handmade computer printer paper chains, paper clips, and some snowflakes awkwardly cut, also from printer paper. It was one of the most beautiful trees she'd ever seen.

"How about I take a picture of all of you in front of this magnificent tree?" Lizzie says.

"I want to be in front, because it was my idea," says Sophie.

"Oh, you definitely have to be front and center," Lizzie says. They all gather around the tree and Lizzie says, "Say, Santa Claus!" and she takes the picture, several actually, and then just stands there for a moment.

"You okay, honey?" Peter asks.

Fighting back tears, she nods. "Yeah, I just love you all so much. You are all what makes Christmas special to me."

"Don't cry, Aunt Wiz, Santa's coming very soon."

Lizzie pulls herself together. "You're so right, Sophie. You know what the song says," she starts to sing, 'You better not pout, you better not cry, you better not shout, I'm telling you why, 'cause Santa Claus is coming to town.'"

"I don't know that song," she looks quizzically at her aunt. "It sounds kind of bossy."

They all laugh. "You're right, it is kind of bossy. We should all feel what we feel, right?" Lizzie agrees. Kids are so darn smart.

"Yup," says Sophie. "And I feel very happy."

"Me too, DoodleBug, me too." Lizzie gives her mom and dad a hug, "I hate to go, but I'm supposed to meet all the guys back at Sea Coast to see what everyone came up with." She buttons up her coat. "Want me to stop at the store to get something for dinner? I definitely feel like I have not been pulling my weight cooking-wise. Oh! Or we could get some Korean take-out at Whistle Pig?" she looks hopefully at her family, grinning. "They have lots of healthy, vegetarian options...just saying."

"Gee everyone, how about some Korean take-out tonight?" Gabby says laughing. "You want to see if Shannon wants to meet up after work, Matt? We could all go to the tree lighting and carol sing together after that."

"Yeah, that could be a real life saver, actually. Would you mind if Sophie comes with you, Mom, and we'll meet you at say,

5? I have an estimate I need to get to a client, and it would be very boring for her."

"Super boring," Sophie concurs, nodding.

"No problem at all," says Gabby.

Lizzie heads to the door. "All of you text me what you want, and I'll take care of it," she says, as she heads back to meet up with the others, curious about what they'll come back with.

It was still snowing on Lizzie's walk back into town. She is being extra careful since they haven't salted the sidewalks yet and it is already getting pretty slippery. She is the first one to arrive at Sea Coast, so she claims a table before the after-school crowd starts pouring in. As she sits, scrolling through her phone she doesn't notice Jack arriving.

"You look very deep in thought," he says, taking off his coat and putting it on the back of a chair. He rubs his hands together to warm them. "I was born here, I am a many-generations old New Englander, why can I never remember to bring gloves anywhere?"

Lizzie laughs. "I know, I do the same thing, and I lose them all the time. My mom on the other hand has gloves from the 1980s." She shrugs. "This apple fell very far from the tree."

"So, I wanted to ask you–"

And then Ben and Sean return.

"To be continued," he says to Lizzie. "Hey!" He stands up, "Cocoa? Coffee? Tea? Scones? Cookies? What will it be?"

Lizzie reaches for her wallet, "I'd love a cocoa and a ginger-bread cookie," she says.

Jack waves off her money, "I got this. And thanks for the reminder about those cookies, I may have to get one too. Gentlemen? What would you like?" he says, turning to Ben and Sean.

"That sounds like the perfect treat on a snowy day, count me in too," says Ben. "Sean?"

"I'm going to be the outlier and have a cranberry scone with my cocoa," he stands up. "You sure you've got this? We can treat," says Sean.

"Nope, I want to do this, but you could help me carry it all," they head off to the counter to order.

"This has been such a good day," Ben says. "It's amazing how something so simple can make you just feel good. I've really loved spending time with you and Jack."

He and Lizzie are quiet for a moment. "Me too," she says. "I haven't done any of these things in way too long. To have gone skating, to the pancake breakfast, doing the scavenger hunt–"

"Don't forget the tree lighting and carol singing is tonight," he says smiling.

"Oh no, I can't forget that. Actually my whole family is going." She sighs.

"Is that not a good thing?" Ben asks, a little concerned.

"Oh, no! It's great! It's all great," she says.

"Yeah, it's awful when that happens, right? When everything is wonderful and great and you're happy? I hate that!" he says, teasing her.

Lizzie swats his arm and he pulls away laughing. "Stop!" she says laughing. "I know! It sounds like a pathetic problem to have!" She sits back. "It's just easier when you kind of block it out and don't–"

"Feel anything so you don't miss it when it's not there?" Ben queries.

"I wouldn't say I don't feel anything," she says, feeling a bit defensive.

""I'm sorry, you're right. Of course you feel things. But you've blocked some people out. And it's hard to keep doing that when they're being pretty great," he suggests.

"Yeah…" she nods.

Jack and Sean come back bearing lots of warm and delicious treats for all.

"Thank you, Jack, this is just what I needed," says Lizzie. She takes the lid off her cocoa and blows on it.

Wanting to get away from the topic of the inner Lizzie, she turns to the guys, "So, did you all find the true meaning of Christmas. In under thirty minutes?"

"This one was hard, no way around that," says Sean. "I don't have the same history you three have, though maybe that makes it easier. Less baggage, more recent memories. This is only my second Christmas here as a year-rounder."

"So what did you find?" Jack asks.

"Well," he pulls out a paper Tall Tales bag and puts it on the table. "I felt a little weird buying something, like maybe it shouldn't be a 'thing' per se, but anyway," he opens the bag and pulls out a copy of, 'Twas the Night Before Christmas. "My parents always read this to us every Christmas Eve, and I got thinking as we start planning to have a family someday, I want to pass on that tradition." He looks at everyone. "Too schmaltzy?" he smiles.

Ben pretends to mock him, rolling his eyes, and then shakes his head. "No, I love it. Who knows, maybe next year we'll be reading it to a kid we haven't even met yet. It's great."

"Did I miss something?" Jack asks, looking confused.

"Yes, and I'll fill you in later," she says. "And I think it's the perfect amount of schmaltz. I love it."

"That is so wonderful, Sean, what a great idea! Okay, you go next," Jack says to Lizzie.

"Okay, so speaking of schmaltzy," she says.

Ben puts his hand up. "Okay, moratorium on worrying about being schmaltzy, it's a Christmas scavenger hunt, it's snowing, we're drinking cocoa...I think schmaltz is kind of baked into the moment. Extra points if you make us cry," he jokes.

"Good point, about the schmaltz," Lizzie says. "Okay, so I ended up at my Dad's office, and when I got there Sophie had insisted that she and Matt bring him the saddest little dilapidated tree so he wouldn't be lonely when he's working."

"Okay, tearing up, we may have a winner," Jack says, raising his hand.

"Just seeing my whole family there, making this little girl's thoughtful idea come to life, I thought, this is it. It's these people who make Christmas special to me." She pulls up the photos on her phone and they all look at them.

"That's so sweet, Lizzie," says Ben. "She will probably always remember that."

"Well, even if she doesn't, I will," she says, fighting back tears. "Okay, someone else go before I dissolve into a puddle."

Jack gestures to Ben. "Why don't you go?" he says.

"Okay, so I wandered around and around and couldn't think of anything." He stops for a minute. "It seemed crazy to me that I couldn't think of anything after having spent more than 30 Christmases here. And then I thought of something. So I went down to Bradford's Market, and bought these." He pulls a bag of Goldfish crackers out of his coat.

Everyone looks perplexed. "Goldfish crackers?" Lizzie asks for the crowd.

Ben laughs. "I know, it's weird!" He takes a deep breath. "Okay, so when I was about seven I had a crisis of faith–"

"About God? At seven?" Jack asks, laughing.

"No," Ben says, laughing as well. "About Santa. This kid in the fourth grade told me on the bus that Santa wasn't real and I was just destroyed."

"Charlie?" both Lizzie and Jack say. Ben nods.

"Why is there always one mean kid who wants to ruin it for everyone?" Sean says. "What happened to them to make them such mean Christmas ruiners?"

"Charlie Tuttle was not a nice kid," Ben says.

"No," both Jack and Lizzie agree, shaking their heads.

"So when I got home I didn't say anything to anyone, I was

afraid to find out the possible truth, so I came up with an idea. I left a trail of Goldfish crackers from the fireplace to my bed, and I was going to stay awake all night to catch Santa following the trail of crackers, because—"

Lizzie nods, "Because, hello! No one can resist Goldfish crackers."

"Exactly!" Ben continues. "But of course I fell asleep, but when I woke up the Goldfish were all gone and there was a note on my bed. It said, *'Thank you so much for the Goldfish, Ben, I get awfully tired of cookies! Merry Christmas, Love, Santa.'* Well, that sealed the deal for me. And it bought me about three more years of believing in Santa. Now, I can never see Goldfish crackers and not think of that."

"That is so sweet, how did I not know this?" asks Sean.

"Maybe because when you're trying to impress a guy you probably don't lead with a story about when a bully told you there was no Santa, it's not exactly a macho story," Ben laughs.

"No, it's completely sweet and adorable," says Lizzie.

Ben points to Lizzie, "And I rest my case. Okay, Jack Cahoon, now it's your turn."

Jack takes a deep breath. "Like all of you it was hard to distill it down to one thing. Christmas is so many things, family, fires in the fireplace, cocoa, so I also wandered around looking for meaning. Something I seem to do a lot year-round. Anyway, I found myself at the church thrift shop, where I ran into Alexis's grandfather. We talked for a couple of minutes, and then I wandered around, hoping something would spark and then I saw this." He pulls a small white bag out of his pocket. He opens it up, unwraps the tissue paper and reveals several old holiday pins. "I saw these and I thought of my grandmother, who was a teacher, and every year at least one kid would give her a gaudy wreath or Santa pin, and she would wear them proudly all through the season, and on Christmas day, come to our house wearing them all." He's quiet. "She made a difference to so many kids who grew up here. She was a beloved teacher, and I know I can never impact all the people she did, but I got these to serve as a reminder about making a difference, loving what you do and wearing something a kid gives you even if it is a giant rhinestone covered reindeer."

"I loved your grandmother," Lizzie says, sniffing. "She was just the best. She used to let us come to her room sometimes during recess and she'd give us treats."

"Yeah, she sure loved you," Jack says, holding back some tears.

"Well, I don't know about you three, but I'm a complete mess," says Sean. "I never knew her, but I wish I had."

"She was an amazing teacher. I had her in second grade," says Ben. "She really cemented my love of nature, plants, and the outdoors." He raises his cocoa cup, "To Mrs. Cahoon!"

They all clink cups and toast Jack's grandmother.

Lizzie's phone dings and she picks it up. "Ah, I have my marching orders for dinner," she reads the text. "Anyone else want to join us for some Whistle Pig Korean before the caroling and tree lighting?"

"Sure, if I'm not crashing," says Jack. "I'll tell my parents I'll meet them at the tree lighting."

"We should go and do a few things to get ready for the wreath making classes, but we'll see you at the square? 7-sharp?" Ben says, getting up and putting his coat on.

"Sounds good," says Lizzie. "Hey, thank you two for making this an amazing day."

"Right back at you," says Sean, giving her a hug. "See you both soon."

"And then there were two," says Jack. He clears his throat and looks uneasy. "So I started to say before, that I'm so happy we've had all this time together. It's meant a lot to me, Lizzie. I'm grateful you'd spend even five minutes with me."

"The past is in the past. We're good," she says, trying to convince herself as well as him.

"I know you're headed back to Boston after the holidays, but I'm really thinking I'm going to stay. I told my boss in California that I want to take a leave, and she's cool with it. She even said I could continue to work remotely if I want."

"That's amazing, things like that don't happen often. There's nothing, no one you need to get back to California for? You can just leave?"

He looks a little confused. "No, it's all good. And they're pretty good about wanting us to be out in the world exploring new projects, it's how they keep evolving and growing. Anyway, I know I completely blew it, but I'd really like to keep spending time together, if you'd like to. I can come up to Boston as often as you'll have me, and maybe you'll come down here sometimes?" He trails off, uncertain of how this is landing.

"Um, I'm not sure, I..." she's flustered and doesn't want to say the wrong thing, or the right thing? "We can certainly keep in touch, keep it loose, and see what happens?" She's still worried he might break her heart again.

Then, he says it. "I still love you, Lizzie. I always have and I always will. I blew it once. I'm not about to do it again. I promise I will never leave you again."

Lizzie doesn't know what to say. She's terrified to say it back, so she doesn't. Instead she looks at her phone. "Uh, I need to call in this order. Stick a pin in this?"

Jack is surprised. "Uh, yeah, sure. Let's do that."

"Cool, so are you okay with mostly vegetarian options? My mom is trying really hard to keep my dad healthy."

"Anything is fine," he says. "I'm good with whatever you choose."

CHAPTER 21

An hour and a half later they are all sitting in the living room, many of them on the floor, surrounded by the remnants of an incredible Korean dinner. They've feasted on a selection of mandu, bibimbap, kimchi, and Sophie's favorite, hotteok (Korean donuts) in front of the Christmas tree.

"You are going to have to roll me to the tree lighting," Peter says, rubbing his stomach. "That was delicious, thank you, honey, for getting all this for us. Sure we can't pitch in?"

"No way, it was my treat, it's the least I can do, you two have been treating me like a queen since I've been here," Lizzie says as she looks at the clock, "What do you all say, are you ready to sing some carols?"

"Is a carol a song, Aunt Wiz?" Sophie asks, working on her second hoddeok.

"It is, it's a Christmas song, like *Jingle Bells*, or *We Wish You a Merry Christmas.*"

Shannon and Matt start cleaning up all the take out containers, dishes and utensils.

"Here, let me help," Jack says standing up from his spot on

the floor. He picks up the rest of the empty containers, grabs some glasses, and carries them into the kitchen, trailed by Sophie in search of some more snacks.

"It's kind of like old times, isn't it?" Gabby says, looking at Lizzie, trying to get a read on her. When Lizzie doesn't respond, she pushes a little more. "You okay, honey?"

"I'm not sure." She looks to see if anyone is coming back into the room. "He told me he loves me. I don't know what to do with that."

Peter sits forward on the edge of the couch. "I suppose what you do with that depends on how you feel about him. Do you still love him?"

"If you'd asked me a week ago I would have said no way, not at all, he doesn't matter to me..."

"And today?" her dad queries.

"Today I'm not so sure." Still seated on the floor she wraps her arms around her legs, pulling herself into a tight little ball. "We've had a wonderful week together. Like old times, only, better in a way. More grounded, less expectations. I've felt relaxed and like myself. I'd forgotten what that feels like–to be completely myself with a guy."

"Can you just spend some time together and see where it goes? It's not like you have to decide anything, right?" says Gabby.

"No, I don't. But I also don't want to string him along and end up hurting him if I can't get over the past." she throws herself back and puts a pillow over her face and quietly yells into it.

"Mommy has me do that sometimes when I get flustereated," Sophie says, having returned.

Lizzie removes the pillow. "You mean frustrated?" she says, smiling at her adorable niece.

"Whatever," she shrugs her shoulders. "Screaming makes me feel better sometimes."

"I think screaming can make all of us feel better sometimes," Lizzie agrees, and pulls Sophie onto her lap. "And hugging you always makes me feel better," she says, squeezing her tight.

"So, I don't suppose anyone here wants to go and see the giant Christmas tree and sing some carols?" Matt asks, looking directly at Sophie.

"Me! Me! Me!" she says, raising her hand.

"All you folks ready? Dad, can you make it off that couch?" Matt teases his very relaxed father.

"Yes indeed, I am ready to go." And, with a bit of a groan, he's up and ready for the next thing. "Okay, I am ready. Boy, covering this festival is feeling like more work every year," he says, zipping up his coat and pulling on his red and green knit cap.

"Too bad you don't know any good writer/editors," Matt says, buttoning up his coat. Lizzie shoots him a look. "What? Oh you thought I meant you? Jeez, Lizzie, way to make everything all about you," he teases. "I'm just putting it out there," he shrugs and opens the door for them all to head out.

"You want to ride over with me?" Jack asks Lizzie as they begin to pile into cars.

"Uh, sure... Mom? I'll ride over with Jack, and come back with you and Dad," Gabby waves to her, and they're all off.

Jack starts his car, they put on their seat belts, all without saying anything. As they drive toward town Jack finally breaks the awkward silence.

"Look, I shouldn't have–"

Lizzie stops him, "Don't worry about it. It's fine. We're all a bit intoxicated by Christmas, being home, it's no big deal. It was Cranberry Harbor talking. I get it." She looks out the window, not at him.

"That's not at all what I was going to say, though that is an interesting angle, Ms. Journalist," he smiles at her.

Now she's embarrassed. "Oops."

"What I was going to say was, I didn't mean to spring that on you. I should have waited. I know you've got a lot going on, and I didn't mean to add something else for you to think about. I didn't say that to add any pressure. I realize you may no longer feel the same way, which is the risk you take when you tell someone you love them."

"Honestly, Jack, I don't know where I am. I just don't know. I decided three years ago when you left that I never wanted to see you again, and that I was done caring about you. Spending time together this week has been really nice, but I still don't know."

"How about we table all of this until after the holidays? Revisit it in the New Year? But just know, I'm not going anywhere, I know how I feel," he says as they pull into the lot near the town square.

"Okay," she says, unbuckling her seatbelt and opening the door, not knowing at all what to do, but yet her heart sort of does.

The town is teeming with people bundled up against the flurries and brisk sea breeze. Lizzie hadn't been home for this in so long she'd forgotten just how many people come together for it. It was completely magical. Two women from the Chamber of Commerce were handing out battery operated candles, while also reminding everyone to drop them afterward in one of the many labeled baskets around the square. Seeing everyone in the snowy scene holding their candles was breathtaking, and actually choked Lizzie up.

"I should look for my parents," she says.

As she turns to leave, Jack's parents, and a young woman she doesn't know find them.

"Jack! There you are," his parents, Jane and David, call to him.

"Hey," he says, and then looks shocked. "Penelope? What, when, why are you here?"

Lizzie immediately recognizes her from stalking her on

Instagram. It's @penelopej. Her heart begins to race, her face feels hot, and she just wants to go.

Jack is obviously flustered, "Penelope, what are you doing..." He looks over at Lizzie who feels like she could cry, and he looks totally shocked.

Penelope wraps Jack in a big embrace. "Surprise!"

Jane and David, Jack's parents, look completely caught off-guard and say nothing, Jack looks totally in shock and is clearly too stunned to talk, and Lizzie wants to leave more than anything in the world. She finally breaks the awkward silence.

Lizzie extends her hand, "Lizzie Martin, Jack and I are old friends. Jane, David, it's lovely to see you, but I've got to go find my family. Enjoy the caroling!" she says, trying to sound perky and unaffected and get away as quickly as possible.

"Nice to meet you! I'm Jack's girlfriend, Penelope Jacek," she says, as Lizzie hurries away.

Jack grabs Lizzie's arm, and looks at her with pleading eyes. "I'll, I'll call you later? I have no idea what this is all about, we ended things–"

"No worries, I think we're good." Stunned, she walks off to find her family. At this moment the last thing she wants to do is sing any stupid, happy carols. Holding her LED candle, she just wants to throw it on the ground and run. How could she have let her guard down? How stupid was she? Her phone rings, she assumes it's Jack so she lets it go to voicemail. A part of her wants to cry, but another, more stubborn part feels like she's cried enough over this man. Her phone rings again and. worried it could be her mom, she answers it this time.

"Hello?"

"Martin? Margaret, here." This was weird, why was her boss calling her?

"Hi, Margaret, Merry Christmas," Lizzie says. Still reeling about Jack, and now perplexed about this.

"Yes, whatever," she says in her typical warm and engaging

way. "I'm sorry to bother you, I know you're on Martha's Vineyard or some insignificant place where you grew up..."

"Cranberry Harbor, on the Cape, that's okay, is something wrong?"

"Yes, well, the thing is the company let too many people take the holiday and I'm here all alone and the mayor is holding an emergency press conference first thing in the morning about an impending strike–the T could be shut down on Christmas and I don't have a reporter to be there."

Without thinking Lizzie answers, "Yes, I'll do it. I'll be there." It's perfect, she can leave town without losing face and avoid running into Jack and Penelope all over town. "City Hall?"

"Yes, 9 am, you're sure you can be there?"

Nary a thank you, but Lizzie doesn't care. "I said I'll be there and I will be."

"Turn the story around as fast as you can, we need it up on the website as soon as possible. I want to scoop those people at the Boston Daily."

"I'm doing a thing now, but I'll head out soon. Promise."

Realizing that if her landlord hasn't finished the electrical upgrades he was doing on her apartment, she won't have a place to stay, she shoots him a text.

Have a work emergency I have to come back to. Is my apartment habitable?

Not expecting to hear back for a while, she's shocked to get a reply right away.

As a matter of fact I just left your apartment. It's all set. Thanks for the leeway in getting it done.

Phew, thank goodness.

No worries. Glad it all worked out. And thanks for the new plugs and switches.

After getting a smiley face emoji back, she puts her phone in her pocket and goes to find her family. And try to forget about the stunning woman, his girlfriend apparently, who was now with Jack.

Lizzie half-heartedly made it through the carols, and even faked a passable, "Woo!" when the tree was lit, but her heart wasn't in it, not at all.

"You okay, honey?" her mom asked, concerned about her change in mood.

"I'm fine. I just got a call from work and I have to go back for a day, but I'll be back by Christmas Eve."

Peter overhears and isn't happy. "Why are they calling you back? That's not right."

"Apparently there may be a big strike of T drivers and the mayor is holding a press conference in the morning. A possible train strike at Christmas is a big story. There's no one there to cover it, so my editor called me. I really don't mind. It's fine."

"You don't sound or look fine," her mom says. "Did something happen with Jack?"

She brushes off the concern, she doesn't even want to talk about it. She just wants to get on the road. "No, everything is fine. Though I do need to get on the road, so-"

"You're driving tonight? It's been snowing, I don't like that, not at all," Peter says, "and I'm not being sexist, I wouldn't want Matt driving to Boston tonight either."

"It will be fine, Dad. I have all-wheel drive. It's only an hour and a half, less maybe with no traffic. I don't want to go in the morning and risk hitting rush hour."

"What about your apartment?" Gabby says as they start walking to the car.

"It's all set, I texted Joe, and he finished today, so, perfect timing." As they're walking she finds herself looking for Jack and Penelope, planning to hide behind anything near if she sees them. Thankfully she doesn't.

Sitting in the backseat of her parent's station wagon she checks her phone. He's called three times and texted four.

Lizzie, we need to talk... she doesn't read any further.

She deletes the texts and the voicemails, without listening to them.

Once they're home she runs upstairs and packs up her computer, her makeup, hairbrush and some, not all, of her clothes. She'll be back before long, so she doesn't need to bring back everything. Or... maybe she won't come back. Avoid Cranberry Harbor altogether for the rest of the holidays. With that thought she decides to pack everything, except all her gifts, so if she decides to stay in Boston it's all good. She picks up her things in the bathroom, stuffs them into her very uninspired Ziploc bag, someday she will have to get an actual toiletry bag and stop traveling like a college student. She does a quick visual sweep, and all of a sudden feels really sad. She was having such a good visit, she was feeling so good, so hopeful, and now that was all dashed. Jack wasn't who she thought he was, or maybe he was exactly who she'd come to believe he was, and her unappreciative and demanding boss was being, well, exactly who she knew her to be as well. She turns out the light, goes down the stairs with all her things.

"Okay, I'm so sorry to leave in a big rush like this, but I know you get it, Dad, duty calls."

Peter hugs her hard. "I do, I just wish that stupid corporation cared more about you, and less about money."

Gabby waves him off and hugs Lizzie. "Okay, now is not the time for a long debate about the future of journalism, honey. We can do that later over some red wine, so romantic," she jokes. "You make sure to call us when you get in, okay?" Lizzie nods. "You've got plenty of gas?"

"Yup, filled it the other day, I'm good."

She opens the door. "Okay, love you guys, "I'll talk to you in a bit."

She walks to her car and her mom calls out to her. "Call us if you get sleepy and want someone to talk to!" she yells.

"Will do!" Lizzie puts everything in her car, gets in, starts the engine, and fastens her seatbelt. As she backs out of the driveway she says out loud, "Damn you, Jack Cahoon, for ruining another Christmas. And shame on me for letting you."

CHAPTER 22

LIZZIE PULLS on to her street in Somerville at exactly 11:04. The snow had clearly only been an Outer Cape thing because the roads were clear and dry all the way back. The street is still busy with folks leaving coffee shops and bars, she gets her things out of the car, and lets herself into her building.

Living on the third floor with no elevator is normally not a big deal, but when carrying a lot of things it is a drag. When she reaches her door she drops her suitcase with a plunk and unlocks the door. As she goes to turn on the light switch to the left of the door, she finds it has been replaced with a dimmer. As she looks around she can see Joe has gone dimmer crazy. She imagines he got a good deal on them or something. Before even taking off her coat she calls her parents.

"Made it safe and sound," she says to her mom who picks up on the first ring, or even half ring.

"Oh good. Good luck tomorrow, will you be coming back after you file your story?"

She doesn't want to lie to her mom, so is vague instead. "Yeah, probably. I'll let you know. You two get to bed. I'll talk to you tomorrow."

"Okay, love you, honey, night."

"Love you too, Mom."

As soon as she hangs up her phone rings. It's Jack. She answers it to tell him to stop calling.

"Hello?"

"Where'd you go? You left so fast–"

"I'm back in Boston. I got called into work. I have to get up early, so I'm going to go,"

"Lizzie, you have to let me explain. Penelope–"

"Jack, you don't owe me a thing. I just can't believe I trusted you. Believe me, that won't happen again. I have to go, good night."

She hangs up before he has a chance to answer. Too tired to deal with her suitcase, she only takes out her toiletries and does a cursory job of brushing her teeth, peels off her clothes and crawls into bed in her bra and underwear. She doesn't want to, but she cries a little, tosses and turns, until she finally drifts off into a restless sleep, feeling so disappointed.

City Hall is bustling already when she arrives at 8:30. She had hoped she could maybe scoop a few quotes from some officials, but is only seeing other journalists and TV crews from all the Boston stations. A strike on the transit system at Christmas was indeed very big news.

The mayor, who was almost always punctual, didn't arrive until 9:17. When she walks in, she does not look happy.

"Thank you all for being here," she says. "I had hoped to come bearing good news, but I've just left a meeting with union officials and they're making demands we just don't have the budget to provide."

Lizzie is recording on her phone, which is balanced on the notebook she is holding, and she's writing as fast as she can. She always wants a backup in case her phone recording doesn't work.

"It's clear we are at an impasse right now, but we plan to keep talking, because we know how important keeping the T and buses running smoothly is for everyone, especially at this time of year. We may not be agreeing on everything, but the one thing we do agree on is keeping Boston moving. I will let all of you know when, not if, we reach an agreement which I hope will be sooner than later. Thank you, and very Happy Holidays to all of you."

Lizzie had been prepared to ask some questions, but the mayor's team quickly ushering her out made it clear that wasn't happening. A part of her is angry, anyone could have written this story from the forthcoming press release, there was no need for her to rush back from the Cape. She could have written this story from there and sent it in. She feels used and unappreciated.

When she arrives at the newsroom no one, not even Margaret. is there, which feels odd. She couldn't remember the last time she was the only one there. Within 30 minutes she has the story put together, even after factoring in a call to a source at City Hall who thankfully was able to give her a good quote about how he felt positive about there not being a shutdown and how Christmas wouldn't be ruined, he even mentioned Santa for good measure. In less than an hour after leaving City Hall it was written, and up on the website, and after a quick online search, she sees she's scooped the other papers.

Looking around she wonders where everyone is, it was still a couple of days until Christmas. She picks up her cell, "Sarah, where is everyone?" she asks the resident of the empty cubicle next to her. As she looks more closely, she sees her cubicle is actually empty. Sarah's photos, her candy stash, everything is gone.

"Hey, I'm sorry I didn't call you, I was too upset."

Panic rises in Lizzie's stomach. "What's going on?"

"I got laid off. Most of us did. You didn't get a call?" Sarah asks, surprised.

"No, except to come in and cover a story. Margaret isn't here either. What the heck is going on?"

"She got laid off too," Sarah says.

Just then her desk phone rings. "Let me call you back." She picks up the phone. "Liz Martin."

"Hello, Ms. Martin, this is Jonathan Toomey from the New York office of Greylock Media."

Lizzie feels her heart racing and her face grow hot. "Yes?"

"Well, there is no easy way to say this, but we are closing down the Boston newsroom, and will be running the paper from here. So your services are no longer needed."

"You're going to run a Boston daily paper with no reporters in Boston? How does that possibly make any sense?" Rather than being upset she's angry. "So you had me called back from my holiday vacation to cover this story why? As a joke? As a last hurrah? Why?"

"We assure you, we don't joke around. We at the corporate office have no sense of humor when it comes to business. I apologize for any inconvenience."

"Inconvenience? I drove two hours in a snowstorm," she decides to add for effect. "I left my family to come here to write a story because that's what loyal employees do, and now you have the audacity to call me, after I did my part, after I lived up to my obligation, to tell me you're not living up to yours?"

"Well…" he's not sure what to say now. "It's not because you haven't done a good job, it's business," he squawks out in business-speak.

"Wow, I'd think you could do better than 'It's not you it's me.' Well since I have nothing to lose, I just want to say, shame on you, and shame on your damn company. You go around and you buy good papers, award winning papers, and then you slowly and methodically kill them, bit by bit until they are shells of what they used to be. The Sentinel is historic, it was here to cover the Great Depression, JFK's assassination, the Boston Marathon bombing, and they did it with the best boots-on-the-ground reporters in the business. But you don't care. You are not news people, you are corporate shills and you should be ashamed, because a true democracy needs newspapers, and it needs journalists who will drive two-hours in the snow to get to a story. You might as well be selling ham, or screwdrivers, the product doesn't matter, money does."

"I'm sorry, Ms. Martin."

"No you're not, because you're a robot. For a regular paycheck and a nice office they killed your soul. Send me whatever severance, buy-out or whatever you're offering. I'm done talking to you."

She hangs up her phone and sits in the once bustling, now empty newsroom and cries.

CHAPTER 23

AFTER A GOOD 15 minutes or so of crying so hard she couldn't catch her breath, Lizzie just suddenly stops. Maybe she's going to roll right through the whole Kubler-Ross stages of grief. She was already angry. She gets up and searches around the newsroom for an empty box and finally finds a printer paper box with a top. There is one ream of paper remaining, which she decides is the least the Sentinel can give her, and begins pitching everything on her desk into it. Old notebooks with scribbled notes of stories? Did she really need those? She knew she wasn't in a place to make any reasonable decisions so errs on the side of keeping them knowing she can always throw them away later. Her RBG mug that she kept her pens in, and her, "Good Punctuation Saves Lives," travel mug with the classic, "Let's eat, Grandma," and "Let's eat Grandma," had to come with her. It had been a gift from her dad who has been drumming proper punctuation into her head since before she could read.

It was pretty incredible that in under 20 minutes she managed to pack up six years of her life into a single box. Feeling a bit like Mary Tyler Moore in the final scene of her show, she puts on her coat, picks up her box, takes one last look around the newsroom and walks out. She doesn't turn out the lights, however. She isn't feeling like saving the company any money.

Lizzie realizes when she gets home that she never called Sarah back. After taking off her coat, she wonders if noon is too early for a glass of wine, decides it is not, and pours herself a glass of a red she's had around for a while. She sits down on the couch with a loud sigh and calls Sarah.

"So what happened?"

"Yeah, I'm out too," Lizzie replies, taking a big sip of wine.

They're both silent, not sure what to say. They've been cubicle mates for the entire time they worked at the paper, hired only days apart.

Lizzie finally breaks her silence as she drains her glass and pours another. "You would have been impressed at my Aaron Sorkin-esque moment I think," she says laughing, already a tiny bit tipsy.

"What? Do tell!" Sarah replies, literally on the edge of her seat.

"Oh I just laid into him about the corporate takeover of newspapers, and how newspapers are the cornerstone of democracy, and how they didn't care, they may as well have been selling ham, or something like that." She starts laughing. "I honestly can't believe I pushed back like that. So not my usual style."

"I'm so glad you did! I'm sure I really intimidated them when I burst into tears," Sarah says. "I was so mad, but that's how it came out."

"Oh, I cried too, just afterward." They're both quiet again. "I can't believe I'm not going to see you every single day anymore. Honestly, that's the only part that makes me sad. Everyone else has been gone for a while, but it's been you and me from the beginning."

Sarah is choking back tears. "I know, that's what hit me too. And the paycheck, as crummy as it was, we need it. We just bought this house. No one's hiring journalists now, all the papers are in the same boat. What a completely useless set of skills I now possess."

"I know, why didn't we go to law school or become dental hygienists?" Lizzie posits. "I don't know what I can do. I was barely able to afford this apartment between my salary and the freelance work I'd pick up here and there." On that note she pours a third glass of wine. "People don't become wealthy blogging anymore, do they?"

Sarah laughs. "I think that was only in the movies. I have yet to meet anyone who made a killing as a blogger." Sarah is hesitant, but then speaks up. "You do have an option you know..."

"Nope, not going to happen."

"You could still be a writer though..."

"No, there is no way I'm going to do that. And besides, he can't afford to pay me, he's barely getting by himself. I think it may even be worse than he lets on."

"Your dad has wanted you to come back and take over the Gazette since you finished grad school. Maybe there are things you could do that he hasn't, a fresh pair of eyes, ones that are more savvy to social media and the internet. It could be something to think about."

"Go back to the Cape, live with my parents, and try to save my dad's paper? I'm suddenly feeling like George Bailey setting out to save the Bailey Building and Loan," she jokes.

"Lizzie, it's not a bad idea. Even if just for a little while, to see what could happen."

"What about my apartment?"

"Sublet. Next question?"

"To whom?"

"Lizzie, plenty of people would love that apartment, as a matter of fact, there's a woman who Adam works with who is here for nine months working on a project and doesn't want to get into a year's lease. Bang! Problem solved! Next?"

"Jack."

"Ex-Jack?"

"Yes, he's moving back to Cranberry Harbor and I'd have to see him all the time and I am currently not liking him very much."

Lizzie gets up and begins pacing around her apartment. She loves this sweet place, how could she leave it? There had to be work for someone with a Master's degree in journalism. Maybe she could teach? That thought sounded laughable, were people still going to school for journalism or had they wised up in the last 10 years?

"I thought things were going along pretty well with the ex, like you were friends?"

"I don't really want to get into it right now, but I'll just say this, Penelope." Lizzie says, a bit sadly.

"Oh, hmmm, okay, well, when you're ready to talk, I'm here. I should go, lord knows what Wyatt has gotten into, he's awfully quiet."

"He won't be after Christmas," Lizzie teases, referencing the guitar she bought him.

"Oh my, you are going to pay, my friend..."

Lizzie laughs, "Talk soon! Love you."

"Love you too, you rat."

Lizzie puts her phone down, and lies back on the couch putting her feet up on the coffee table. She knows she needs to call her parents, clearly after three glasses of wine she's not driving back to the Cape. But first she decides she's going to take a nap and hope everything looks better after.

CHAPTER 24

NOTHING LOOKED BETTER, but it did look darker when she finally woke up. She picks her phone up off the table, looks at it and can't believe it's 4:45. She slept for three hours. There are several texts from her mom, and another one from Jack. She deletes that one.

Not wanting to get into what happened at work with her mom on the phone, she decides to send her a text instead of calling. She's worried that hearing her mom's voice will make her start crying again. Between Jack, Penelope and work it had been quite the 24 hours.

Hey, All is well, just got done with work, going to stay overnight. Will check in before I head back tmrw. Love you.

She feels a little bad lying, but there was no need for her parents to get upset. There would be plenty of time, more than plenty of time it seems, to talk when she gets back to Cranberry Harbor. Her mom writes back immediately, saying she's glad she's okay, and that they'd miss her. "Not for long," she says out loud. "You're going to get plenty sick of me."

As soon as she says that out loud, she thinks that perhaps she is giving up too easily. She hasn't even tried to think of other

CANDACE HAMMOND

things she can do for work in Boston. Grabbing her laptop she writes an email to a friend from grad school who is a very successful freelancer, writing for papers and magazines all over the country. If he can do it, why can't she?

Email sent, she realizes she hasn't eaten anything all day. A diet of just wine probably wasn't the healthiest thing in the world. Grabbing her coat, she decides the best remedy for a broken heart and spirit is some pizza from Mama Gina's, and dessert from Gracie's, her favorite ice cream shop. She knows she could have it all delivered, but she needs to get out and walk to try to shake off all that's happened.

The brisk air hits her as she leaves the building. She buttons up her coat and pulls up the collar around her neck. She should have grabbed a scarf, but hadn't. Her ungloved hands remind her of Jack saying how he was a generations-old New Englander and never remembered to wear gloves and she feels sad.

As she walks she thinks about what it would feel like to leave the city, to go back home. She has to admit it feels like failing, even though she knows it's the industry she works in, not her work, but still, she can't help but feel it is her fault.

Everyone walking around Somerville looks so young, she tries to imagine what it would be like to live back on the Cape in the land of retirees. Which makes her think about Jack and his good ideas. Why couldn't it be someone else, anyone else, who wants to revitalize the community? She quickens her pace as she begins to think about how she'd begun to let herself have feelings for him again, and is furious with herself. For three years she'd done a good job of putting all those feelings aside. Sort of a good job. Who was she kidding? All she'd done was push them deep inside, they were always there. And now, here she was, back where she started. No, I'm not back where I started, I'm not the same person I was three years ago. I am stronger, I am capable, I am better. She laughs a little at how

210

she's now sounding like a parody of a very cheesy self-help podcast.

Before she knows it she's at Gracie's. Anger walking often gets you places more quickly. Getting the ice cream first made sense because it was so cold outside, so it shouldn't melt too much.

She walks in and looks at the chalkboard with the daily flavors and decides on a pint of blueberry cinnamon, and is out and on her way to get her pizza in just a couple of minutes.

Mama Gina's is pretty busy. She orders a plain cheese, which is always amazing there, and waits. As she sits at a high-top table waiting for her number to be called, she hears her name.

"Lizzie?" Oh dear lord it's Ed, and his new girlfriend. Seriously, could this day get any weirder or worse? It was beginning to feel like the worst cosmic joke ever.

"Ed, fancy running into you here," she says, barely making eye contact. She looks at the woman on his arm who's avoiding looking at her too and introduces herself. "Hi, I'm Lizzie," the woman barely smiles and nods, and doesn't give her name. Okay. Two days running now she's found herself introducing herself to ex-boyfriend's girlfriends. That has to be some type of record.

"I thought you were on the Cape for the holidays?" he asks, when she just wishes he'd go away into the night with whatever her name is and his pizza.

She nods, "Yup, headed back tomorrow, had to come in for a work thing." She doesn't share the work thing was being let go. Thanks to luck or divine intervention, her number gets called quicker than she expected. "Well, that's me, see you around! Merry Christmas."

As she walks back home with her pizza and ice cream she realizes there is no escaping your past no matter how long you've lived someplace. And what the heck? How could Ed already have found another girlfriend? He doesn't even like dogs!

After eating three pieces of pizza, and settling on rewatching *Elf* for probably the one thousandth time, she pulls the ice cream out of the freezer, gets a spoon, no dish, and digs in. Why is it when your heart is broken that the perfect remedy is cream and sugar, and the magic that happens when you freeze it? It's a classic cure for a reason, it may not make the pain go away, but it does numb it for a while. Was there something inherently unlovable about her? Was she just a bad chooser? She knew Ed wasn't the right person for her, but him moving on so fast still stung. She was teary as she kept eating her ice cream.

Mid-pint her phone alerts her that she's got an email. It's from her freelancing friend.

Good to hear from you! So sorry about the job, that sucks. I'm afraid I can't be of much help with the freelance gig. I gave it up last year and am working at a bank. Real exciting, huh? I am writing, working on a book, but my advice is get something steady, and don't rely on freelance, it's way too much pressure and not dependable.

Sorry to not give you better news,

Hope to see you in the New Year, wherever you land,

Jon

She puts down her phone, and picks up the ice cream. Okay, looks like the Cranberry Harbor Gazette and home it is.

Thanks to a three-hour nap and a lot of carbs and sugar she is still wide awake after midnight. If she is going to go to work with her dad she needs to have a plan of action. She takes her laptop off the table, swings her legs around to the length of the couch, and opens it up.

Going straight to Google Docs she creates a new folder, "Cranberry Harbor Gazette Reboot" and starts typing out ideas.

Number one is building a strong online presence as well as

keeping the print edition going. Engaging younger readers means having a strong web edition and utilizing social media, especially Instagram. Her dad had been resistant for years to having people read the paper online, insisting that the only true way to read a newspaper is to get actual ink on your fingers. But times have changed, and so many people now only get their news online, it's important to be a positive, reliable source in the endless stream of shoddy and unverified information.

Number two was making sure to have a lot of diverse voices in the paper. She immediately thinks of Jay and Anika Patel at Tall Tale Books. They both had such impressive backgrounds she had no doubt they could add a lot to the paper with a monthly column. The same with Leah, Hope's granddaughter, with her passion for the environment and a keen eye on meshing being environmentally responsible and a good business person, she knows she could offer a lot as well. She wasn't sure how to pay them right away, that was something they'd have to figure out, but where there is a will there's a way. She would not expect people to write for free.

Next would be future-building for Cranberry Harbor. Whether it is housing, jobs, businesses, or protecting the community from being harmed by climate change, it is important to have voices that are letting people know about the real risks and what can be done right now. Alexis would be the perfect person to put on this topic, her background and studies in community planning will be ideal.

As she continues to write she finds herself getting excited. More excited than she's been about her work in a really long time. Rather than being a cog in a corporate machine where she has no say or control over anything she writes, this is a chance to have control and a stake in what she's doing. She knows her dad will certainly listen to her, but she also wants to respect that this is his paper, his business, that he's kept going for over thirty years. She needs to be cautious and not come in pretending she has all the answers and disrespect what he's been doing success-fully for a very long time.

In terms of her own writing, she thinks she could perhaps bring the perspective of a local coming back and wanting to make a go of it, and how the community needs to be welcoming of new ideas and things they might not have considered before. Like Jack's ideas of someday re-utilizing the old, abandoned base down-Cape, and looking at the benefits of employment that goes beyond the traditional Cape service industry jobs which aren't well paying and are seasonal. Then she writes a segment, a fairly decent sized one, arguing against the Norman Rockwell angle–the 'we can't change anything that removes any amount of quaintness and that picture-perfect-postcard facade'. But, people don't live in postcards, they live in real towns, and have real bills, and need real houses, not one Edward Hopper painted decades ago. She wants to help Jack get his housing idea approved by the town, no matter what her personal feelings are.

By the time she's written most of her proposal it was near two o'clock. She closes her laptop, pulls the afghan on the back of the couch over her and drifts off to sleep thinking about how maybe the worst thing that could have happened may end up being the absolute best thing.

CHAPTER 25

WHAT A DIFFERENCE 24 hours can make.When Lizzie woke up at about 8:30, much later than normal, she felt happy. Such a novel feeling! She quickly straightened up, gathered the little bit of trash she had to throw in the building's trash on her way out– she didn't want anything sitting around smelling bad, folded up the afghan on the couch, fluffed the pillows, and packed up her computer. She quickly brushed her teeth, but skipped a shower, choosing instead to get on the road asap. She grabbed another suitcase and threw more of her clothes in it. No matter what, she'd need to come back after the holidays, but she wanted to have a few more clothes to choose from. Sarah had an extra key to the place, and once she knew how things are going to go with her father she'd tell her that they can show his co-worker the apartment to possibly sublet. Who knows, maybe in nine-months she'd be back, but for now it would be nice to know the rent would be covered.

By 9:30 she was organized enough to get herself out the door, and sent her mom a quick text telling her she was heading out.

But before she leaves, she walks around the cozy, pretty

apartment. She'd fallen in love with it the first time she'd seen it. It was the three windows that bumped out in the living room that had sold her, and the claw foot tub and shower. It was a lovely old building, and Joe kept it up beautifully. It was her first roommate-free apartment. She'd never lived alone before and this had been a perfect place for her. For the second time in less than 24 hours she was saying goodbye to something important to her, but it was feeling okay. Somehow, she had a feeling that everything was going to all be alright.

She closed the door and locked it, and after a stop to pick up some coffee for the road she was on her way.

Before she knew it she was back in Cranberry Harbor having hit next to no traffic. It felt different this time. Now as she drove through town she knew she had a mission, a purpose, in being there. She debated about what to do, whether to go right to her dad's office, or wait to talk to both of her parents together. She decided the best thing to do is to get them together, and she had a plan. She calls her mom.

"Mom? Hey, I'm back, did you have lunch yet? I was thinking of picking up some sandwiches or salads at Bradford's and thought you and Dad and I could all have lunch at the office? Or the house... whichever is best!"

"Hi honey! No, and I just talked to your dad, he's stuck at the office and asked if I'd mind while I was doing errands dropping off something, so that would be perfect." There's a pause. "Everything okay?"

"Yeah! I was hungry, and thought it would be nice to all have lunch, everything is great."

"Great, huh? That's nice!"

"Yes, it is. So I'll get an assortment of sandwiches. Healthy, vegetarian things, and meet you at the office in say, a half hour?"

"Sounds good! Thank you, honey!"

Lizzie pulls into Bradford's, goes in and happily takes a cart. Happily that is until she rounds the corner and the first person she sees is Penelope. She does a quick 180 and heads out of that aisle, but it's too late. "Lizzie?" she hears. She turns and smiles.

"Oh! Hi!," she says with a forced smile. "I'm sorry, I didn't recognize you." Liar, liar, liar, she thinks. You've been looking at her Instagram so much you definitely know who she is, heck you even know that coat she's wearing, she wears it in a lot of photos.

"Fancy running into you," Lizzie says, wishing a hole would miraculously appear and swallow her up.

"Well, it's the only grocery store in town, so I imagine the chances are probably pretty good of running into people."

"Very true...Well, I'm supposed to meet my parents for lunch soon, and since I'm bringing the food, I'd better get going. I hope you enjoy your Christmas here."

"It's quite lovely here, I can see why Jack is so fond of it," Penelope says, clearly not taking the hint.

"Yes, it's very pretty, well…"

Penelope cuts her off. "You know, once Jack gets this out of his system, after he gets his little project off the ground, I'm sure he'll come back to California. He belongs there, not here. This place is way too small for him," Penelope says emphatically.

"Well, that's great. I'm sure you two will be very happy. In California," she says, not wanting to prolong this conversation. "Well, it was very nice seeing you, but I do have to get going."

"Of course, it was nice seeing you again, Lizzie," she says, in that way that really means she was anything but happy to see her.

Lizzie hurries to get all the things she needs, hoping not to see Penelope in another aisle, pays and gets back in her car as quickly as she can.

As she starts her car and begins driving, she wonders why Penelope made it a point to talk to her, that whole encounter was just weird.

For the moment though, she has more important things to

think about than Jack Cahoon and Penelope J. She has to try to sell her dad on maybe not all, but at least some of her ideas. She doubts it will be a hard sell, but she wants to be professional, not just rely on nepotism, she wants him to do this because her ideas are good, not just because she's his daughter. She pulls in, parks, gets her computer and the bag with their lunch, takes a deep breath and heads up to the Gazette office.

"Hey, Dad," she calls out as she enters the room. He says hello back, but is deep into something on his computer. She looks around at the empty office. At one point during her childhood the office was busy and full of people. Three fulltime reporters, two ad sales people, a photographer...things had certainly changed. She lays everything down, and puts out the food on the seldom-used conference table. She takes off her coat, "I can't believe I beat Mom," she says, her dad still not paying much attention. "Everything okay over there?" she asks as she walks to his desk and peaks over his shoulder.

"It's this darn formatting software, it's not letting me upload a story I just wrote, and I want to get it off to the printer."

"Do you mind if I take a look?" she asks.

"Not in the least! I'd welcome the help," he gets up and gestures for her to take his seat.

Lizzie sits down, and in a few clicks she's solved the problem. "There you go, it's all sent."

He kisses her on the head, "Oh my dear, you are a godsend, I had been messing with that for an hour. Thank you!"

"Sometimes it just takes a fresh pair of eyes," she says getting up. "I got an assortment of things, hopefully you'll find something you like. Is Mom due here soon?"

"Yes she is," Gabby says as she arrives, dog in her arms, who she quickly sets down, and takes off her coat. "Sorry it took a while, this one," she says giving Daisy a stern look, "decided to chase a squirrel and got away from me, took me 15 minutes and the enticement of treats to get her to stop running all over the yard."

"Daisy, that was not a good thing to do," Peter says, scolding her, sounding more proud than angry. "Lizzie, this looks wonderful, thank you." He chooses a veggie wrap and green juice that Bradford's makes fresh on the premises in reusable glass bottles. "So how was Boston? The press conference? I heard on the radio this morning that they hope to avert a strike. The mayor sounded hopeful." He takes a bite and sighs happily. "This is delicious, honey, thank you!"

"You're very welcome," she says, choosing a whole wheat hummus wrap and freshly squeezed orange juice. "It was very frustrating, one of those things where a phone call would have sufficed, heck a press release would have sufficed, but I did it, got it filed."

"They don't seem to be very organized," Gabby says, putting down her sandwich. "That seems incredibly inefficient, why have you drive all the way back there for no reason? Maybe you can sit down and talk with your boss when you get back about how they can use your time better."

Lizzie is quiet. It's harder than she thought it would be to tell her parents she's lost her job. She feels like she's letting them down, as much as she knows that's not true, it still feels like she did something wrong.

"Well, the thing is, she's not my boss anymore. When I got back to the newsroom it was empty. Sarah's desk had been cleaned out, no one was there. Not even Margaret, my boss."

"That sounds really strange, are you sure everyone wasn't just gone for the holidays?" her dad asks.

"No, I called Sarah and she said she'd been laid off, and so had Margaret and everyone else."

"Oh my God, they did that just days before Christmas? What kind of people are they?" Gabby innocently asks.

"Not nice ones, Mom." she sighs and pokes at her sandwich.

"While I was talking to her my office phone rang and it was some guy telling me I had been let go, too."

"Oh honey, I'm so sorry, but I have to say, good riddance to those corporate idiots who don't know the first thing about journalism," says Peter.

In spite of her trying to have a good, plucky attitude Lizzie starts to cry. "I am so sorry, Mom and Dad, you worked so hard to put me through school, helped me with my Master's, and then this happens. I'm so sorry to disappoint you."

"Lizzie, the last thing we are is disappointed," says her mom, jumping up and coming over to hug her. "We have never been anything but proud of you, so stop that nonsense right now, okay?"

Lizzie blows her nose into a napkin and nods. "I just naively thought it wouldn't happen at a paper like the Sentinel. It's been there forever." She wipes her eyes. "They're closing the newsroom. They are going to run the paper, once one of the best in the country, from New York, and use some freelancers, I guess. It breaks my heart. There have been so many Pulitzer prize winning writers to come out of that paper. It's just awful."

"It sure is honey, and I'm so sorry you're now one of the casualties," he takes her hand. "But you are going to be just fine."

"Well, that's what I wanted to talk to you about," she looks at both her parents nervously. "Sarah knows someone who could sublet my apartment, and I was thinking–"

Before she can even finish the sentence her parents jump up and hug each other, and then both hug her. "Yes!" they both yell.

"I am so sorry for the reason, but to have you back here, that would be the Christmas miracle I've been wishing for!" says Gabby.

"Dad?" Lizzies asks. "I have some ideas, if you'd like me to come on board and help."

Now it's Peter's turn to get choked up. "Are you kidding me? I have never wanted to pressure you into coming back and taking over this antique of an operation, but I would be so happy, and well, grateful for the help. I know I'm stuck in the last century on so many things and would welcome any and all ideas."

"I don't want to step on your toes, Dad," Lizzie says, wanting to make sure he knows she's not planning a takeover. "You started this paper, it's yours—"

"No, honey, it's ours. From now on it's going to be ours."

"Really?" she starts to cry again, and soon all three of them are crying.

Peter is quiet for a minute. "I have to be honest, we're not in the best shape". Now it's his turn to be nervous. "I'm a month behind on the mortgage, and they've been nice, but I don't know what I'm getting you into."

Lizzie knew things were worse than he'd been letting on. "I don't want to make you hang on if what you really want to do for your own well-being is sell the paper. Dad, please be honest."

"No, selling is the last thing I want, if for no other reason than to have one last independent voice on this spit of land, I want to do anything I can to keep it just that, independent. And I'm betting between your youth, talent and energy, that is a lot more likely to happen than it would if it's just me and Stan."

"So you're really sure? This isn't a pity hire?"

"Well, you may feel it's pitiful when you get your first paycheck," Peter says, "No, you're saving me too."

All three of them begin to cry. "Jeez, we really are the schmaltz family, aren't we?" Lizzie jokes. Just then, as they're all bawling, Matt walks in.

"Is everything okay?" he says, concerned.

Peter sniffs, "Yeah, Matty, it's better than okay, say hello to my new business partner. Your sister's coming home."

CHAPTER 26

As soon as Matt gets the gist of what's going on he's crying too. "We really are a sappy bunch, aren't we?" he says through his tears. "Aw, Lizzie, it will be so amazing to have you around, and not just to babysit."

"Ha ha," she says. "I definitely look forward to spending more time with Sophie, and Shannon too. I am a little nervous about reconnecting here, it's been a long time since I spent a winter here."

"It's like riding a bike," Peter says. "Or a sled. You'll find your rhythm." He stops for a minute. "Look, I know you've loved living in Boston, writing for a city paper, but I'm hoping you'll see the impact that local journalism can have."

"I know that Dad, I really do. What I'm hoping we can do, with your go-ahead, is to bring in some fresh voices to write about building community and how we can plan for the future. Maybe we can get Ben to write a recipe column! I just thought of that!"

Peter puts his arm around her. "You are exactly what's been missing from this place, honey, we need a shot in the arm, some new ideas and energy. I really think this will work."

They finish up their lunch, wrap up the leftovers, and Gabby and Matt head out.

"I'll be home in a little while," Lizzie says as her mom is leaving. "I haven't even showered yet."

"I'm going over to the Marshview Inn for the wreath making, want to meet me there? I'm betting you forgot, no wonder with all you've had going on," she smiles, noting the surprised look on her face.

The idea of going to this event feeling as gross as she does isn't exactly how she saw her afternoon going, but she'd promised Sean and Ben she'd be there. "Yeah, what with losing my job and all it kind of slipped my mind," she laughs. "But yeah, I should go. How about I come with you?" She picks up her coat. "We can put all the leftovers in my car, it's cold enough."

"Sounds good, and Peter?" He looks up from his computer, "I'm leaving Daisy here with you for an hour, okay?" He nods, and goes back to work. "Are you absolutely sure you want to work with that every day?" Gabby jokes, opening the door.

"I heard that," Peter calls after them, laughing.

"Love you, honey," Gabby calls before the door closes.

Once again Lizzie is wowed by how pretty the Marshview Inn is as they pull up.

"Why aren't I ever blasé about this place? Every time I come here I am awestruck," she says, getting out of the car.

"I think it's good to never lose that sense of awe and beauty," Gabby says as they climb the majestic front steps. "It means you're awake and paying attention," she hooks her arm through Lizzie's and they open the front door.

"Yay! I'm so glad you made it back," Ben says, giving Lizzie a hug. "Dr. Martin, it's so good to see you, I'm so glad both of you came." He leads them to the large farmhouse-style kitchen where everything is laid out in neat piles. "Let me take your coats, and help yourself to some cocoa or some hot cider, and there are scones and shortbread cookies on the counter."

"Ben, how'd you know I was in Boston?" Lizzie asks as she pours herself and her mom some cocoa. "It was such a quick trip, I didn't think anyone knew."

He shrugs, "Huh, oh, I think Jack told me? I wondered where you were when we met up this morning for coffee."

She doesn't know why, but she's annoyed. She doesn't want Jack talking about her or her whereabouts to anyone. She's not his concern. Period.

And then, suddenly, he's there, carrying in some firewood along with Sean. Their eyes meet, but Lizzie quickly busies herself looking at the huge assortment of greens, berries, ribbons, barks, pinecones, shells and herbs on the giant table.

"Gabby, it's nice to see you," he says to her mom. "Lizzie, glad you made it back okay in time for this, and of course, the rest of the festival events." He's being very formal which feels weird, though she has to admit nothing he can say or do will be right at this point. She nods, and gives her best 'I can't stand you, don't dare talk to me anymore' smile. If she was Southern she would have said, "Bless your heart." He takes the hint and moves to the other side of the table. Adding to Lizzie's discomfort is the knowledge that she hasn't showered, slept on her couch, and is not at her sartorial best. It never fails that when you want to be wearing the best outfit ever, you are instead one step above being in public in your pajamas. Truly, it is like some law of physics.

Ben and Sean introduce themselves, give some history of the inn, and the materials they've chosen for the wreaths. They're all local items, all grown in and around Cranberry Harbor, the couple of exceptions being the cinnamon sticks and dried orange slices. Even in her foul mood Lizzie has to admit everything smelled wonderful. At this point there are eight people in the group gathered around the table, and as Ben demonstrated how you can build your wreath, Lizzie found herself enjoying the project. No matter what had happened with Jack, she was going to make the best wreath ever, and then strangle Jack with it. No, that is not in the Christmas spirit, she tells herself.

Gabby is struggling with her wreath a little. Asked to suture up a sliced hand, she's your person, but she was never particularly crafty. She and Lizzie laugh about how she is all about the mathematics of the project–the orange slices to cinnamon sticks ratio, balance and symmetry– she doesn't really allow herself to think about just what looks pretty. Lizzie on the other hand is all about the feel of the wreath, and if it would look welcoming and friendly in the house.

Jack is at the far end of the table, and it's clear Ben and Sean are a bit confused about what has happened since two days ago when they were all happily doing the scavenger hunt. They keep shooting looks at each other, but with so many other people to guide through the project they don't say anything.

In the end Lizzie has created a wreath she plans to hang inside, and has intentionally chosen the most aromatic additions to it. The lavender, orange, cinnamon, dried rosemary and thyme will smell great indoors, she thinks. Her mother's wreath is very symmetrical, very organized and balanced. They both laugh. "This is like a psychological look inside us, Mom–mine, slightly messy, a bit disorganized–"

"But very artsy and pretty," Gabby says, "Mine looks like a science project made with plant products. Even when I try, I cannot seem to just let go and be creative."

"Mom, it's lovely, and you will be the perfect person to teach robots how to make wreaths when AI takes over." Lizzie laughs, and Gabby feigns a frown. "Oh, Mom, it really is perfect."

"But art isn't supposed to be perfect," Gabby says.

"There is great beauty in symmetry, Gabby," Sean, who walked over to see their wreaths, says. "Studies show that symmetry relaxes people and makes them feel calm, it's true! There is no 'right' way to create, so stop being so hard on yourself."

"See Mom? My crazy dream-catcher of a wreath will make people feel stressed and anxious, and yours will calm them down," Lizzie says, laughing.

She's actually having fun despite having Jack there. The idea that she's going to be home for a while is beginning to sink in and it's not feeling terrible. It's actually feeling kind of good. She really wants to help her dad save the paper, and is excited that she'll be doing work that is more meaningful and appreciated, and have good friends like Ben and Sean to spend time with. And Alexis, and her parents and brother. She's resisted the idea of coming back here for so long, but now without too many other options, she's seeing that it might actually not be bad, even with the annoying ex.

Jack holds up his wreath to show Ben, "What do you think? I've never done anything I needed a glue gun for in my life, but this doesn't seem too terrible, does it?"

"'Not too terrible' isn't exactly giving yourself a rave review," Ben jokes. "I think it's awesome, I like that you used so many of the shells, and that you mixed them up, and paired the pieces of quahog shells with purple with the lavender, and chose a ribbon with cream and lavender woven in, very much on-theme, sir."

"I had no idea I'd done any of that," he laughs. "It's all a happy accident," he looks over to Lizzie. Hoping to catch her eye. She doesn't look his way.

In an hour they've all managed to create truly one-of-a-kind wreaths, eaten far too many cookies, and Lizzie is feeling a bit buzzed on hot chocolate.

"Let me help you guys clean up," Lizzie offers as the other crafters begin to leave.

"No, don't worry about it, we've got it. There's another

group coming tomorrow, so we'll just be adding more stuff," Sean says. "Did you have fun?"

"I did! It makes me realize how much time I spend in my head and not doing things with my hands. I need to learn to knit or something! I feel like I'm mostly always on some sort of device with a screen, I need to give my brain a break and cut back. Maybe I'll be able to find some balance now."

"Now? What's going on?"

"Oh, well, um," she's a little flustered saying it out loud for the first time to anyone in town. "I'm coming back to Cranberry Harbor, at least for a little bit. My dad and I are going to run the Gazette together," she finds herself smiling, beaming even.

Ben hears this and comes running over and picks her up in a big bear hug. "What?! You're coming back?!"

At this point Jack has heard the congratulations and wanders over. "Really? You're coming back? You parents must be thrilled!" He looks excited, despite their recent falling out. "So what changed your mind?"

Not wanting him to think for one second it was because of him she quickly says, "My entire newsroom was laid off, that's what changed my mind." She looks around for her mom, who she sees is still fussing with her wreath. "Well, we should be going. Thank you both so much for hosting this. It was so much fun! We'll have to get together soon."

Gabby comes over, wreath slung over her arm. "Yes, this was a complete delight. I hope you do it again next year!"

Lizzie hustles them both out, even though it's clear Jack wants to talk to her.

On the drive back to the office, the car filled with the lovely aromas from their wreaths, Gabby asks the question she's been wanting the answer to for two days.

"So what happened? You went from having a wonderful time with Jack to freezing him out overnight. If you don't want to tell me, I understand, but it's just such a change."

"Something didn't happen, someone did. Someone named Penelope and she's his girlfriend," she says looking out the window as they drive back to town. "It's all good, I've gotten over him before so I can get over him again."

Gabby isn't so sure, and wonders just how complicated the next several months are going to be.

CHAPTER 27

THE NEXT MORNING Lizzie is up bright and early ready to get a start on her first day at the Gazette. She's up before both her parents or Daisy, and has coffee made, oatmeal warming, and sliced fruit ready for everyone when they finally pad downstairs.

"Well, if I knew this is what having a new business partner would be like I would have twisted your arm years ago to come back, thank you honey," Peter says, giving her a peck on the cheek. Lizzie is at the table, drinking coffee, going over notes and creating a budget for this weeks' paper. A budget in journalism-speak is figuring out all the content.

"So Dad," she says as Peter sits down with his coffee and oatmeal. "I had an idea to add some new contributors, would you be open to that?"

"Yes! Of course! That's a great idea!"

She hands him her notes that she printed out in his home office earlier. "My idea is to add some younger and forward thinking voices. To get people thinking about the future of the town, and how we can grow and evolve, work on climate change, housing, jobs, retaining young people..."

He's reading, "What are you going to do in your second week?" he jokes. "Wow, this is ambitious, for sure."

She's nervous that maybe he doesn't like it. "Too ambitious?"

"Not at all. I think this is the kick in the pants this place has needed for a long time. We need young, fresh voices and ideas. I love it. I truly love these ideas. And hopefully all you're planning will bring more money in and we can pay them. In the meantime, I can at least give Sea Coast and Tall Tales free ads. "

"I thought the same thing. Yeah, Alexis would be great. She's almost done with her Master's in community development and planning, and she has the passion, but also the knowledge and nuts and bolts tools on how we can bring about change. And the Patels, with their shared knowledge and experience, I think they would be a fresh voice about diversity, books, the environment, even law."

"Those are both great ideas," he pauses. "I don't want to bring up a sensitive subject, but what about Jack? I've been hearing rumblings about him having some ideas he wants to bring to the area that sound really exciting. Possibly some big projects?"

Lizzie is quiet for a minute. She knows if he brings in the money and people he's talking about it will be big news. Really big news. She can't avoid him. "Of course, this is about more than personal feelings for sure. If he gets to create the projects he's talking about, like creating the eco-friendly housing on that unused land, wastewater reduction, or down the road, the carbon capture facility at the old base, of course we want to cover those. And maybe he'd even want to write some pieces, though he says he's not a writer." She thinks back to their talking about her helping him and feels a little sad.

"Those are incredible ideas that we'd definitely cover, and I think it would be great to get him involved with the paper, maybe even give him a tech column once a month to educate people."

Lizzie panics, "Please don't say anything to anyone in town, about his idea for this project, it's not my idea to tell. Where did you hear that?"

"His dad told me a bit about it when we were each recycling last week. He's going to have his work cut out for him though. This place moves forward at a glacial pace. There's always the contingent that already made their money, retired here and can't understand why anything has to change."

"Maybe when they realize that no one under 65 lives here anymore because they can't afford to, it will sink in," Gabby says, joining them at the table.

"Exactly," Lizzie says, getting up and pouring another cup of coffee. "If I didn't have you here I wouldn't be able to afford to come back, not right now. It's crazy that the rents on year-round rentals are comparable to what they are in Boston, but there aren't jobs that pay Boston-level salaries."

"I feel very frivolous bringing this up, but today is the Main Street Cookie Stroll," says Gabby.

"Is this a new event? I don't remember that one," Lizzies asks.

"Yeah," Peter says, "The Cranberry Harbor Merchants Co-Op started it two years ago to try to counter how much shopping people were doing online. It's a way to entice people into the local shops, which hopefully they've been supporting all season, and get them to shop local."

"I love this, if I go early and get some shots I can get it up on the paper's Instagram and Twitter accounts, bring more people in," Lizzie says, quickly getting up and taking her dishes to the sink, rinsing them and putting them in the dishwasher.

"We don't have an Instagram account, or Twitter," Peter says, a little chagrined.

Lizzie takes her phone out of her pocket, "Yeah, you do now, I set it all up last night and we already have close to 1000 people following us," she smiles at her dad. "I tagged a few folks with big followings who love Cranberry Harbor that I've interviewed in the past. Super easy," she smiles.

"Wow, now if this was me, I'd be thinking how we could never get any news out at the last minute because the paper comes out today and it's too late."

"It's a melding of the two worlds, Dad, embracing and respecting the importance of a newspaper you can hold in your hands, but also being able to be immediate in your response to what's happening in town, and in the world. My goal is to make our social media and website the landing spot for people to check on to see what's happening here and off-Cape as well. Hopefully, we'll be able to get a lot more people out to the Cookie Stroll because maybe they didn't know about it, or maybe they just forgot, but we're going to be the place that reminds them."

"God, love you, Lizzie, you are just what this antique of a publication needed."

"Dad, it still needs you, and it still needs Stan. You two are the backbone, the ones who know everyone and how everything works. What I hope to do is to shine a brighter light on what was already there, what was already special about the paper and Cranberry Harbor," Lizzie says. "Okay, so I'm going to take a quick shower, and then get myself to my very first Main Street Cookie Stroll, if that works for you, boss?" she teases.

"Sounds good to me," he stops for a second. "Thank you honey, I haven't felt this hopeful about the Gazette or the future of this town in a really long time."

"My pleasure," she says as she dashes up the stairs.

CHAPTER 28

WHEN LIZZIE ARRIVES on Main Street, ready for the Cookie Stroll, she thought Cranberry Harbor is looking even more beautiful than usual, but maybe it was merely reflecting how she is feeling about being there. There were a fresh couple of inches of lovely ocean-effect snow covering everything, and with the sun now out in a cloudless bright blue sky, it is sparkling as well. Lizzie smiles to herself and shakes her head, it's like Hollywood came and dressed the town for the day. She starts taking pictures right away, thinking their Instagram feed is going to look amazing. If you weren't already in Cranberry Harbor this morning, you were going to want to hop in your car and get there immediately.

Her first stop was Jess's Vintage Bridal Shop where of course she had lacy looking snowflake cookies which were sparkling in the sunshine on a beautifully adorned table outside the shop. While nibbling on the cookie she wanders in, and then quickly changes her mind, a bridal shop is not where she wants to be today.

"Hi!" a very friendly woman, she assumes is Jess, says. "Can I help you find anything?"

Lizzie continues chewing the cookie in her mouth, holding up a finger. "No, thank you, I just wanted to compliment you on these gorgeous cookies. And this beautiful shop," She swallows the rest of the cookie in her mouth. "I'm Lizzie Martin," she shakes her hand. "I'm going to be working with my dad, Peter Martin, at the Gazette."

"That's so wonderful! I'm Jessica Taylor, and this is my shop. "Your dad and Stan have been so wonderful to me since I opened. They really helped me to get the word out about my business."

"I'm so glad to hear that. Now that I'm here I want to do a lot more with social media, as well as the print edition, so we'll have to talk about how we can help each other."

"I'd love that, especially in the off-season, we really need to keep shining a light on all these great year-round local business-es." She goes over to the counter, "Here's my card. It's my cell and email, after the holidays we'll have to get together, maybe have coffee sometime or something?"

Lizzie puts the card in her pocket, "I'd love that." She has moved past her bridal shop panic and takes the store in. "This really is exquisite," she says looking around. "I love that you have vintage and new, and all the accessories. It's pretty amazing a bride can get everything she needs right here in Cranberry Harbor. Back when I was…" she stops herself. "Well, it used to be you definitely had to go to Boston, so this is great."

"There's lots of wonderful businesses right here, we just have to get people to come to town and then we've sold them!" She says, smiling.

"I have to keep moving to get some more photos, but I'm so glad I got to meet you. I'd give you a card too, but I just started this job yesterday, so no cards yet," she laughs.

"No worries, I know where to find you," Jess smiles. "I'm sure I'll see you around town. Or maybe you'll be back soon shopping for your own wedding gown," she teases.

CHRISTMAS IN CRANBERRY HARBOR

Lizzie laughs, "No immediate chance of that happening, but maybe we'll see each other getting a caffeine fix at Sea Coast. I'll see you soon, Jess. Merry Christmas!"

She's about the run across the street to the town toy store, Kid Works, when she sees Jack walking in her direction. She tries to go back into the bridal store before he sees her. It doesn't work.

"Lizzie!" he yells, "wait!"

She starts to open the door when he catches up with her. The last thing she wants is to have a conversation with him, especially in front of a bridal shop.

"Lizzie, we need to talk," he says, touching her arm. "Just let me explain..."

"No. Not now, I have work I have to do. I'm fine. It's all good. You don't owe me a thing, Jack. I hope you and Penelope will be very happy." She turns to cross the street. "Merry Christmas," she says, and quickly crosses the street to the toy shop. She stands outside for a moment, trying to pull herself together. She refuses to turn around to see if he's still standing there, but she senses he is. "Forget about it, forget about him," she says to herself, and then she heads into the store.

It had been a long time since she'd gone into Toy Works, it had opened when she was in middle school just on the cusp of not playing with toys anymore, but still liking games. She doesn't recognize the woman behind the counter, which isn't surprising.

"Hi," she says, "I'm Lizzie Martin, from the Gazette, and we're just getting some photos for social media of the Cookie Stroll. Your jam thumbprint cookies look amazing by the way."

"Hi, Lizzie, I'm Justine, my aunt and uncle own the shop, and I can take no credit for the cookies," she jokes.

"That is very forthcoming of you," she jokes back. "With no one else here you could have taken total credit and I would have been none the wiser."

Justine shrugs. "I would not want the weight of that deception on me, it would be far too much." She then points to a row of boxes of *Elf on a Shelf*, "And with all of them watching me, well, I have to be good, or you know…"

Lizzie likes this young woman, she's funny. "Oh, can you imagine the implication of lying in front of…" she begins to count, "…seven elves?! That could ruin Christmas for you for years." She wanders around looking at all the Hello Kitty swag, Legos, and games. Lots of things have changed in the toy world, but it was nice to see that some things hadn't. "Are you okay if I take a few photos for our Instagram and Facebook?"

"Of course, go right ahead. Wait, the Gazette doesn't have any social media, or it didn't before."

"Yeah, it's been live a whole 12 hours, so please follow us, and I'll tag you in the photos."

Justine takes out her phone. "Done!"

"Thanks so much Justine for letting me poke around," Lizzie says as she gets ready to leave. "It's nice to see other younger adults here. Now that I'm moving back I'm a little worried about not having anyone my age around. There's a few people I went to school with here, but knowing three or four people does not a social life make."

"I hear you! There's several of us who do yoga together a few times a week, and we even started a book club, as weird and maybe old as that sounds," she laughs. "but we take turns picking books from light fiction to more serious social justice titles. You should totally join us!"

"I'd really love that, thank you. After the holidays I'll definitely stop in and see you." She suddenly remembers she needs some things for Sophie and decides to create a small collection of fun things like sparkly stickers and a little book to put them in, a stuffed cat, and two puzzles.

Justine wraps them all together beautifully in a reusable bag, and ties it with a big red ribbon. "There you go," she says, handing it to her. "I'm so glad you came in!"

"Me too, I just ran into my ex out there, so this has been a nice mood changer," Lizzie says.

"Make sure to take a cookie! Cookies make everything better." Justine says as Lizzie walks to the door.

"I will! Thank you again, I look forward to doing yoga and reading serious and not-so-serious books together!" Lizzie says as she leaves.

Back on the street she decides to stop by Sea Coast to sit down and do some social media posting. She looks around to see if Jack is there, and once she deems the coast clear claims a table with her coat and goes to the counter to order some coffee.

Once back at her table, she quickly gets her posts up, tags all the businesses, and hopes she's done alright with all her hashtags. She makes a mental note to talk to Leah sometime, she seems to be the queen of social media, and get some tips. She's drawing the line at creating a Tik Tok account though, that's one generation below hers and she doesn't want to look like she's trying too hard.

She takes a few photos inside Sea Coast too, encouraging people to stop in and warm up with a beverage, because it's all part of the spirit of the Cookie Stroll. It's a lot of work, but it's the kind of work that helps the community. At least she hopes it does. She's getting a bit of a late start this year, but next year this will all be in place and she can promote the town earlier. She stops for a moment and thinks, am I really planning on being here a year from now? Apparently the answer is yes.

"Hey you," she hears Alexis call to her as she walks over and sits down with her coffee. "So rumor has it you are going to be here for a while."

"Boy, I forget how small this town is," she laughs. "Why am I even bothering with social media, I can just come here and tell two people something and in an hour everyone will know."

"Yeah, but it won't have pretty pictures to go with it," Alexis says, laughing.

"To answer your question, I am back, for how long I don't know, and well, I wanted to see if you'd ever be interested in writing a column, maybe once a month?"

"I can't say I consider myself a writer, but I'm up for anything! What would it be?"

"I was thinking about you writing about housing, community, the need for younger people and diversity. Things like that."

"That sounds really good, I might even be able to work in some of the things I'm doing to wrap up my Master's into this. I'm definitely interested, thank you for thinking of me!"

"Are you kidding? Of course! I want to make the paper interesting to all ages and all of the community, that starts with bringing in fresh voices, like yours," Lizzie says, excited that her ideas are so far working out. "We don't have a lot of money right now, but I can give you a free subscription," she jokes. "I promise it won't be working for nothing for long. I hope."

"I'm happy to contribute. I think it's fantastic, and just what this place needs." She looks down at her coffee and slyly looks back up at Lizzie.

"What? I know that look, it's the same look you gave me when you talked me into sneaking into the drive-in with you, that look is dangerous and makes me do stupid things," she laughs.

"Oh, I'd forgotten about sneaking into the drive-in. We got caught pretty quickly as I recall," Alexis says.

Lizzie nods, "Yup, and our families made us write letters of apology."

"That your dad put in the paper! Oh my gosh, how could I forget that! Okay, so this has nothing to do with trespassing or any law breaking at all, well, unless you consider being tone-deaf a crime," Alexis mysteriously says.

"Okay, so what are you talking about?"

"A bunch of us - Sean, Ben, and um, Jack, were going to go to Murphy's Pub tonight for some Christmas karaoke, and you have to come, it won't be nearly as much fun without you."

"Ugh, I don't know. For one," she points to herself, "totally can't carry a tune, and two, Jack and Penelope being there? I don't think I'm up for that."

"Where have you been? Okay, Penelope left, and have you forgotten, we stood next to each other in the middle school chorus and you can totally carry a tune."

"What do you mean, Penelope left? I saw her yesterday at Bradford's. So she's gone back to California to wait for him to come back? Is Jack leaving too?"

"No, he's not. Ben told me that Jack was shocked that she showed up here. He'd ended things months ago, but she thought putting in the effort of showing up here would change things. He was not at all happy that she just swooped in. Apparently she's very much a West coaster and made it clear she would never, ever want to live in Cranberry Harbor. And that was always his goal. To settle down here."

"I had no idea, I thought—"

"He told Ben he kept trying to reach you and you wouldn't take his calls, or answer his texts." She's quiet for a moment. "He was pretty devastated that you wouldn't let him explain."

Lizzie is stunned. She sits back in her chair, speechless. "I have been a total jerk." She feels like crying. "I thought he'd had this girlfriend all along and was just being all nice to me out of guilt or something. He must think I'm terrible. And I am for believing the worst without even giving him a chance to explain."

Alexis puts her hand on Lizzie's, "I think he's confused. And

241

yeah, hurt that you wouldn't even let him tell you himself what was going on."

"There's a reason they tell people to never assume, huh?"

"Maybe some karaoke would be a good way to break that ice between you two?" Alexis offers.

"I don't know, seems like a recipe for public humiliation all the way around."

"I'm not going to twist your arm," she says as she gets up to go back to work, "I'll just say we're all going to be there at 8 o'clock, and I'd love for you to come. And sometimes what you can't say you can sing," she shrugs and smiles at her.

"Okay, I'll think about it. And Lex, thanks for telling me about Jack, I really appreciate it."

"I've always got your back, friend, forever and always."

Alexis heads back to the kitchen and Lizzies sits a little longer thinking about how badly she's handled things. If she were Jack, she wasn't sure she'd ever want to talk to her again.

CHAPTER 29

AFTER LEAVING SEA COAST, Lizzie headed to the Gazette office to check in with her dad. She didn't want to be seen as coasting because she's the daughter. She knows this job is not going to be endless days of just wandering around Cranberry Harbor eating cookies, taking pictures, posting them online, and sipping coffee with friends. Okay, maybe some of them are. She is also going to have to pull her weight writing, editing, finding stories and selling ads. They needed revenue and this was an all-hands-on-deck everyone doing everything operation. When she walks in she's surprised to see Stan at his desk, arm in a cast, but looking chipper as ever.

"Stan, what a nice surprise!" Lizzie says, giving him a hug as he stands up. "How's that arm?" She takes off her coat and tosses it over an empty chair. "Oh, hey Dad," she nods at him. Truth is, she's worried. Worried about Stan feeling displaced.

"So your dad has been filling me in about what's going on, and I just want to..."

Lizzie jumps in, "Stan, I don't want to step on your toes at all, really, I totally respect all you've done, and I'm not here to take away anything from you. Not at all. Not one little bit." She's shaking her head emphatically, wanting to make sure he understands.

Stan laughs, "Are you kidding me? Do you know how long I've wanted to step back? I couldn't be more delighted, I just didn't want to leave your old dad here in the lurch. You are welcome to cover anything you want. I am so happy you're here."

"Oh my gosh, I'm so relieved!" She lets out a big sigh. "I do hope you'll want to keep doing some stories though, you're our resident expert on all things marine and environmental."

"Of course, I would love that. I'd love to work on some longer form stories and be able to put more time into things. For instance, these projects Jack Cahoon is talking about, that's the kind of big project I would love to sink my teeth into."

Lizzie's stomach clenches. "The Jack Cahoon projects?"

"Yeah, your dad was telling me how he's talking about a carbon capture facility at the old, empty base, and working with the marine center on the wastewater issue and nitrogen removal. Oh! And his ideas for that big parcel on the town border. Boy, all that could be huge for the community, and for the environment. I'd love to explore writing about that."

Lizzie shoots her dad a look.

"Yeah, but that's not etched in stone yet, Stan, don't say anything to him, or anyone yet," Peter says. "I only mentioned that to you in passing."

Stan looks at them both, "Oh, I didn't know I shouldn't mention it to him. I ran into him at the hardware store this morning and he did seem surprised that I knew about it. Sorry about that, guess I misunderstood."

Stan and Lizzie exchange a horrified look.

Lizzie is trying to calm down, Jack didn't want her or Alexis telling anyone anything yet, it had to be under wraps until he got funding, he hadn't even formalized what he was going to present to the town. This could ruin everything. Still, she smiles at Stan, trying to be cool. "I'm sure it's fine, just don't say anything to anyone else, okay?"

Stan is quiet. "Well, always the reporter, I did ask Tom Jenkins if he'd met with Jack yet, shoot, I guess I shouldn't have done that."

"Tom Jenkins, the town manager?" Lizzie asks. This is getting worse and worse.

"Yeah, he didn't know anything about it, acted real surprised."

"What did he say?" Peter asks tentatively.

"He didn't seem real keen on it, you know how he is, nothing new, nothing innovative. Goshdarn it, I feel terrible about spilling the beans here, Lizzie. I didn't know it was such a big secret."

Lizzie is trying to keep herself calm and from shaking Stan. "It's okay, I'll talk to Jack, and hopefully Tom didn't say anything, or in the craziness of Christmas forgot all about it." Never going to happen she thinks, but one can dream. "So Dad, is there anything you need me to be working on? I'm going to head home for a little bit, then I'm maybe going to Murphy's with Alexis, Ben, Sean and a few other people tonight."

Her dad looks at her, he knows what a 'few other people' means. "I think I'm okay. Maybe at some point you can take that column you wrote about the Cape and the need for change, and rework it to add that you're coming back here, and going to be a co-editor with me?"

"You really want to do that? Co-editor? I figured I'd just be a staff writer until you get so sick of seeing me every day that you'd retire."

"For one, I will never, ever get tired of seeing you every day, and second, this is what I want, I want you to be co-editor, and I want everyone to know."

"You'd better accept it, Lizzie, poor guy, he offered it to me through the years and I said no thanks so many times he stopped asking," says Stan.

"Well then, I accept," she says, shaking his hand. "Thanks for the opportunity, Mr. Martin, I won't let you down," she gives a little bow, puts on her coat and heads to the door. "So Stan?"

"My lips are sealed from now on until you give me the say so," he says.

"Sounds good, see you two fellas later."

She gets into her car, starts it and sits back for a minute. How the heck is she ever going to explain this to Jack? Not only has she screwed things up by assuming he was with Penelope, her family and Stan may have also sabotaged his project.

CHAPTER 30

LIZZIE DEBATED, paced and fretted for an hour and a half in her room about whether or not to go and meet up with everyone at Murphy's. The thought of going was hard enough when all she had to concern herself with was having completely misjudged Jack on the Penelope matter, but now he was going to think she wasn't trustworthy with all his plans and ideas. She never should have discussed it with her dad at all. It was stupid and thoughtless, and..."Argh!" she barks out loud, loud enough that her mom hears her as she walks by her room. The door is slightly ajar and Gabby pokes her head in. "Is everything okay, honey?"

Lizzie throws herself on her bed like she's 13. "No, it's not, I think I've really screwed things up." She rolls onto her side and clutches her ancient stuffed teddy bear that is missing a leg and an eye. "Is it too late for me to change my mind and go back to Boston? Or for you to ground me and tell me I can't go out tonight?"

Her mom sits down on the bed next to her and runs her hand through Lizzie's hair. "'Fraid so, honey. I really hate that term, 'adulting' but I guess it sort of applies here. Anything you want to share? If not, I totally respect your privacy."

Lizzie props herself up on her elbow. "Dad will just tell you anyway. Well, at least the newspaper part. He doesn't know the personal part."

"Tell me both, one or neither, I'm good with whatever."

"Were you always this chill when I was a teenager? You seem so relaxed."

"I was not. The nice thing about this phase of life is as long as you are not in any kind of serious danger, which I can see you are not, you're an adult and I don't have to think about fixing your problems. You are more than capable of doing that yourself. I get to be a supporting player now, not a featured cast member," she smiles.

"If I live to be 110 I will never be as Zen as you. I didn't get that gene."

"It comes with age, honey, I may not have the legs I once did, but this is a nice tradeoff. So, what happened?"

"Well first off, I totally screwed things up with Jack. I jumped to the conclusion that he and Penelope were an item when they were not, and he kept trying to reach out to me to explain, and I was a jerk and wouldn't talk to him, and now I'm sure he hates me."

"I'm one-hundred percent sure he doesn't hate you. He may be frustrated, hurt perhaps, but I'm positive he doesn't hate you. What's the next thing?"

She sits up, crosses her legs in front of her, picks up the teddy bear again and clutches it into her stomach. "Ugh, this is even worse." She takes a deep breath. "Stan ran into Jack..."

"Oh boy, any sentence that starts with, Stan ran into someone, is not good. He is not the best keeper of secrets. When your dad took me to Paris for our thirtieth anniversary?"

"Yeah, the big surprise trip?" Lizzie's eyes get big, "No! He told you?!"

Gabby nods. "He didn't mean to, he was so excited. Anyway, he's not good at keeping secrets. So now who's anniversary did he spoil, metaphorically?"

"Not an anniversary, but Dad had told him about some of Jack's plans-"

"No," she shakes her head in disbelief. "Of all the people to tell something like that to."

"I know, so anyway he ran into Jack at the hardware store this morning, and he's going to think Dad and I ruined his prospects with the town."

"Oh no," she smacks her forehead with her hand.

"Yup, told him how excited he was about all the plans for the town he had, and wanted to talk to him about it. But it gets worse."

"Oh no, who did he tell next? I shudder to think," Gabby says.

"Yeah, and oh, it's bad, he told Tom Jenkins, who I'm sure will make it his mission to use every legal string he can pull, along with all the heartstrings of the old timers, and new people who don't think about the economic or environmental future of the town, and will try to kill anything he wants to do. But before that happens Jack will never, ever speak to me again."

"Well, I've seen the way that guy looks at you, and I think the chances are very good that he will speak to you. Eventually."

"Somehow that is not very reassuring, Mom, thanks a lot," she tosses the teddy bear at her and they laugh. "I cannot believe that here I am, 32-years-old, and I'm still sitting here on my bed talking about boy problems with my mom." She throws herself back on her bed. "Maybe coming back here was not a good idea."

"Coming back was a great idea, don't ever think it was not, and," she lies down next to Lizzie and takes her hand, "I love having you here. I've missed you so much, and while I don't ever wish any problems on you, I can assure you it's all going to be okay."

Lizzie turns and hugs her mom. "Promise?"

"I promise." Gabby suddenly sits up. "So if you're going to wow them at karaoke tonight, you're going to need a cuter outfit than that," she teases. She gets up and starts looking in the closet. "Here, this is perfect!"

"Really? That's what you want me to wear?"

Her mom nods, "I will leave you to get ready. Love you, sweetie."

"Love you too."

CHAPTER 31

LIZZIE KNEW she was obsessing way too much over what she looked like to go to a neighborhood bar. The last time she'd gone to Murphy's she'd worn some old cut-off shorts, flip flops and ripped T-shirt. It is not exactly a dressy place. She hopes her mother hasn't steered her wrong.

Thankfully it hadn't snowed in the last few hours, and even then it was only light, so she is gambling on wearing dressy shoes and not boots, which she carries down the stairs, just to be safe.

Her mom is sitting at the kitchen table putting the finishing touches on a very fancy looking package.

"So, you still think this is right?" she asks her mom, giving a little twirl.

Gabby puts her hands over her heart and sighs. "Oh yeah, that is perfect. You look so beautiful." She reaches over and takes a gorgeous, cream-colored, cashmere shawl off the chair next to her and hands it to Lizzie. "Here, this will look wonderful and keep you warm. Murphy's can be drafty."

"Mom, this is the shawl you bought in Paris, I can't!"

"I will not take no for an answer. Beautiful things are meant to be worn and used. I want you to take it."

"Well fine then," she wraps it around her. "This has to be the softest thing I have ever felt, thank you. So you're one-hundred percent sure this is not too much?"

"It's just enough. Now go, have some fun, and sing something wonderful."

"Oh, you must have me confused with someone else, you know, someone who can carry a tune," Lizzie says as she buttons up her coat, pulling her hair out from collar and putting it to one side.

"It's not about sounding like Lizzo, it's about sounding like Lizzie and having fun."

"Did you just reference Lizzo?" Lizzie laughs.

"You don't know everything about me, young lady," she smiles as she curls the ribbon on the gift. "I keep up."

"Apparently I do not. That present is so pretty, who's it for? Sophie?"

"Nope, you hurry along, it's getting late."

"Wish me luck," she calls as she heads to the door.

"Break legs!" her mom calls after her.

Murphy's was right on Main Street, down at the end, past the Gazette office. As Lizzie drives by the office she looks up and can see her dad is still there. She snags a parking space not too far from the door for which she is glad, it has been a while since she's worn heels and she is a bit out of practice. After she parks, she takes one last look in the lighted visor mirror, takes a deep breath and gets out.

The place is packed, and she sees lots of familiar faces, but is not seeing the one she is looking for. "Lizzie! Over here!" Alexis calls out to her. Looking around she feels overdressed and is tempted to leave her coat on.

"Yay! I'm so glad you're here!" Alexis says, giving her a hug. "Take your coat off and sit down."

She nervously unbuttons the coat and slips it off.

"Holy Audrey Hepburn!" Alexis says. "That is totally the best little black dress I have ever seen. You look way too good for the likes of us!"

Ben and Sean, also sitting at the table, are equally impressed. "I wanted to wear a dress shirt and Ben told me I didn't have to, now I really wish I had, you look fantastic," says Sean.

"I feel really weird," she says looking around at the array of thick sweaters and jeans in the room. "My mom picked it out." As soon as she says that she feels stupid. Like in just one day living at home her mom is dressing her. "It was my Grandma's, from the 1950s. It was her favorite dress but she almost never wore it because she didn't want anything to happen to it. Funny how we do that, isn't it? We love something so much we don't enjoy it?"

"Yup, I do the same thing," says Ben. "I do it with cookware which is ridiculous. I'm a chef, but there are certain pans that I think are too nice." He takes a sip of his beer. "This is a really good reminder, thank you. I am definitely going to take those pans out and start using them," he raises his glass. "Here's to not waiting until it's too late to use the things we love, and not letting ourselves enjoy them!" They all toast, except Lizzie, who doesn't have anything yet.

Alexis signals the waitress who comes right over, "What do you want? My treat," she says.

"Oh no, you don't have to."

"I know I don't, I want to. What will it be?"

"Um, a glass of whatever red you have?" Lizzie says to the waitress.

"The bartender just opened a nice cabernet, would that be okay?"

"That would be perfect, thank you."

"I love your dress," she says as she walks away. "It's a total classic."

"See? Everyone loves it," Alexis says. "Stop fidgeting," she smiles.

"So, is this everyone?" Lizzie asks, wondering if Jack didn't come because he heard she was going to be there.

"For now anyway," says Ben. "Is everyone ready?" he looks excitedly around the table. "I can't wait."

"Of course you can't wait, because you're really, really good," says Sean. "I however do not possess your talent or confidence."

"I don't either," says Lizzie, taking a sip of her wine that has just arrived. "I really admire people who, even though they can't sing, can just relax and have fun, they really don't care. Me on the other hand? I care way too much about what people think, and then that makes it all worse, and I just sound terrible."

"Maybe we can sound terrible together," Alexis offers. "I can't sing either."

"That's not true," says Ben. "I was with you in chorus and you were good."

"Maybe when I was twelve, but not anymore."

Lizzie takes another sip of wine, and screws up her courage, and tries to sound all casual, "So is Jack coming? I thought you said he'd be here?" she asks the table.

"He said he might be late, something about a conference call with California or New York? He said to not wait, it could be a while."

"Oh, okay," she says, feeling slightly relieved, but also disappointed.

A young woman steps onto the makeshift stage at the front of the bar. "Hi Everyone! I am Evie, your host...I know, go ahead and make some Christmas Eve-ie jokes. I'll wait." The crowd laughs. "Okay, so now that we got that out of the way, I want to welcome all of you to the Second Annual Christmas Karaoke Night at Murphy's!" Everyone applauds, there's even a few whistles. "Everyone is welcome to sing, it doesn't matter if you think you can't sing, tonight is all about Christmas spirit and having fun, right?!" The crowd claps and cheers in agreement. "So put aside any doubts you may have, any stage fright that stops you from normally doing anything like this, and know we are all in this together!" She walks to the edge of the very small stage and whispers into her microphone. "So, who is going to be brave enough to be the first person up here?" The room goes silent. Sean elbows Ben who shakes his head. Finally, a meek voice from the back of the room says, "We'll go." Lizzie turns to see who it is, but can't.

As they make their way through the crowd, Lizzie sees that it's six boys and girls, they look to probably be early high school age. They also look very nervous, awkward, and completely adorable. They're dressed in black and white, each with an accent of red, a tie, a scarf, and a head wrap. The crowd grows quiet, and they hand Evie a tape with their background music on it. Apparently they are not doing karaoke, but instead going old school and singing on their own, unassisted by the karaoke machine. Just in case this is something special, Lizzie pulls up her phone and starts to record. The kids look at each other nervously, and then one of the boys, there's only two, begins singing the opening of the Springsteen version of *Santa Claus is Coming To Town*. There's an audible gasp from the crowd, and after that you could have heard a pin drop. Lizzie, Alexis, Sean and Ben all exchange open mouthed looks with one another. By the time they finish the entire place is on their feet cheering for them. Evie jumps back on stage as they're about to exit.

"Wait, you can't go yet," she says, calling them back. "That was amazing, wasn't it?" She looks to the audience, and they applaud and cheer some more. "You have to tell us who you are!"

The kids all reluctantly introduce themselves, and say they're freshmen and sophomores at the high school, and recently started a band, so recently they don't even have a name yet.

"They are amazing!" Lizzie says, leaning over to Alexis. As the kids walk by, she jumps up. "Hey, that was fantastic. I'm Lizzie Martin, with the Gazette, are you okay if I put the recording I did of this on our social media? I'd love to share it." They all look at each other and nod, "Yeah, that's cool," the lead singer says, and keeps walking. "That kid is going places," Lizzie says to Alexis. "He's probably 14 and already has swagger. Amazing."

She was so busy posting the video she didn't even notice the next person had stepped up. She recognizes her from Bradford's Market, she'd been the one to check out her groceries yesterday.

"Hey, I'm Millie Maynard, and I'm going to sing *Santa Baby*, thank you." She steps back a little, clears her throat, and starts to sing, again, another amazing rendition of a beloved classic song.

Lizzie leans in to everyone, "Okay, this clinches it, there is no way I am getting up there in front of this town and singing anything. Are we in some alternate universe where everyone living here is actually a star who is secretly living here while not on tour with their rock band or on Broadway? This is not normal. How can this one little town have all this talent?"

"All I can say is it wasn't like this last year," Alexis says. "That night it was a parade of the most off-key people I'd ever heard. I'm getting very nervous."

"Oh come on, not everyone is going to be that good," says Ben. "You promised you'd do it, you have to."

Evie crooks her finger at Ben, signaling him to come up, after Millie has left the stage.

"Here goes nothing," he says, standing up and jumping onto the stage. "Hey, everyone, Merry Christmas, and thank you to everyone who has made this festival, and this whole year so wonderful for all of us in Cranberry Harbor. We are so grateful to call this our home. Which leads me, perchance, to my song choice, *There's No Place Like Home for The Holidays*. I only hope I don't mess it up too much," he laughs.

Far from messing it up, there is not a dry eye in the house when he is done singing. Evie hugs him, she's crying too, "Thank you, Ben, ugh, I swore I wasn't going to get all sentimental, and cry, but here I am, crying already. That was beautiful." She looks down at her list.

"I didn't know you had to sign up ahead of time," Lizzie says, finally able to relax. "Oh well, maybe next year," she sits back with her wine glass and smiles. Yes! No karaoke for her tonight!

"Oh, don't get too relaxed there, we're on after this next guy," Alexis says, grinning an evil grin at her.

Lizzie sits bolt upright, puts down her glass and suddenly feels nauseous. "I thought you didn't want to do it! No, no, no, no, no!" she says to Alexis. "You did not sign me up without my permission."

Alexis shrugs her shoulders, "Eh, I've changed my mind, what's the worst that could happen?" she pats Lizzie on the hand. "It will be fine, I'll be up there with you. And I have the perfect song picked out, you're going to love it."

"What, what is it? And how am I possibly going to love it when I'm unconscious having passed out from stage fright?"

"Don't be dramatic, it's going to be fine. We're doing *Last Christmas*."

"The Wham song? I cannot do that. I could maybe eek out *Rudolph*, or *Jingle Bells*, but a pop song? I just can't!"

"Yes you can, and as soon as Tommy Finnigan is done butchering *Jingle Bell Rock* we're up."

"I think I'm going to be sick," Lizzie says, fussing with her hair and smoothing her dress.

"No you're not," Alexis says, dismissively. "You're going to be fine." She turns and looks at her friend who is a shade somewhere between light green and white. "You need to learn to have fun, to relax, and be okay with not being perfect at everything you do."

"I don't like not being perfect."

"Get over it," she takes her hand and pulls her up on stage.

"Hey, Evie, this is so fun, thanks for doing this again this year."

"I am thrilled to do it again," she says. "And I see you have a friend with you."

"I do! This is my best friend, Lizzie Martin, from all the way back from second grade. She is not thrilled that I dragged her up here, so let's give her some good Cranberry Harbor support, okay?" Everyone cheers. "Lizzie has just moved back to town to help her dad run the Gazette, how cool is that?!" Everyone cheers again.

"Well, I will let you two get to it, you are singing, one of my all-time favorites, from Wham, *Last Christmas.*" The audience applauds, and someone even yells, "You got this, Lizzie!"

As Evie starts to walk away, Alexis grabs her hand, "Feel free to stay and join in, the more the merrier!"

"Okay, that would be great!"

Lizzie is still just standing there, feeling so nervous in her Audrey Hepburn dress, and then the song starts, and the three of them are crowded around the mic, *Last Christmas I gave you my heart, and the very next day, you gave it away, this year, to save me from tears, I'll give it to someone special...*and then, suddenly, she starts to laugh, and let go, and have fun. She feels like Cameron Diaz in *My Best Friend's Wedding,* who, even though she knows she's not good, gets the crowd with her and they begin singing along too. When they get to the last verse, *Once bitten, and twice shy, I keep my distance but you still catch my eye,* she looks out and sees Jack standing in the back. She can't tell looking at him if he's angry, happy or something in between, but she just keeps singing. By the time they finish a third time on the chorus at the end, the crowd is standing and cheering.

Alexis yells above the din to her. "See? Letting go can be really fun!"

"You're so right!"she says as she makes her way back to the table. She looks around for Jack, but he's gone. Was she that terrible? Or maybe he's just that mad. She decides she has to let it go. She doesn't have a time machine to go back and undo anything, so she's just going to relax, and revel in breaking through a really big fear.

"To us!" She toasts the table. "I'm so grateful to be here and to have such good friends." They all clink glasses, and Lizzie reaches over to Alexis and hugs her. "Thank you, my friend, it is really good to be home."

CHAPTER 32

JACK NEVER DID MATERIALIZE at their table, but Lizzie had a wonderful Christmas time... to quote Sir Paul McCartney. At the very end a whole bunch of them, including Lizzie, got up and sang a rousing, or ear shattering, depending on one's perspective, edition of *We Wish You a Merry Christmas*. Lizzie couldn't even say it was the wine, she hadn't even finished that one glass and had switched to club soda.

As she and her table of friends spill out into the parking lot, they exchange hugs and good wishes. Ben hugs her, takes her by the shoulders and says, "I'm so glad you're back. This town needs you. We need you. And whatever is going on with Jack? It's going to be okay. I just know it."

Lizzie sighs. "I sure hope you're right," she says, squeezing him back. "I'm really glad I'm here too. I never, ever thought I'd come back, but it feels right."

"I'm glad," he says, giving her a kiss on the cheek and letting her go. "If we don't see you before the big day, Merry Christmas!"

"Merry Christmas to you, too!" Lizzie says back. Alexis is parked next to her, and about to get in her car.

"You did really well tonight, Martin, I'm very proud of you. And I hope someday you will forgive me for forcing you on that stage," she smiles a 'sorry, not really sorry' smile at her.

"Already forgiven. I need someone to push me out of my comfort zone once in a while, so thanks for being that person." She presses the button on her keys and unlocks the door. "Hey," she calls to Alexis, "Was it my imagination or was Jack there, in the back, and then left without even saying hi?"

"I saw him too, I don't know what happened."

"I do. He's mad at me."

"Stop making assumptions, look at the trouble you got yourself into doing that. You don't know what he's thinking, so don't project your worst fears onto him, okay?"

Lizzie takes a deep breath, lets it out, and watches it form a cold cloud in front of her. "You're right, I will try to not do that, though I am very good at it."

"There is no try, only do," Alexis laughs as she gets into her car.

"Okay, good night, Yoda," Lizzie says, starting her car and heading home.

As she gets into bed, after carefully hanging up her grandmother's dress, she checks her phone one last time to see if Jack has called or texted. Nope. She turns out the light, curls up on her side, and eventually drifts off to sleep.

Early the next morning Lizzie is startled awake by her phone ringing, and receiving texts at the same time. She picks it up off the nightstand, and groggily says hello.

"Hey, it's me, can you meet me at the property in a half hour?"

As she wakes up she realizes it's Jack. She looks at the clock, it's 7:45. "Can we say, 8:30? I'm still in bed, and–"

CHRISTMAS IN CRANBERRY HARBOR

"Fine, 8:30. I'll see you there, bring your dad, okay?" and he's gone.

Lizzie shakes off her sleepiness, picks out some jeans and a sweater, and heads to the bathroom. She washes her face, brushes her teeth, and puts on a little makeup. What the heck could this be about? Why so cryptic and clipped?

When she gets downstairs her dad is already dressed, drinking coffee and reading the Sentinel. "I am not renewing our subscription," he says by way of apologizing for reading the paper that dumped her. "But, while it's still being delivered, why not read it before it goes into the recycling bin?"

"It's fine Dad, you don't have to apologize." She pours herself some coffee. "So I just got a weird call from Jack, he wants us to meet him at–"

"The property outside town? Yeah, he texted me too. Any idea what it's about?"

"Not a clue." She looks at the clock on the oven. "We should head out in a couple of minutes. This is not how I expected to spend Christmas Eve, that's for sure."

"Me either, it's kind of fun, our first journalism adventure as a team," he says, finishing the rest of his coffee.

"Yeah, I just wish I could shake the uneasy feeling I have, like he's going to sue the town, or they're suing him, something not good and involving lawsuits," Lizzie says, concerned.

"You need to stop watching all those procedurals, things don't always involve lawsuits, prosecution or jail time, honey," he says trying to calm her down.

"You say that now," Lizzie says as she finishes her coffee and puts the mug on the counter, "But mark my words, something's going to happen. I think I've spent too much time covering politics, not a beat that instills positive feelings about towns, cities and government."

"There's only one way to find out, let's go," Peter says, putting on his coat and hat.

As Lizzie puts hers on too, she is suddenly aware her mom isn't around, nor the dog. "Where's Mom?" she asks as they head into the garage.

"I'm not sure. She said she had a quick errand to run, but wouldn't say what."

They get in Peter's car. "Yet another mystery to be solved," Lizzie says, fastening her seatbelt.

When they arrive, there are a few cars there, including one that's quite fancy, like something a rock star would travel in. Peter pulls the car over to the side, behind the other cars and one truck.

Jack sprints over. "Thank you both for coming here on such short notice. I didn't know Grace and Ellis were going to be coming here until about two hours ago." Lizzie has never seen Jack so nervous. Well, except when he proposed to her four years ago. On Christmas Eve, coincidently.

"Grace and Ellis? Grace and Ellis Parker? The billionaires?" Peter asks, not quite believing it.

Jack nods.

"Before we go over there, Jack, I just want to apologize-" Lizzie says, trying to smooth things over.

Jack stops her. "No, it's all good. It actually proved to be kind of fortuitous. You'll see. Come on, I want you to meet them."

"Grace and Ellis Parker, this is Peter Martin, the owner and editor of the Cranberry Harbor Gazette, the best paper in town."

Peter laughs and extends his hand, "The only paper in town, it's so nice to meet you both, but Jack misspoke, I am now the co-owner and co-editor, this is my daughter, Lizzie, who now runs the paper with me."

"Hello, it's lovely to meet you," they both say, shaking their hands.

"When Jack reached out to us we happened to be on our way

to Truro for Christmas with our son and his family who live there, so the timing was perfect," says Grace.

Lizzie is feeling a little agog. She has read about the Parkers, of course, everyone has. She even watched Grace's TED Talk several times about climate change and their commitment to doing what they can to help the cause. It was inspiring, they are inspiring.

"We absolutely love the Cape," says Ellis, a diminutive man with salt and pepper hair, and a warm, engaging smile. "When our son moved here five years ago we started to get to know another side of the Cape, the year-round side. Through him we got to know the struggle for housing, for work, and of course, concern about erosion, wastewater and all that comes with climate change and not putting the environment first."

Jack steps in, "The Parker's and I have some mutual friends, hard to believe, but we do," he laughs. "When they heard about this project that I've been working on they told him they'd like to see the property, and possibly invest."

"So here we are," says Grace.

Tom Jenkins, the town manager emerges from one of the cars. Lizzie's heart sinks, figuring this will be the kiss of death to the project.

"I just got off the phone with the members of the select board, and they've agreed that the community would most definitely benefit from this project. We just need to sell it at a special town meeting. I can't promise anything yet, but we're willing to explore the project idea. That is if, Mr. and Mrs. Parker, you want to proceed?"

Peter and Lizzie look at each other, Tom Jenkins had never been this cordial in all the years he'd been in office. Lizzie suspects he's a little awestruck by the Parkers as well. Whatever the reason he's being so agreeable, she is not going to question it.

Ellis and Grace look at each other and nod. "We're in," Ellis says. "But wait, there's one other thing."

Everyone looks concerned. Ellis turns to Lizzie and Peter. "Jack filled me in about the struggles you're having at the paper, Peter and Lizzie. It's a really tough time for independent newspapers, I know. I have friends who are some of the ones buying them all up."

Lizzie and Peter look at each other and wonder where this is going. "Grace and I are planning to spend more time here, a lot more time, and want to find ways, like with this project, to help the community. One way we think to do that is by investing in local, independent journalism."

"I used to be a features writer, way back in the day," Grace says. "I love newspapers and think they're vital to the communities they serve." She looks at her husband, "So, we were thinking that we, along with some other friends, would like to invest in the Cranberry Harbor Gazette so we can insure its future. If that would be okay with you both? We want no say in the content, we will be completely hands-off, we just want to make sure it is viable and financially healthy and able to continue."

Peter and Lizzie are stunned, and speechless. Finally Peter says, "I am..." he can't find the words. "I am shocked. Well, first, thank you, and oh my god, yes, thank you, we'd love to work with you! I never in a million years would have thought of something like this."

"Honestly, we hadn't thought of it either. It was Jack, he really sold us on the importance of the Gazette to the community."

Lizzie has been silent, and is completely stunned that it was Jack who made this happen for the community, and for her family.

As everyone is shaking hands and congratulating each other she walks over to him.

"I can't believe you did all this," she says, still in shock. "I can never thank you enough for helping to save the paper. You are..."

"I did it because it's the right thing to do. This town needs the paper, it needs your dad, and it needs you."

"I can never repay you for this," she says, beginning to cry. "You have helped save what my dad has worked so hard for, for decades. Thank you so much."

"I'd do anything for you, Lizzie, you have to know that. This was something I could help make happen, something that was good for everyone, and for the town too."

She wipes away her tears, and suddenly remembering her role as a journalist, she asks the Parkers and everyone else to squeeze in for a photo.

"I'm glad one of us is thinking straight," Peter says to Lizzie, hugging her. "Can you believe this?" he whispers to her.

"No, I can't. It really is a miracle, dare I say a Christmas miracle?" She laughs and hugs her dad.

"I'm not going to argue with you on that!" he says.

Lizzie also manages to have enough presence of mind to get a few quotes from the Parkers before they take off to their son's house.

"You're a lot more with it than me," her dad says. "Thanks for doing our job."

"No problem, I don't want to lose my job just as I've gotten it," she quips. She wanders off, taking a few more photos.

Jack walks over to Lizzie, who's standing on a spot that looks out to the bay. "Hey," he says.

"Hey, yourself," she says, turning toward him. "I am so excited for you, for the town, this is going to be incredible. I can't believe you got the funding, that you helped us, it's amazing." She looks out at the water and screws up her courage. "Look, I want to apologize again, my dad never should have-"

"Stop, it actually may have been to the benefit of the project. When Tom called me, irate of course, I decided to cash in my chips earlier than I had planned to, and it may have been, no I know it was, serendipitous. My friend caught the Parkers as they were leaving New York for here, and they loved the idea. So it was good, it got me to stop agonizing and going over plans again and again, and just say what the heck, and go for it, for all of it. I'm not good at that."

She nods in agreement. "I'm not good at that either. I over-think. A lot. Like a whole lot, a lot."

"Well you've made a pretty big change, you don't seem to have over-thought that too much."

"I didn't really have a choice. The change came to me," she says, looking over at her father.

"I think it's going to be really good. We're both going to make some big changes here, for the better, I hope," he says, turning around and surveying the land. "It's going to be a lot of work, but I think it will be really good."

"I do too. But you know, the Gazette is going to be holding your feet to the fire, we're going to be on you to make sure you're living up to your mission. And now that we won't have to sell or go under, we're going to be around for a long time," she teases.

They start walking back to the cars. "Oh I know, just don't sic Stan on me, I don't think I will be able to take the grillings he will most certainly subject me to, especially at the hardware store," he laughs.

Everyone is starting to disband, it's beginning to lightly snow, and it's getting colder.

"Listen," Jack shakes his head. "Why do people say that? Anyway, what are you doing tonight?"

"Um, it's Christmas Eve, so Christmas Eve stuff I guess? Why?"

"Well, Tall Tales decided at the last minute to have a Christmas Story Slam, but it's early, so everyone can get home and wait for Santa," he smiles. "I think we should go."

"You do?" She can see her dad getting into the car, but he signals her not to hurry. She looks down at the ground, "Look, about the whole Penelope thing, I was a jerk, and I'm so–"

"There's no need, I understand why you were upset, and why you didn't want to talk to me given our history. She and I ended things months ago. She never wanted to live here, so she thought maybe if she showed up and seemed game we could get back together. It was never going to work." He pauses and looks at her, "So what do you say? Let's move past that, okay? Bring your parents too, I've heard your dad tells a good story."

"I will ask them, I'm not sure what they have planned, I'll let you know."

And then, there is a moment, a perfect moment for a kiss, and they hear, "Jack? Can I ask you a few questions?"

"Stan," they both say, laughing.

"I will let you know," Lizzie says walking back to the car.

She gets in and is smiling. "Well this sure isn't the way I expected the day to go," she says as they head to the office.

"Those can end up being the very best days," her dad says looking straight ahead.

"So what do you think about going to a story slam at Tall Tales, later? Sounds like the place to be," she says.

"I'd love that, let's run it by your mom. I've got a million stories," Peter says.

"I am sure you do, Dad, and I can't wait to hear them."

CHAPTER 33

BACK AT THE Gazette office Lizzie quickly writes up a short story to put up on the website, and puts a link on their Facebook page, and on Instagram, along with a bunch of the photos she took.

"I cannot tell you what a difference you've made here already, honey," Peter says from his side of the partner desk. "I would have struggled to get the story written and up on the website, nevermind all the new social media spots. You have no idea how much stress this has taken off of me, and it's only been two days! And this angel investment from the Parkers and their friends? It's going to take so much pressure off of us. I still haven't fully absorbed that yet."

"I know, me either. I think that's going to take a while to sink in. To think we can maybe hire a photographer, and another reporter. I'm so glad to be here Dad, but I feel like such a jerk that I wasn't doing more to help before this. I didn't realize how dire things had become, and I'm so sorry."

"You needed to do what you needed to do. I get it, you needed to get away from here, and I'm really glad you did it."

"I know, but I should have been more help," she shakes her

head. "Anyway, I'm here now, so you can count on me." She spins around in her chair. "After the holidays I may bring in some plants, something to brighten the place up a bit, would that be okay? I think with this new chapter in the paper's history we need to spruce things up a bit, make it warmer."

"You do whatever you want, Stan and I have really let the place go. We have a local team come in and clean once a week, but other than that we don't do a thing. I'd love to bring it back to life. It's felt pretty dead for a while now."

"Well, we'll change that, we need a workspace that makes us feel good, that's cheery."

Peter slaps his desk, and startles Lizzie. "I think since it's Christmas Eve and we've already put in a few hours of work, we should close down the office and get out of here and go tell your Mom the good news. What do you say?" he says, standing up.

"I think it's a bad idea to argue with the boss, so I say, yes, let's call it a day."

Before they walk out the door, Lizzie turns and hugs her dad. "Merry Christmas, Dad, thank you for being here when I needed you. You really saved me."

He hugs her back, hard. "Nope, it's the other way around, you saved us. Thank you! And thank Jack!"

She wipes her eyes. "Ugh, Matty is right, we really are the schmaltz family!"

He turns out the lights, "Yeah, but I think there are far worse things than being that."

Gabby is as stunned as they were with the news about the new development, and of course, the investment in the Gazette. A great sense of relief fills the air. Those unspoken stresses weighed on everyone, even when they weren't talking about them, especially then.

Later, after they've all calmed down from the big news,

Gabby is happily putting gifts under the tree, while Christmas music fills the house, and the aromas coming from the kitchen are positively intoxicating. Lizzie feels so happy, so content. Looking at the tree, her parents, the fire in the fireplace, she feels more at peace than she has in a long time. She sits on the couch as her parents head off in different directions in the house, and curls up. Daisy comes running in, wagging her tail, jumps up, and curls right next to her.

"Hey girl, you want to have a snuggle with me?" she says, scooping the little dog up and hugging her.

"Well you sure look cozy," her mom says, bringing them each a cup of tea. "You sure Daisy isn't bothering you?" She sits down in a rocking chair near the fire.

"Are you kidding me? I love this." she rubs her face into Daisy's fur and sighs. "She is just the best. You really lucked out adopting her."

"We sure did."

"I am totally having a Dorothy Gale moment here," she says to her mom.

"Dorothy as in the *Wizard of Oz* Dorothy?"

"Yes, a total and complete, 'there's no place like home' feeling."

"It's really nice to hear you say that," she says, sipping the steaming tea carefully. "I kind of thought we'd lost you for a while there."

"I think I kind of lost myself too. After Jack and I broke up I didn't know what to do because we'd made all these plans, and it was sort of back to the drawing board," she says, looking at the fire. "And I guess in the midst of that I cut everyone out to a certain degree that reminded me of what I wasn't going to have. But I'm good now, no matter what happens I've found my own center, and my own purpose. Regardless of romance, I'm in a really good place. I'm sorry it took me so long to get here and if I hurt you and Dad at all."

"We weren't hurt, we just missed you. I always believed when you sorted everything out you'd be back, maybe not back like this, but back with us. I wasn't worried. We have a pretty strong bond."

"Yes we do," Lizzie says, still snuggling a now sleeping Daisy on her lap.

Gabby sits forward on her chair, and looks around to see if Peter is in earshot. "So I had an idea, but before I finalized everything I wanted to run it by you."

Lizzie is very curious. "What kind of idea? A surprise for someone? Someone in this house?" she laughs.

"Shhhh... yes. But I need to know if you're okay with it."

"Are you getting another dog? If so I vote yes and will totally have your back if Dad fights you on it."

Gabby laughs and shakes her head. "No, Miss Daisy here is plenty for me. Your dad and I haven't taken a vacation in years, not since that trip to Paris. We could never get away because the paper was like a baby he always had to tend to. It was too much for Stan on his own. But I was thinking, now that you're here..."

"Oh my gosh, yes! Of course! I would be thrilled to be able to run things while you go away!" Her excitement startles the dog and wakes her up. A few pats and she's back asleep. "What are you thinking?"

"Well, I have two tickets on hold for two weeks in Ireland, is that crazy?"

"No! I think that's fantastic! When would you go?"

"Not till spring, end of April. You're sure you'd be fine, running the paper, taking care of the house, Daisy?"

"I would love to do it. Go and finalize those tickets, and then you and Dad can spend the winter figuring out all the places you want to go. So this is what you were so mysterious about, and the gift you were wrapping?"

"Yes, I'm still sort of old fashioned, and I went to see Marge."

"Who used to have the travel agency on Main Street? I remember her."

"Yes, most people do their own tickets and everything now, but she still works out of her house, so I went to see her, she just needs my okay to buy the tickets. Eek! I've never done anything like this! I usually give your dad a sweater, or some new slippers. This is so extravagant!"

"And so well deserved. Go, go call her and tell her yes, buy those tickets. But do yourself a favor?"

"Don't tell Stan?"

"Exactly!"

Gabby gets up to go make the call.

"Oh, Mom? Would you be okay if we went to the story slam at Tall Tales at 4? Jack mentioned it, and he said we should go, but I understand if it interferes with dinner, or other plans."

"It doesn't interfere at all. Matt and family are staying home so they can get Sophie to bed early, so it's just us three, that sounds fun." Gabby turns around before she leaves, "So apparently he does not hate you," she says looking at Lizzie. "Told you so. I'll be right back."

"Mom is always right," she whispers to Daisy.

CHAPTER 34

CONSIDERING how last minute the event was, and that it's on Christmas Eve, Lizzie is surprised at how many people are at the bookstore. The three of them find some seats near the back.

"I'll be right back," Lizzie says, going to say hi to Anika and Jay. "Hey, it's so nice to see you again, what a fun way to spend Christmas Eve!"

"We thought, why not, a few people had asked so we decided to do it. We'll keep it short," says Anika. "Make sure to help yourself to coffee, cocoa, tea, Leah brought over a bunch of things from Sea Coast."

"Thank you, I'll see if my parents want anything. Merry Christmas, by the way!"

"And congratulations to you on partnering with your dad, we're really excited to have you here," says Jay.

"Thank you, I will be in touch after the holidays, I have some ideas I'd like to run by you and both," she says, and they nod.

When she returns to her parents, she finds that Jack has joined them, and she sees Alexis, Sean and Ben in the back. They all wave. "Do you mind if I sit with you?" he asks. "My parents were knee-deep in Christmas prep and couldn't come."

"Of course, the more the merrier," Lizzie says. "There's hot drinks, cookies? Does anyone want anything? I'm happy to get it."

Peter looks at Gabby, "Two cocoas?" Gabby nods.

"Jack?"

"Let me come help you," he gets up. "So are you going to tell a story?"

"Me? No, I shamed myself enough at karaoke last night, I am here as an observer only." She pours three cocoas. "You?"

"I'm going to get some coffee," he says. "Oh! You mean telling a story. I'm not sure. I might."

They are each carrying two drinks, and manage to avoid any more cookies. Lizzie vowed to herself to join the other young women in town at the yoga studio after the holidays, this endless drinking of cocoa and eating cookies had to come to an end.

Jay gets up and tells everyone about the theme of the afternoon, *Holiday Hopes - Realized or Dashed,* and asks if anyone wants to start them off. Lizzie was not surprised, from everything she's heard, when her dad puts his hand up.

"Peter Martin, come on down!" Jay says as everyone applauds.

"Thank you, it's so nice to see so many of you here. I am especially glad to have our daughter here, this has been a wonderful Christmas season. So as most of you know, I started the Cranberry Harbor Gazette over thirty years ago. I was just a kid, had no clue as to what I was doing, but I had a journalism degree and a dream."

Peter proceeded to tell an elaborate tale of the first Christmas he was running the paper, it was printed in town back then, and when a storm hit no one could get to the print shop to get the paper out. He'd only been in business for a month, and he didn't want his first Christmas issue, one he had painstakingly worked on, to not get out, so he did everything.

He had written all the copy, printed hundreds of copies, and set out to deliver them all in his dilapidated old truck. He stayed out all night, got back to the office, fell asleep at his desk, and was awakened by the phone ringing. It was a subscriber complaining that he didn't get his paper but his neighbor had. It was then he said he realized two things, "No good deed goes unpunished, and I had created something that people really wanted. Thank you."

"Peter, as usual you are the best. Thank you. Anyone else feeling brave?"

Jack's hand goes up and Lizzie is surprised. Jay calls him up. "Jack Cahoon, welcome, this is your first time up here, but from rumors swirling around here, it sounds like you may be here for a while."

Jack nods, "Yeah, I'm very excited to be back. I've missed this town, this community so much."

"Well, I will let you get to it," Jay steps aside, and Jack sits down on the tall stool.

"I know lots of you here, but there are also new faces. I am an actual native Cape Codder, as most of you know, even if you moved here as a baby, unless you were born here you will always be a washashore. The Cranberry Harbor school system was not regionalized when I was growing up, and was quite small, so you always knew everyone. Well, I sort of knew everyone. In tenth grade I got partnered with Lizzie Martin on a project for English class. We had to write an article for the school paper. It had to have certain elements, interviews, facts and be newsworthy. I figured I had it made - Lizzie's dad ran a newspaper, she wrote for it sometimes, I thought this would be a super easy A." The crowd laughs, and Lizzie smiles, remembering the incident. "What I didn't bargain for was how she was not going to let me off that easily. She was going to make me work. Which I thought was incredibly unfair. She loved this stuff! I was a math and tech guy, I wasn't a writer."

He pauses. "So we decided to do a story we could both get into, a new tech lab at the school. I could write the technical part, and she could finesse the prose, weave in the quotes, and it would be great. Except I was just not good at it. I was great at explaining to other computer people how something worked, but not at breaking down how this would be beneficial to everyone. I kept wanting her to take it over and just write it, but she wouldn't. She kept telling me I could do it, and that she wasn't going to do my part for me. I felt so frustrated, but then, all the things she had told me about writing suddenly made sense, and I got it. She thought I could do it, and made me feel like I could too."

He takes a deep breath. "I know this isn't a Christmas story, but in some ways it is. Four years ago on Christmas Eve I asked her to marry me, she said yes, and then I blew it a year later on Christmas Eve. So no, I am not going to stand here and propose to her on Christmas Eve out of an abundance of caution, and I wouldn't do that to her." Everyone laughs. "But what I am going to do, in keeping with the theme of Christmas hopes realized and dashed, is to tell her that I love her, and that I promise I'm not going anywhere this time, because I think together we can accomplish anything. And I'm here for the good, the bad, and everything in between. I want to be a team player."

By now Lizzie is crying in her seat, the audience is applauding, some of them are also crying, and there's nothing else for Jack to do but go to her, which he does. He takes her hand, grabs their coats and leads her outside.

She's still crying as he wraps her coat around her shoulders. "Well I pity the poor person going up next, that is a hard act to follow," she says, wiping the tears away with her hands. "That was amazing. And, in case you didn't know, I love you too."

"I was hoping you were going to say that, or else this would have been a really, really embarrassing thing to have done."

She laughs, and takes a deep sigh, pulling her coat tightly

around her as it starts to snow. Cranberry Harbor is really pulling out all the stops. "So we're starting over, huh?"

"Yes, if you are willing to take me on. I know I'm not always easy," Lizzie interrupts him.

"And neither am I. But I think we're better together than we are apart."

"I do too," he says, kissing her.

Lizzie didn't know just how much she'd missed him, how much she missed this, kissing him felt so perfectly right. She smiles and pulls back, "But don't think this means I'm not going to be all over you on all these big projects, I'm a professional," she teases.

"I'd expect nothing less. And I know because of that, it will make everything worthy of that A we never got."

"I know! That was so ridiculous, how could she not see what we'd done!" Lizzie starts in, getting riled up.

Jack pulls her in close, "Just kiss me, we'll make everything perfect later, I promise."

The End

ACKNOWLEDGMENTS

While being a writer means spending lots of hours parked alone with a laptop, creating a book does not happen in a vacuum. It indeed does take a village. I have so many people who have been supportive and gone way beyond what anyone could expect, and I'm so very grateful.

To that end I want to thank my team at Sea Crow Press. Mary Petiet is a joy to work with. I truly feel I didn't just find a publisher, I found a friend. Thank you Mary for seeing something in my work, for whipping it into shape, for designing an amazing cover, and pretty much doing whatever needed to be done!

To my editor Anastasia Drost, thank you for catching all the things I did not, for making me look like I know where commas go, and for just making me look good.

Maggie Marr, thank you so much for your expertise, patience, care, and helping guide my career. I wouldn't be here without you.

After I slog through a first draft, believing in my heart it's the worst thing ever written, I read it, and make much-needed, can't be ignored changes. I then send it to the best first-reader ever, my dear friend, Sarah Shemkus. She sends me back the best notes any writer could ask for. Even bullet pointed! Thank you, thank you for all your insights and catches. You make me a much better writer, make my stories better, and you totally get me.

My good friend, mentor, teacher and cheerleader, Claire

Cook. You've been Inspiring me for years, thank you for always being there.

Barbara Tierney, thank you for reading, editing, and for the very much needed Hot Chocolate Sparrow breaks that get me out of the house and help me keep my sanity. I can't tell you what they, and your friendship mean to me.

To the amazing writers whose books I love, who offered to read my book and had nice things to say about it, thank you! Claire Cook, Kristen Meinzer, Abbi Waxman and Sally Gunning, you are women and writers I so admire. I know how busy all of you are and your generosity with your time is something I am incredibly grateful for.

Joanne Powers and Ian Ryan, thanks for meeting with me on Zoom for all those long Covid months reading the early chapters and drafts. Our weekly meetups kept me writing and kept me sane. Mostly sane.

And lastly, a huge thank you to my Cape Cod writing, theater, radio, and creative community. *Christmas in Cranberry Harbor* is a love letter to the people and places of my beloved Lower and Outer Cape. We are indeed fortunate to live here, surrounded by some of the most talented, generous and fun people on the planet. I certainly don't live on Cape Cod for its affordability, (ha!) or its interminably gray winters. I'm here for the community I am so very fortunate to be a part of. Love to you all.

ABOUT THE AUTHOR

Candace Hammond grew up and still lives on Cape Cod, but will forever be considered a washashore for not having been born there. She is a journalist, playwright, and novelist, who also hosts an arts podcast/radio show on WOMR out of Provincetown, because people in the arts have the best stories. She is the mother of three adult children who are scattered around the globe, and grandmother to one amazing little girl. She lives with her musician partner and their very large cat on the Lower Cape.

ABOUT THE PRESS

Sea Crow Press is an award-winning woman-run independent book publisher based on Cape Cod in Massachusetts committed to amplifying voices that might otherwise go unheard. We publish creative nonfiction, literary fiction, and poetry. Our books celebrate our connection to each other and to the natural world with a focus on positive change and great storytelling.